Forever with the CEO

The Whitley Brothers
Layla Hagen

Copyright ©2025 by Layla Hagen

All rights reserved.

No portion of this book may be reproduced in any form without written permission from the publisher or author, except as permitted by U.S. copyright law.

Contents

1. Chapter One   1
2. Chapter Two   9
3. Chapter Three   16
4. Chapter Four   26
5. Chapter Five   44
6. Chapter Six   51
7. Chapter Seven   58
8. Chapter Eight   69
9. Chapter Nine   80
10. Chapter Ten   87
11. Chapter Eleven   95
12. Chapter Twelve   103
13. Chapter Thirteen   114
14. Chapter Fourteen   119
15. Chapter Fifteen   126
16. Chapter Sixteen   134
17. Chapter Seventeen   140
18. Chapter Eighteen   150

19.	Chapter Nineteen	159
20.	Chapter Twenty	167
21.	Chapter Twenty-One	173
22.	Chapter Twenty-Two	183
23.	Chapter Twenty-Three	191
24.	Chapter Twenty-Four	197
25.	Chapter Twenty-Five	208
26.	Chapter Twenty-Six	218
27.	Chapter Twenty-Seven	231
28.	Chapter Twenty-Eight	244
29.	Chapter Twenty-Nine	255
30.	Chapter Thirty	265
31.	Chapter Thirty-One	271
32.	Chapter Thirty-Two	280
33.	First Epilogue	289
34.	Second Epilogue	297

Chapter One

Nick

"I'm heading out," I said to the receptionist as I passed the front desk of my fitness club.

"Hey, brother," Leo greeted me. He was just coming in. "You're leaving already? Short day, huh?"

"Yes. I'm going to visit Allison and the kids."

"Right. Okay."

All of my brothers trained at my flagship gym, and I usually liked to hang around with them after the training to catch up. But I'd promised those kids I'd see them today, and I didn't want to disappoint them. Ever since my best friend, Jim, and his wife, Nora, passed away, I tried to see the little ones as often as possible.

"How's Allison doing?" Leo asked. Allison was Nora's sister. She immediately took the kids in, moving them into her home to live with her.

"Coping."

"Still as hot as I remember her?"

I frowned at my brother. "You're engaged."

"What's one thing got to do with the other? I wasn't asking for myself, obviously."

I groaned, shaking my head. "Whatever, bro. I said I'd drop by with dinner, and I don't want to keep them waiting. Have a good workout."

With that, I left. Leo knew me too well. If I lingered, he'd figure something out.

Obviously, I'd noticed Allison was hot, but I'd never had much to do with her over the years. I saw her maybe three times total before the tragedy. These days, I saw her at least once—sometimes twice—a week.

The first time I met her was at Jim and Nora's wedding. She'd looked stunning, so of course she caught my eye. But I'd always been a player, and she was Jim's sister-in-law. Therefore, she was off-limits. These days, even more so.

I helped out whenever I could and tried to keep the ogling to a minimum. I focused on the kids as much as possible when I visited. Damn, they'd been through a lot.

Allison owned a house in South Boston. It was supposed to be a starter home—"plenty of space for one person," as she put it. But with two small kids, it became a little crowded. Annie and Jack were four-year-old twins. They'd been everything to Jim and Nora. The whole situation was just gut-wrenching.

I dropped by the pizzeria two blocks from Allison's house and ordered everyone's favorites. Annie liked cheese, and Jack loved a lot of bacon on his pizza. Allison favored the extra mushrooms.

A half hour later, I pulled up in front of the house. It was a two-story building plus an attic and a basement. The lower part was painted white, the upper part exposed red brick. There were three wide windows on each floor and two in the attic.

As I walked up the stairs to the front door, I heard Annie's and Jack's voices, which meant they were in the backyard. I went back down the steps and around the house, heading straight to the back.

"I come with pizza!" I announced.

The twins yelled with joy and immediately came to me, hugging my knees.

"Cheese?" Annie asked.

"Of course, and extra bacon for Jack."

"You really are their favorite person," Allison said. Her voice was soft and melodic. She was always calm and composed, which totally amazed me. With all that she was juggling now, Allison took things in stride. No wonder the kids felt so at ease around her.

As usual, I took in a deep breath before looking at her. Yeah, that was right. I'd been coming to this house with dinner twice a week and still had to brace myself to look at this woman because she was *that* damn hot. She had long, thick brown hair. Usually, she wore it loose down her back, and it reached all the way to her ass. I'd fantasized more than once about fisting her hair and tugging her head back just so. Tonight, she'd pulled it up, so it only hit her shoulders. Her green eyes were large and enchanting. You could easily tell that Annie and Allison were related, as they looked so much alike.

"You know, they're starting to think that Wednesday is pizza day," she said, taking the boxes from me.

"Isn't it?" I asked.

She laughed, throwing her head back.

"Or if inviting myself over every Wednesday's too much, you can just tell me and I'll fuck off."

Allison winced and looked at the kids, but then she waved her hand. "They hear me swear plenty, so I don't think there was any harm done. They're still too young to really know what we're saying."

We moved toward the wooden table and chairs she had out here and set everything down on it. As she got things ready, the twins ran around the yard with a balloon they were using as ball.

"Hey, it's dinnertime!" she called to them, but they didn't respond right away. "I think they want to finish their game first. They're going to be late for bedtime again." She sighed, her shoulders drooping. "My sister wouldn't be happy."

"Allison," I said, stepping closer to her. It was truly impossible not to be smitten with how gorgeous she was. She had freckles on her nose, and her fragrance drew me in. But that's when I noticed her beautiful sage-colored eyes were a bit red. She'd obviously been crying, and I hated that they all were going through this. Losing a sibling would be unbelievably hard. If something happened to one of my brothers, it would cut me deep.

"You're doing a great job," I told her.

"Let's see how long I get to do it," she whispered.

"What are you talking about?" I fixated on her freckles again and then cast my gaze away. She even had freckles on her cleavage.

Nick, whatever you do, don't hit on her. I'd been repeating this mantra ever since the first time I came here—which was two days after the funeral.

"Bob and Sophie's lawyer contacted me."

They were Jim's parents.

"Why?" I questioned, maybe a bit too harshly.

I'd met Jim when we were in college, and we hit it off right away. I'd only met his parents a few times, and they weren't the warmest people I'd ever encountered. In fact, they were more academic and snobbish and totally different from the upbringing I had with my mom. Plus, they'd never approved of Nora, and they hadn't been too happy about him marrying her.

"They want custody of Annie and Jack!" Allison's voice shook as she told me.

"What the fuck?" I said a bit too loudly, and the twins looked up. "Shit," I whispered.

Allison said nothing.

"Have they mentioned anything like this before?"

"No. I'm not even sure why they're bringing it up now. I never got the sense that they wanted to spend too much time with the kids," she whispered and then grabbed her hair. She pulled at something, and it fell to her waist. She needed to play with her hair, I realized as she took a strand and wrapped it along her fingers. The impulse to reach out was even stronger.

"Did they see them that much? I mean, even before the accident?" I asked.

"No, not really. That's the thing. Mostly just on Christmas and Jim's birthday. That's the only time they came to Boston. And even then, they didn't really spend time with the kids, so this is very out of the blue." She shook her head. "Nora rarely spoke with them, and neither did Jim, so I'm guessing phone calls with their grandkids were minimal too. I don't know. I'm still trying to process this."

She pulled at the thin straps of her dress, rearranging them, and I caught a glimpse of her breasts. I nearly groaned.

"They don't have a case." I sounded far more confident than I was. I was extremely good at business—I'd grown a failing company into the most successful chain of gyms in the country—but I was no lawyer.

"I don't know. I've asked a colleague at work. He doesn't specialize in family law, but he said it all depends. It's circumstantial."

"What the hell is circumstantial? Your sister passed away, and she and Jim specifically put it in their will that they want the kids to be with you. And you didn't even hesitate in taking them to live with you."

She was a fucking amazing human being. Not many people would do that. Some people, like my own father, even had an issue taking responsibility for their own damn kids.

"You have a fantastic job," I continued. "You own this house. How could you possibly not be fit to have custody?"

In addition to being drop-dead gorgeous, Allison was also a brainiac. She was a CFO of a huge fashion label.

"Yes, I do. But as the lawyer pointed out, I have a great income for myself, not necessarily for myself and two kids."

"That's bollocks," I said.

She laughed. "That's actually a British swear word."

"I know. I was hoping they don't know what that means." I nodded toward the youngsters.

"You're right, they don't." But then her smile fell again. "So... back to the lawyer. He insisted that I don't discard their demand as baseless. I wonder if the fact that I moved the twins out of their parents' house can count against me."

"What's going on with the house?"

"The mortgage is simply too large, so I rented it out as fast as possible. Jim and Nora had a good life insurance policy, but they wanted it to be used for the kids' college, not the mortgage. I'm executor of the estate until the twins come of age, and then the house belongs to them. Renting it out takes care of the mortgage."

Jim and Nora's house was a sprawling mansion in Beacon Hill. Jim had made a lot of money as an investment banker, but even he complained once or twice that the mortgage was eating up most of their money.

"Oh, Nick, I can't lose them." Her face crumpled, tears threatening to spill over.

Besides the funeral, this was the first time I'd seen her inconsolable.

"You won't. Now come on, let's eat. Then we can put our heads together and think some more about this."

She nodded, wiping her eyes. "Annie, Jack, come on," she called after a moment. "The pizza's getting cold."

"Yes, Auntie Allison," Annie said. She spoke a bit more than Jack, who understood conversations but would only reply with yes, no, or very short sentences after Jim and Nora passed away.

While they were eating, I asked how their daycare was going. Annie dutifully filled me in on her favorite toys. Mr. Beagle was still up there, holding the first spot.

Allison was looking at them like they were her whole world. Who in their right mind would take these kids away from her, and why?

After we finished the pizza, Jack started to wail. He was obviously tired. Then Annie followed suit.

Allison sighed. "Nick, I think it's best if you go. Putting them down for the night will take longer than usual."

"I can help," I said even though I didn't know jack shit about the kids' bedtime routines. I had a nephew, Ben. He was my half brother Spencer's kid. We spent a lot of time together, but I'd never been with him in the evening.

She laughed. "Trust me, you don't want to do that."

"Listen, I know a family lawyer. He's a friend of mine. I'll talk to him."

Her eyes brightened. "That would be amazing. I started to look for one, but work is madness. I have zero time. My day is divided between drop-off at daycare, my job, picking them up from daycare, and then bringing them back home."

"I have no fucking clue how you do it," I said. Damn it, I should have asked her in more detail if she needed help with day-to-day things. "What can I do to help?"

"Dropping by with dinner twice a week is amazing," she said.

Annie's wails became even louder, so Allison picked her up on one hip. Then she took Jack by the hand as they went up the steps.

I was rooted to my spot, watching her.

Would there ever be a day when I wouldn't look at Allison Holmes and immediately think inappropriate things?

I didn't think so.

Chapter Two
Allison

"Allison, I just need your signature before you leave for the day," my assistant said, poking her head into my corner office.

I eyed the clock. It was 5:20 p.m.

"Sure. Put it here on my desk."

"Sorry it took so long. I wanted to have it ready for you at lunch."

"No worries." I signed everywhere she'd put a Post-it. "All right, here you go. Sorry, but I've got to run."

She gave me a sympathetic smile. "Sure. Thank you."

Before everything happened, I usually left the office around seven. But many things had changed since I lost my sister and Jim. This wasn't even the worst of it. I worked from home after the twins went to bed to make up for leaving at five. So far no one had complained. Then again, I didn't expect them to, given my executive position—and because I was very good at my job.

Everyone else in my department was still working as I gathered my things to go. There was a common joke in the company that when everyone else left for the day, finance was still here, and it was true. But numbers made the world go round, as far as I was concerned, and the later hours never bothered me.

My office was downtown in a huge skyscraper that housed over ten thousand employees. The best part was that we had a daycare in the building. I'd been unaware of it until I was desperate for someplace for the kids that wasn't far away from the office. I felt a bit guilty for leaving the twins there for so many hours a day, but what else could I do?

My sister had only taken them to daycare for three hours in the mornings. The rest of the day, she did a lot of activities with them, from baking to painting to playing games. She'd been an amazing mom and sister. Nora had simply been amazing all the way around, and I missed her like hell.

No, no, no, Allison. Don't think about Nora. Not now.

Because every time I did, I teared up. She and I had been as tight as sisters could be. She was my best friend and my everything. She'd been three years older, and I'd worshipped her ever since I could remember. Some days I still couldn't believe she was gone.

When I arrived at the daycare, there were only five other kids left. I sighed at the sight.

"Hi," the daycare worker said. "These two have been great today." She pointed to Jack and Annie.

They seemed to love this place, but I couldn't help feeling guilty anyway. When they noticed me, their faces broke into smiles, and they ran toward me.

I lowered myself onto my haunches. When they wrapped their arms around my neck, I instantly forgot about the spreadsheet that had been percolating at the back of my mind. I hugged them both tightly, enjoying the feel of them and their little kid smell.

"Ready to go?" I asked.

"Yes," both of them chorused.

With a grin, I took their hands and led them out to the car.

We arrived home forty minutes later. We still had some leftover pizza from yesterday, which I heated up along with steamed broccoli and chicken from the night before. Cooking was never my strong suit.

Honestly, before I had to care for the twins, I didn't even give dinners much thought.

We ate at the dining room table tonight because it was too cool to eat outside. June could be fickle in Boston. I loved my house. It was much smaller than the one where they lived before, but there was enough space for us. The only crux was that I had two bedrooms, so they had to share. That was fine now, but down the road... Well, I'd figure something out. I was a CFO, for God's sake. I made good money, and I'd do whatever needed to be done.

"All right, little guys," I said once we were done with dinner. "Let's go upstairs so you can brush your teeth."

They both started to wail at the same time.

"Can we watch cartoons?" Annie asked cheekily.

"We read books before bed," I reminded her. TV was too stimulating, and they'd never want to go to sleep. Reading to them always did the trick.

"Okay." She looked so much like my sister when she pouted that it took my breath away. It instantly transported me back to my own childhood, which had been loving and warm. I thought fondly of those days. Even though we were born to older parents, we never realized that because they played with us constantly.

My mom used to joke that their age caught up with them the second I left for college. After my sister passed away, they asked if I wanted them to move to Boston to help with the kids, but they were far too frail for that.

To my astonishment, we were done with the routine only forty minutes later. Normally, putting these two to bed could take up to one and a half hours. I kissed their foreheads before leaving their room and heading downstairs.

I yawned as I sat on the couch. Before, I spent my evenings going out with friends or binging TV series, but right now, I still had to catch up on work.

As I opened my laptop, I couldn't help but wonder if Nick had already spoken to his lawyer friend. Before I dove into spreadsheets, I decided to call him.

"Hello," he answered on the first ring.

My stomach somersaulted. His voice was unbelievably sexy. But it fit him because he was, hands down, the best-looking man I'd ever met.

"Hey," I whispered.

"What are you doing?"

"Funny you should ask. Eating leftover pizza. Don't worry, I actually found the twins something very healthy to eat. Leftover steamed broccoli and chicken."

"Damn, I'd take the pizza over that."

That made me grin. "Me too. My cooking skills aren't fabulous, but I'll continue to work on them. I wanted to ask if you talked to your lawyer friend."

There was a pause, and my chest constricted. I didn't know Nick too well, but he didn't seem like the type of guy to hesitate unless he didn't have good news.

"I did, but just briefly. He did say that he needs some more details to make recommendations."

"But what does he think? Do they have a case?"

"He said that custody cases are always complicated. He wouldn't just outright dismiss it."

I felt as if someone had put a stone on each of my shoulders. "That was not what I was hoping to hear. But of course it's better to know the truth and prepare. What kind of details does he need to make recommendations?"

"He'll be in touch soon. I caught him before a business trip, so he didn't have much time to chat."

I took a deep breath. "When's he coming back from the trip?"

"Next week."

Suddenly, I felt like maybe I shouldn't be waiting that long.

"But I asked him explicitly to work on it while he's away, and he said he would," he added.

"Thank you, Nick. I truly appreciate it. I can reach out to a lawyer too. Get a couple of opinions."

"I'm sure. But why don't you let me take this off your plate?"

"Thank you. You're my favorite person right now."

"Only right now?" he teased. "How about the rest of the time?"

"I don't even see other people, so you're the only one in the running."

"Ahhh, so I have no competition."

I laughed. God, it felt good. I'd been a bit on autopilot these past few months. The only time I seemed to be able to relax and laugh was when Nick was visiting.

"Oh, Nick, I've been living a *Groundhog Day* lifestyle for a while now. The same day is on repeat all the time."

"Come on, that can't be true. What do you do to relax after the twins go to bed?"

"Well, funny you should ask. I catch up on work."

"Allison!" he practically growled.

I groaned. "Hey, I feel like you're about to judge me."

"Not judging you, but that's... a lot."

"I have a demanding job. Which was never a problem before, but now the hours I spend at the office are simply not enough."

"I have a proposition for you. You do have a sitter, right? You mentioned something a few times."

"Yes. About once a week so I can work the second I get home. Doreen gives them dinner and puts them to bed for me."

"How about you book her for Saturday evening?"

"Why?" I asked, frowning at my laptop.

"Because I'm taking you out."

I straightened up on the couch as if electricity ran through me. "Wow. Why?"

"Because you deserve a break."

I thought hard for a second, guilt hitting me immediately because I was actually considering it. "Let me think, okay? I don't know if I should... I mean..."

"Just say yes."

"Why can't I think about it?"

"Because you'll guilt yourself into saying no."

I bit the inside of my cheek. How did he know that was what I was doing? "There is a high risk of that." I paused a minute and then threw caution to the wind. "You know what? I'll do it."

"Hell yes!"

I chuckled. "Nick, thanks. This means a lot to me. I mean, everything you do means a lot—that you drop by with dinner, you ask the twins about their daycare. You actually remember their favorite toys. It makes me feel less lonely."

"Allison, you're not alone. I should have helped you more all along." His tone had softened with a tinge of sadness.

"No, you shouldn't. This is not your responsibility."

"Maybe not, but I don't mind in the least."

I vaguely wondered why Nick had been as involved as he had been. No one else had shown nearly as much interest. Nora and Jim were social people, and they had a ton of friends. But after the first few weeks, the calls stopped coming. Why was Nick different? "So, what are we doing on Saturday?"

"I'll think about it and let you know. I promise you'll have fun."

"That's all I need. Actually, you know what? Surprise me. I don't want to know anything."

"Now we're talking." I could hear the grin in his voice.

I felt more alive right now than I had in months. My entire body was vibrating with excitement. It hadn't even occurred to me to book Doreen and go out. It had felt completely wrong.

But my thoughts immediately jumped back to where this smoking-hot man was going to take me.

Oh, Allison, take him being hot out of the equation, okay? Just look at Nick as Jim's best friend. That's all. The last thing you need right now is any guy trouble. You've got enough on your plate as it is.

"What time are we leaving?" I asked.

"Whenever you want. I'm at your service."

"Careful, Nick. You don't know me well enough to make such an open invitation."

"True, but I'd love to get to know you better. And what better way to start than by spending Saturday together?"

Chapter Three
Nick

On Saturday, I went to my grandparents' house for brunch. Even though several of us had huge houses where we could host it, my grandparents always preferred we come to their place.

Jeannie and Abe Whitley were both in their nineties but still sharp and agile. Eons ago, my grandmother insisted on preparing elaborate dinners whenever we came over, but since the family had grown over the past few years, we convinced them that brunch was the better option. Everyone could bring something. My contribution today was bacon. I was a lot like my brother Jake that way; we both loved bacon.

I had three pans on the stove because frying bacon for eighteen people was a damn lot. Yep, that was right—*eighteen*. I had two brothers and five half brothers, and everyone was engaged or married. I was the odd man out. And then came my nephew, Ben, who loved bacon as much as Jake and me. So yeah, I needed all the pans Gran had.

"Do you need any help?" Gran asked, popping into the kitchen. Most of the family had arrived already and were in the living room talking up a storm.

"Do you have any more pans, Gran? This might take a while."

She laughed. "No. Goodness, what a great problem to have, huh? I love having a full house."

I knew what she meant. Things in the Whitley family hadn't always been like this. Just a few years ago, they'd been tense as hell. The reason

I had brothers and half brothers was because our dad led a double life. He had a family here in Boston and us back in Maine. He was married to my half brothers' mother, and our own mom had been his side piece. Neither knew about the other until Jake discovered that something was amiss. Then everything came tumbling down like a house of cards.

My grandparents had been left to pick up the pieces after Dad got out of Dodge. The coward. He left both families to crumble. The company, Whitley Industries, had been in shambles, too, due to his mismanagement. But nowadays, it was thriving, with each of us was running a branch.

Fortunately, the bacon didn't take as long as I thought it would, and chatting with Gran while we waited for it to cook was always enjoyable. I didn't get to have her all to myself all that often, so this was a treat.

"All right, bacon's done!" I put everything on a platter and then grabbed it before Gran could. She was fit, but still, the woman had to slow down.

As we went to the living room, I realized the rest of the group had arrived too.

"My favorite part of brunch: bacon," Jake said, kissing his daughter's head. She was at that odd age when she wasn't a baby anymore but also not a toddler. She loved being carried around by her father.

"I made enough for everyone," I assured him.

Colton immediately reached out and grabbed one of the crispiest bits. Our relationship with him had been especially strained. Some days it still seemed like a miracle that we could all gather like this.

Colton, Jake, Spencer, Cade, and Gabe were our half brothers. Leo and Maddox were my actual brothers, although I'd always considered Gabe to be my brother too. The two of us had been the youngest of the group when our family life imploded. When we'd met, he and I instantly became friends. Then again, when you're a kid, you don't think too much—you just act.

"We have a feast again," Grandad said. "It's good to see you all."

"As usual, it's best to take turns to grab food," Gran reminded us.

"Uncle Nick, bacon," Ben said, running up to me. He looked more like Spencer every day.

My brother was a very decent man. Ben's mother had practically dumped Ben on his doorstep. Spencer had stepped up to the plate and done a great job raising him.

"Sure! And I'll tell you a secret. I kept a few bits for us in the kitchen. They're the crispy ones."

Colton looked like I'd just committed a betrayal of the highest order.

"Dude," he said.

"What?"

"You do this every time—snatch the best part."

Gabe and Spencer laughed. "You really do. You're a bit of an ass because of that," Gabe said.

"I'll get them from the kitchen," I told Ben.

"No, I get. I big."

I mean, he wasn't *that* big. He was only three and a half.

"I'll go with you," Penny said.

Spencer was the luckiest man, I swear to God. Penny had been his temporary neighbor when he met her, and things worked out seamlessly. Then again, they did so for all my brothers. The women they were with were just perfect for them and the family.

"You look wistful," Gran said. I realized she was watching me intently.

I cleared my throat. "What do you mean?"

"Oh, nothing."

"Quick, someone change the subject," Maddox said.

Thankfully, I could always count on him to have my back, because I knew where this was going.

"Oh, nonsense. Why are you so defensive, you boys?"

"Were you or were you not looking for signs that Nick is ready for you to matchmake him?" Leo asked.

Gran just shook her head. "He hasn't been ready for years now. But I have a theory about that."

"And what is it?" I asked. I was genuinely curious.

"If there's one thing I've learned after all my experience with your brothers, it's that no one is truly ready. You just get ready when you meet the right person."

"There is some merit to that theory," Colton said, frowning.

"So, I've learned that everything happens when it's supposed to. There's no reason to start pushing and setting you up with granddaughters of my friends," Gran concluded.

Leo whistled. "Dude, that's one of the finer advantages of being the last one to find someone. You don't have to go through any matchmaking attempts."

I opened my mouth to say, *"Thank fuck,"* but then Gran added, "Make no mistake. I *will* try as soon as I get a whiff that he's ready."

Wait, what just happened?

My brothers all started to laugh.

Gran winked, then went to the kitchen. She, Penny, and Ben returned almost immediately with the crispy bits I'd set aside especially for him. I was still in a bit of a daze as I went to the table and loaded some food on my plate.

My grandparents came up to me. "Son, how is that girl coping with Jim's kids?" Granddad asked.

He'd met Jim a few times when we went together to watch baseball games.

"She's got a lot on her plate."

"I'll say. She's doing so well after all that sorrow," Gran said, affection in her voice. "She must be a wonderful girl."

"Yeah, she is. But she's got some issues with Jim's parents. They've recently hinted that they want custody."

"What the hell?" Leo asked, putting some boiled eggs on his plate. I hadn't realized he was within earshot.

Gabe and Maddox were right next to him. They'd met Jim's parents a few times. No love lost there either.

"My reaction exactly," I told him. "So I've spoken to Hugo."

"That's good. He's excellent at family law," Maddox said.

We'd gone to college with him, but he went on to law school. He was one of the best in his field.

"You've been stopping by regularly, haven't you?" Gabe asked.

I glanced at Maddox, who held up his hands in self-defense. Even though I considered all seven to be my brothers, there was, of course, no denying that I was closest to Maddox and Leo. They'd been the only ones I'd told about my comings and goings to Allison's house. Out of the two of them, Maddox was most likely to blab to Gabe. The look of guilt on his face confirmed as much.

"I try. Twice a week. We have dinner, and I play with the kids. I'm not sure how much help I'm being, though."

"I'm sure Allison appreciates it," Gran said. She was looking at me intently with an odd expression that I couldn't decipher. Maybe it was best if I didn't.

"What's everyone doing today?" I asked, deciding to change the topic because I felt like I was on thin ice.

I didn't know why. It was just an instinct, and I'd learned never to ignore it.

Everyone spoke at the same time. It was hard to keep track, but it didn't matter. I liked hearing snippets of what everyone was doing. We all got together maybe once a month, though I saw my brothers a bit more often. Each of us was handling a different branch of Whitley Industries. My grandfather had set it up in his youth and had successfully added branches over the years. Then my father took over and started adding even more. The problem was, he didn't do so profitably, so when he literally left the country, most of them were in danger of bankruptcy.

I'd taken over the fitness branch, which hadn't been developed at all. It had been mostly an afterthought, but I knew it had potential. Maddox was running a company designing office plans. Leo was the head of Whitley Real Estate. Colton, the oldest, was running the biotech branch. Spencer took over the publishing arm. His mother had been operating that one; she passed away from cancer shortly after finding out about the double life her husband led. Cade ran the coffee business, and Gabe had started with a craft distillery and went on to add a bar. Now he'd opened a hotel with Maddox. We were all successfully growing our grandparents' legacy, and I knew they were proud of us.

"What are *you* doing today?" Natalie, Jake's wife, asked me.

"I'm taking Allison out."

The chatter died instantly.

"What do you mean, 'out'?" Leo inquired.

"She hasn't had any time on her own since everything happened, so I offered to go out with her."

"Very interesting," Gran said.

She glanced at Leo, who had a Cheshire cat grin on his face. Gran's eyes simply lit up.

Fuck. She was going to jump to conclusions fast. I was sure of that.

"Give her our best," Gran said. "And please tell her that even though we don't know her, we're all ready to help in any way we can. I think I speak for the entire family when I say that."

All right, that was a decent reaction. I really should give Gran more credit. Her mind wasn't always on matchmaking.

Although, to be fair, Jeannie Whitley had been an actress back in her day. She could fake it if she wanted to.

Leo frowned, clearly just as perplexed by her blasé comment as I was.

Thankfully, no one mentioned Allison or my outing with her for the rest of the day, although by the looks Maddox, Leo, and Gabe gave me, they did want to give me shit about it. I appreciated that they held their tongues.

I left the house early in the afternoon, as I was picking Allison up at five. On the way, I decided I'd call Hugo. Initially, when I brought this all up, he'd asked me a few details about Allison, like what her job was and other information. He had enough to go on, but I put the two of them in contact, as he needed more details. Now I wanted to know if he'd made any progress.

He was excellent at what he did, but he was also swamped with work. I wanted to make sure he was able to stay on top of this, friend or not. Thankfully, he answered after several rings.

"Hey, Nick."

"Hey. Sorry to call you on a Saturday. Figured I'd have better odds at reaching you."

"I suppose you want an update on the whole Allison thing?" he said.

"Did she send you all her information?"

"Yes. She was very open about it and eager to cooperate, which is always helpful."

"So, how does it look?"

"I'd like to know a bit more about the in-laws, but..."

I didn't like that pause.

He sighed. "Grandparents usually have a good fighting chance."

"But Nora and Jim specifically wanted Allison to look after the twins. They put that in the will."

"Wills can always be contested. They can try and prove they're better candidates. That's why I said from the get-go that you can't dismiss it. Several things are taken into account, of course, such as their age and income."

"They're around fifty-five. They had Jim very young."

"All right, so that won't be an impediment. Do you know anything about the financial situation?"

"They're well off, from what I know. They put Jim through college, so he didn't need a loan. They even helped with the down payment on the house he and Nora owned," I explained.

"Right. I'll investigate this a bit more before making a recommendation."

"When will that be?"

"Sometime next week. I promise that I'm on top of this case."

"Look, no offense—" I began.

"Nick, what do you know about me? I don't overpromise or underdeliver. I told you I can see Allison through this. At the very least, I'll come up with some recommendations. Can you give me the in-laws' full names and as much as you know about them? I'll look them up. I have people who do that."

"Excellent," I said, rattling off their names. "Thank you, Hugo."

"No problem."

I didn't have a good feeling about this. I'd assume this would be a slam dunk, and he would simply tell Allison that if she did A, B, and C, she was going to keep custody for sure.

I decided to push the issue to the back of my mind for now. I was fucking excited about going out with Allison.

My phone rang again. I figured maybe Hugo wanted to add something, but then I saw it was Maddox. I answered right away.

"You've been keeping secrets, brother. I'm with Cami and Leo," he said without further ado. It was silent in the background, which meant he wasn't at Gran's house anymore.

"About what?"

"Allison."

"Hey, you're going on a date," Cami, his fiancée, said. "That's huge news."

I groaned. "No, we're not. Jesus, that's what everyone thinks?"

"Uh, yeah," Leo said.

"That's not what this is at all. I'm just literally taking her out. I figured she could use it."

"Really?" he asked. "She couldn't just go out by herself?"

"If she'd wanted that, she would have done it already," I pointed out.

"I see. So that's the solution you came up with." His tone was laced with amusement. "Could have offered to just watch the kids so she could go meet a friend or something."

He had a point. It never even crossed my mind. "Please tell me that you didn't give Gran any ammunition to harass me."

Cami laughed. "Nick, you know your gran. She doesn't need anyone to give her ammunition. She finds it by herself. She was over the moon after you left."

"You're all making too much of this."

"No, we're not," Leo said. "Maybe you don't see it, but we do. This is a huge deal for you. Actually, so are all the things you've done since Jim passed away, especially going to Allison's house."

"I care about those kids. Don't be a jackass."

"I wasn't implying that you didn't. But I think that's not the only reason you keep dropping by."

"Right. Well, I'm at Allison's house now, so I need to hang up."

Technically, I was still two streets away, but I needed to end the conversation. It was making me question myself, and I didn't like that. I wasn't prone to introspection or whatever it was called.

After hanging up, I couldn't help but wonder. Why *did* I offer to take her out?

Oh, for fuck's sake, Nick. Get your shit together.

And I did.

I parked right in front of the house. When I got out of the car, Allison's voice filtered through the windows. I looked up. She was on the second floor, moving around and... singing?

This woman was something else.

My imagination immediately went haywire. I could imagine her nipples peeking through the fabric of her shirt. Or was it a dress?

I realized on the spot that Leo was right. I hadn't just offered to take her out for her own benefit. It was self-serving as well.

Chapter Four
Allison

I was singing at the top of my lungs while looking at the outfits I'd laid out on the bed. I was determined to have a good time tonight and wasn't going to let anything put a damper on my mood even though the short call I'd had with Nick's lawyer, Hugo, yesterday, hadn't been the good news I was hoping for. Still, for now, things were great. The kids were downstairs with Doreen, whom they adored. She was in her midsixties and very good with them.

I focused on my clothing options. Summer was definitely my season. I loved Boston year-round, but there was something special about summer. I'd narrowed it down to a red dress, a yellow one, and a blue one. Even though they were all different styles, I chose based on color. Red was my favorite. The dress was simple: thin straps and a V neckline. It was pretty snug around my body, but so what?

I put it on just as I heard Nick's voice drifting up from the backyard. *How late is it?*

I glanced at the clock and gasped. Shit, it was already five o'clock. How was I not ready?

I ran to the hallway window that overlooked the backyard. Opening it, I prepared to call down to Nick, but my voice got stuck in my throat. He was on all fours carrying the twins on his back. They were having the time of their lives. Doreen was standing to one side, looking at them with glee. It was definitely a sight to behold.

Finally, I found my voice. "I'll be right down. I'm sorry."

Nick looked up. "Take your time. We're having fun."

"Yes!" Annie clapped her hands.

It was so good to see those two smile. The first month had been crushing. They were crying themselves to sleep every night. I wasn't much help because I was crying with them more often than not. I'd go in to comfort them, and then all three of us ended up having a sob session. They kept asking when Mommy and Daddy were coming back. It seemed like they were finally accepting that they weren't.

My heart started to feel heavy at the thought, but I quickly nipped it in the bud.

Nope, Allison—tonight is for fun. Don't think about any sad things. Nora would want you to have fun.

I headed back to my room, glancing at myself in the mirror before pairing the dress with black ballerina shoes. I wore heels at the office, but I simply refused to put my feet through that torture in my free time. Grabbing a very light jacket, I ran a hand through my hair. It was still damp, but I didn't like using a hairdryer. I also had a very small backpack that matched my shoes.

After one last look at my reflection, I dashed down the stairs, feeling more excited than I had in months. I joined everyone outside and noticed a huge paper bag on the table.

"What's that?" I asked.

"Nick brought takeout," Doreen said.

She smiled wholeheartedly. She'd heard of him from the kids but hadn't met him until now. By the way she smiled, I could tell she liked him. That was good. I always trusted the judgment of the elderly. There was nothing quite like life experience.

God, the kids were so cute. I could just stay here for the rest of the evening to watch them. But then they both hopped off Nick's back at the same time, and he rose to his feet.

Don't ogle him, Allison. It was impossible not to, though, because Nick Whitley was absolutely breathtaking. He was wearing a dark blue shirt, the top button undone. No judgment there—it was hot outside. He'd also crumpled his sleeves up to his elbow. Not rolled, just carelessly pushed up. His jeans had a few light grass stains on his knees from crawling around, and I loved him for it.

"Ready to go whenever you are, Allison," he said.

I turned to Doreen. "Is there anything else you need?"

"No, dear. Go have fun. You need it. I'm glad you're doing this."

Her words took me by surprise. Doreen and I weren't close. We mostly had a transactional relationship, although I did ask her for advice about this and that on occasion.

"Thanks." Slowly, I looked at Nick. "I'm all yours, then. Let's go."

He flashed me an absolutely gorgeous smile. Were his smiles always this amazing, or was I noticing this one more for some reason?

"Come on, let's go."

We walked back through the house. A shiver went through me as we reached the front door. This was the first time I was spending time with Nick alone. Even when he stayed after the twins went to bed and it was just the two of us, it was different because there was someone else in the house. But now it was going to be just him and me, at least in the car.

"What are you thinking about?" he asked me as I closed the front door.

"Oh, this, that... By the way, I need to take a selfie of us."

Nick's eyes bulged. "Why?"

"For my mom. She didn't quite believe that I was going out tonight, so she wants photos to make sure it happened."

"Then by all means." He cracked yet another devastating smile.

I took the phone out of my bag and held it toward me as Nick moved to stand behind me.

I smiled, too, and almost gasped as I felt his hand on my waist. He tilted his head closer to my shoulder to fit properly in the picture. I felt his hot breath on my cheek and his chest against my back. I swallowed hard and momentarily forgot what I was about to do.

Oh right, selfie.

I took a few pics. In the first one, Nick just smiled. In the second one, he was looking at me with a huge grin. I turned to face him.

"Why are you looking at me?" I asked as I kept clicking.

"Because I can. Isn't that reason enough?"

Huh. What a strange thing to say.

I lowered the phone, and he let go of me, huffing out a breath. His eyes widened as if he couldn't quite believe where his hand had been. He cleared his throat, looking at the ground for a beat.

"Let's go to the car."

"What are we doing tonight?" I asked.

"Everything in due course."

It was so refreshing to be taken by surprise. I'd had to plan every minute of every day lately. It was good for someone else to take the lead so I didn't have to think about logistics or anything else. The anticipation was amazing, and I was ready to have a fun evening.

Nick walked behind me, close enough that I could feel the heat of his body. I swear, I could still remember the way his muscles felt against my back. They'd been as hard and defined as I always imagined. Then again, he ran the most successful gym business in the country. Being fit came with the territory.

"You're silent again," he said.

I looked up, smiling sheepishly. What could I tell him? *"I was just reaffirming to myself how hot you are"*?

As I got in his Lexus, I thoroughly relaxed against the black leather seat. He joined me a few seconds later, and as soon as he closed the door, I felt something shift in the air. For the first time ever, we were truly alone.

Why was I so obsessed with this? Perhaps because my skin simmered in places it had no business simmering. My pulse was more rapid. I licked my lips, glancing out the window at the porch. Was this all because of that selfie we took? Because we'd been so close?

Jesus, I wasn't a teenager who'd never been close to a boy. Why was I reacting like this? Maybe because I hadn't touched a man in God knew how long. Obviously everything was going to fire up.

Yep, that was a plausible explanation.

"Allison, are you having second thoughts?" Nick asked, and I realized that perhaps he was interpreting my silence as not wanting to go.

"Not at all. This is a good thing."

"Then why are you talking as if you're trying to convince yourself?" He gunned the engine, and we started down the road.

"I wasn't always like this. I was more social. I went out with friends, especially on the weekends. But ever since the twins came to live with me, I've had this urge to spend every free moment with them. I feel guilty if I don't."

"Tonight, you're not allowed to feel guilty." Stopping at the traffic light, he took my hand and looked me straight in the eyes.

That simmer intensified, and I had no idea how to stop it.

"You think I need your permission for that?"

"Hell yes. I'll make you a deal."

"Huh?"

"Every time I see you drift off, I'll assume it's because you're feeling guilty. So then I'll do something outrageous to take your mind off it."

I cleared my throat. "You wouldn't."

He grinned. "I would. You don't know me too well, Allison. Jim never told you some of our stories?"

My smile fell.

He shook his head. "Sorry. We won't speak about Jim and Nora."

"It feels wrong to say that," I whispered. They'd passed away three months ago, and all I wanted was to talk about them—even though it saddened me.

Nick hesitated. "It's not, though. We both cared about them a lot. Avoiding a topic that brings up difficult feelings isn't wrong. Let's just try, okay?"

I was wondering if he was doing this for his benefit as much as mine, but he did have a point. Besides, we were going out to have fun.

I nodded. "All right. Let's jump back to what you said before. Can you define outrageous?"

"You'll know it when you see it," he assured me, and then he concentrated on the road again. "We're having a barbecue along the waterfront."

"Oh, that's a great idea. The weather is so nice. I didn't want to be cooped up inside."

"I figured you wouldn't."

"How?" I asked.

"Because when I drop by on weekends, you're always soaking up every bit of sun you can."

"I'm an outdoorsy person. I like to bike. I used to do that as my workout every morning."

"You go to the gym?"

"Why? Are you trying to sell me a membership at one of yours?"

He gave me a cheeky smile. "They are the best in the country."

"So I've heard. Shame I've never been inside one of them."

"It's never too late. Let me know when you'd like to go."

"I'll keep that in mind," I said, but I immediately realized it wouldn't be doable. There was no way I could add a trip to the gym to my schedule, no matter how close to my office or house it was. I decided to share this with him so he didn't think I was rude when I didn't follow up. "I don't think I'll have time, though. Right now I'm doing a workout three times a week at home. It's very efficient."

"I get it," Nick said. "No worries."

"So, how did you even find this barbecue? What does it involve?"

"You'll see. It's very laid-back. I've been a few times with my brothers, and we enjoyed it."

"Are any of them going to be there?"

"No, just us."

I clapped my hands together. "I can't wait!"

We spoke a bit about the location as we drove along, and a short while later, Nick announced, "We're here."

I spent a lot of time by the water, since I lived nearby, but I hadn't been around this side of the harbor. It wasn't exactly a harbor, though. The nearest marina was pretty far away.

"I can't believe I didn't know about this place." It looked like a beach. There was sand, lounge chairs, and umbrellas. "Nick, I think you've found my new favorite spot in the city."

"Glad to be of service."

The unmistakable scent of grilled meat was wafting through the air. I looked around, trying to trace its source. There was a bar on the left side, and right in front of it was a grill station.

"Yum," I said, rubbing my belly. I wasn't even hungry, but the smells were delicious.

Nick nodded in that direction. "Let's take a look."

There were several tables around the grill station, but most people were eating while standing at the huge counter. I could feel my limbs relax, as if they'd been holding tension for all these months and it was finally starting to melt away.

We glanced at the menu together. Nick put an arm around my shoulders, and I slowly warmed up. He was a touchy-feely person. How had I not realized it before? And why was I enjoying it so much? And his scent... wow. His aftershave was really something.

Goodness, Allison. You need to climb a man, stat, but that man will not be Nick Whitley. He's basically the only other person in the twins' life. No way in hell can you mess that up just because your hormones are working overtime.

"I want one of those mixed kebabs."

As far as I could see, the cooks were the ones taking the orders as well. I wondered how they managed with so many people, but the system worked.

"Same for me," Nick said.

"Coming right up," the guy replied. "The drinks are on the other side."

To my astonishment, we got our food only a few minutes later.

We each grabbed a skewer at the same time. I grinned, pressing mine to his. "Cheers!"

"Cheers, Allison. To a memorable evening."

"Memorable? Why? Because of all these outrageous things you plan to do?" I waggled my eyebrows.

He chuckled. "I don't plan to do them. I'll just spontaneously come up with something if I have to."

"So that's the plan? You fly by the seat of your pants?"

"I've been doing that forever."

I took a bite of the skewer. It was delicious.

"I wouldn't have pegged you for that, being the CEO of such a huge company and all."

He shook his head. "I plan things in business. There's no way around that. But not as much as some of my brothers. And not at all in my private life."

"What did you do today?" I asked him.

"Had brunch at my grandparents' house."

"Wow. Your grandparents are still alive? That's amazing. How old are they?"

"Well into their nineties, but you wouldn't know it."

"And you've got a lot of brothers, right? I'm sorry, I'm not really up-to-date with your family. I know the Whitleys are prominent and known all over Boston, but I guess I've either not paid attention or have been living in my closet." We both laughed at my joke.

When he set down his half-eaten skewer, I noticed the veins on his forearm move with the motion. I had no clue how I could find that sexy, but I did. Clearly I was losing my mind.

"There are eight of us. I have two brothers and five half brothers."

"I think I read something about the Whitley family, but I really don't remember the details."

Nick frowned. "My father had a double life."

I gasped. "Oh, I didn't put two and two together. Wow. I assumed that maybe... You know what?" I cleared my throat. "Let's not get into that. Sad topic and all that."

Nick curved up a corner of his mouth. "That it is, but I don't mind telling you."

Now I was curious. "Okay. But only if you want to."

"The story had an unfortunate beginning, but all of us brothers are on very good terms right now, and we're especially close to our grandparents. We get together as often as we can. Most everyone's married.

The only ones who are still engaged are Maddox and Leo, so it's always a full house."

"That must be something."

"Yes. By the way, my grandparents actually offered to look after the twins if you feel like you need help at any time."

I jerked my head back. "But they don't know me or the kids."

"I know that. That's just how they are. Obviously, you'd get to meet them and everything, but it's just something to keep in mind."

I was touched in ways I couldn't even express. These perfect strangers just offered to spend time with the twins when not even Nora's best friend ever had. I swallowed hard, thinking how kind Nick's family was.

"Thanks. I like your grandparents already."

He winked at me. "Something tells me they like you too."

"How come?"

"That's a story for another time."

It didn't seem like a sad story, just one he was keen to avoid for now.

We finished our skewers, then left the counter. It seemed to be an unspoken agreement between everyone that once you finished the meat, you moved away to make space for the next customers.

"Let's get a drink," Nick said.

"Yes, please. Something with alcohol. Not too much, though."

He smiled. "Don't worry, Allison. I'll take great care of you tonight."

"Just don't get me drunk."

"Would never dream of it."

After checking what they had on offer, he said, "White wine?"

"You've read my mind. I've never really been a cocktail girl."

Nick ordered my wine and a beer for himself.

"Let's go a bit closer to the water," he suggested after we received our drinks.

"Great idea." I liked the vibe of the place, but it was a bit too crowded around the bar. They'd set up swings near the water, and I pointed at them. "That's so cool. I want to sit on a swing."

"Your wish is my command."

"Just for tonight or always?" I teased. I was in a very teasing mood today, but why shouldn't I be? The weather was amazing. I was here with the hottest man on the planet, which was absolutely irrelevant but still worth mentioning. I'd had an excellent barbecue, and now I was relaxing with a glass of wine.

"You can always count on me, Allison." He leaned in closer. "And if you need some entertainment, you can call me," he said as I sat on the swing.

Only after he sat did I realize that it was meant for couples. Our thighs were touching, and my stomach somersaulted. Being this close to him, it was impossible not to notice the effect he had on me. My pulse quickened. My mouth was dry, and my skin seemed on fire *everywhere*.

I tried to pretend this wasn't affecting me at all because what else could I do? So I took a sip of my wine and then another one, closing my eyes.

"Relaxation looks good on you."

My eyes flew open, and I felt my cheeks go completely hot. He was watching me.

"It's nice. I forgot what it felt like."

He turned slightly toward me, then resumed his position, probably realizing there was no way to turn without completely climbing over me.

Which you wouldn't mind, would you? a naughty voice said at the back of my mind.

"I'm going to take time for myself more often," I promised him. "Although it'll be in another shape, such as me taking a hot bath with rose petals and rubbing all sorts of scrubs over my skin."

He started to cough.

"Are you okay?" I asked.

"Sure, sure." And then he immediately rose from the swing.

I moved to the center of it because it was weird to be on one side by myself, plus it tilted with the loss of his weight.

He cleared his throat, looking at his beer, then gave me a cheeky smile. "There's not much I can do to help with that, but it sounds like you've got the hang of it."

It took me a second to realize what he meant. Oh. *Oh.* I might have gone a bit overboard describing my bath to him.

"I promise I'll call you for anything that I can't do by myself."

His eyes bulged.

Wait, that didn't sound right. *Ugh.*

I looked at my glass. I definitely hadn't drunk enough to warrant a loose tongue. Clearly the combined effect of Nick and the wine was going to my head. I decided to pretend I hadn't said anything.

"So, what would you like to do in your free time?" he asked.

I tilted my head. "I'm not even sure." Going with friends for drinks until late in the evening didn't sound appealing at all. Neither was shopping with my best friends—especially since I hadn't heard from any of them in months. "I'm not sure. I guess I'll have to think about it."

"Do that and let me know. I'd love to join you if you need company."

"Nick, are you serious?"

He stepped closer but didn't attempt to sit back down. Instead, he put his hand on the metal bar above me, his muscles flexing with the motion. Yum. This man was truly something else. "Yes."

"But why? I'm sure you've got a million things to do."

"I'm good at setting priorities, and I'm making *you* a priority. I should have done more from the very beginning."

My heart warmed—along with other places on my body. "You're doing more than everyone else, frankly."

"Still not enough. I want to be more involved."

"You know the kids' godparents are pretending they're not even the godparents?" I asked, apropos of nothing.

He scoffed. "I always wondered why they chose Phil and Lola as godparents."

"Oh, I know why. Because they were the only friends who had experience with kids at that point. That's what Nora said. They were hoping that maybe the kids could play together. But I know for a fact that she would have loved for you to be their godfather. I believe her explanation was 'Pity he's never been serious about a woman. I don't want to make his current date the godmother, only for her to then be replaced by others.'"

Nick blinked repeatedly. "Jesus. I have no defense because I don't even remember who I was dating when the kids were christened."

I burst out laughing. "Oh, Nick."

"Is that bad? Don't answer! I can see it on your face," he said with a laugh. "It is bad."

"No, it's not. Just the way you are," I said. "Nothing wrong with that." I took a few more sips of wine.

After a while, I started to shiver, so I put my jacket on. "Do you want to sit back down? I can move over. Sorry, I didn't think of asking earlier."

"Nah, these things are tiny."

Did that mean that he'd felt just as on edge as I had when he'd been sitting next to me? Now that I'd drunk my entire glass of wine, I wasn't able to keep my thoughts in check any longer. If he sat next to me, I could find an excuse to climb onto his lap. After all, we'd both be much more comfortable.

Oh, man, I truly was a danger to myself and also to Nick.

"I think I should head home."

"It's not that late," Nick said.

"I know, but I've been gone a few hours already. I'd feel more comfortable if I went back."

"Of course. The last thing I want is for you to stress out. That would ruin the point of this evening."

"Which has been a success!" I attempted to get up from the swing... and failed. I fell right back onto my ass. "Whoops! I drank the wine a bit too fast. And I haven't had a drink in months."

"Why not?" he asked, setting his empty beer bottle on the small table next to my glass.

"It felt weird drinking, knowing I have kids under my care."

"I'll help you up." He held out his hand.

I put mine in his, feeling how strong and calloused his palm and fingers were as they slid against mine. Was it from weights or other training equipment at the gym? Had to be. I couldn't imagine him doing other manual labor.

"And up you go." He pulled me up, and I managed to trip over my own feet, slamming headfirst into Nick's hard chest.

I straightened up quickly as Nick grinned. Next thing I knew, both of his hands were on me: one on my upper back, one at my side. I felt his touch so intensely that you'd think I wasn't wearing any clothes.

What's happening to me? I was usually composed.

"Fuck," he exclaimed.

I stepped back, looking up at him and smiling sheepishly. "Truly sorry. Did I hurt you?"

"Don't worry about me." His look was feral, but I didn't think it was because I'd made him mad. He then said, "I'll take you to the car."

"I'm not inebriated, really. I'm not even sure what happened."

"I think the sand moved away from under your feet." His voice sounded odd.

I was feeling a bit embarrassed. He didn't need to chaperone me. I was a damn grown-up.

Once we were in his car, though, I relaxed a bit.

"Last chance to change your mind. Want to head home or—"

"Do something outrageous?" I finished for him, feeling even sassier than before.

"I would have said 'continue to have fun,' but now that outrageous is on the table, fun sounds boring. So, what do you have in mind?"

I grinned, shrugging. "I don't know. I haven't done anything outrageous in a while. Tonight is not the night to start, though."

He laughed as he pulled out of the parking space. "You still have time to decide before we arrive at your house."

It was tempting, but I knew it was time to call it a night. Even though it seemed like we had only just arrived, we'd spent three hours here. By now, the twins were in bed.

God, it was as if I couldn't shut off that part of my brain. I was constantly thinking about them. Were they safe? Were they happy? Could I do more?

When we finally arrived home, Nick said, "And? Change your mind?"

I bit the inside of my cheek.

"We can leave outrageous off the table for now and continue with the original plan—fun," he added.

"It's getting late, but thanks a lot. This evening was amazing."

A strange expression crossed his face. "How about making this a standing thing?"

"What?"

"You and I going out on Saturday evenings."

My eyes widened. "Nick, I'm sure you've got much better things to do on Saturdays."

"As I said, I'm very good at setting priorities."

God, this was so tempting for a million reasons. But I had to exercise at least some self-restraint.

"I'll think about it."

He nodded. "Good enough. Can I come in and say hi to the kids?"

"That's very sweet of you, but they're already in bed by now. It's past their bedtime."

He cocked a brow, looking at the car's digital clock. "Really?"

"Nick, they're young."

He chuckled. "Yeah, not sure what I was doing when I was their age, but I'm pretty damn sure I wasn't in bed. Mom always used to say that we drove her crazy every night."

"Nora and Jim were very strict about their bedtime routine. Said it was the only way they would be rested enough and not ornery the next day. It was nice seeing you, Nick."

"I'll walk you to your front door."

I shook my head. "Really, don't."

"Now, listen—"

"Nick, I'm not drunk, okay? Or tipsy. I just lost my balance somehow." I was even more embarrassed than before.

"All right, if you insist."

"I do. Thanks a lot for everything." I got out quickly and then hurried up the front steps. As I reached the door, I turned and waved at him. He nodded before driving off.

I was smiling for no reason as I stepped inside the house. It was eerily quiet, but a light in the living room told me that Doreen was watching TV on mute. She immediately stepped into the foyer.

"Back already?"

"I've been gone a long time."

"Hon, I thought you were going to come back at midnight at the earliest."

"Oh, I couldn't..."

She moved closer to me. "Look, I haven't said anything because it's not my place, but this is good for you. You look relaxed, and you're smiling. Everyone needs time for themselves now and again."

My shoulders slumped. "I know. But everything is so new."

"I know. And I'm not saying this for self-interest, but I'm at your disposal no matter when, all right? I don't have much going on with my kids and grandkids all grown up. All my book clubs and old-people activities happen during the day when you're at work and the kids are at daycare. But I'm free on evenings and weekends."

I gave her a soft smile. "Thanks, Doreen. That means a lot to me."

"Just don't go blabbing about what I told you to anyone else, okay? I don't want to be at everyone's beck and call."

"So, you're making an exception for me?"

"You need me the most, child." Her words hit deep.

"Thanks, Doreen. Have a good night."

"You, too!"

After she left, I locked the doors, turning off the outside lights as she got into her car and drove away. Doreen really was a sweet woman, and I was lucky to have found her.

I tiptoed up the stairs, peeking in the twins' bedroom. God, these little angels. I wanted to wake them up just to kiss them and tell them how much I loved them. But I knew better than to do that or they'd keep me up for hours. So instead, I just closed the door, leaned against it, and smiled.

This evening had been amazing. And Nick had offered to do it every Saturday, huh? Well, now I was even more tempted to take him up on it. But I had a feeling that it was a dangerous idea.

Chapter Five

Allison

On Monday afternoon, I was still on cloud nine. I couldn't believe what effect an evening with Nick had on me. Yesterday, I'd been full of energy and took the twins to the zoo.

But right now, I was ready to call it a day. I'd been with a client after lunch, and now I was heading back to headquarters to pick up the twins from daycare.

On the way, my phone beeped with a call from the lawyer. I immediately answered.

"Allison. This is Hugo."

"Hugo, hello! One second." I immediately straightened in my seat, looking around for a parking spot. Driving wasn't my favorite activity, and I couldn't really multitask. That included talking on the phone while I was behind a wheel. I figured this conversation was going to require focus, so I pulled into the first free spot I found.

"Do you have news for me?" I asked after I'd parked. "Once again, thank you for agreeing to advise me on this."

"Of course. I did some research on your sister's in-laws. Your late sisters' in-laws," he corrected. "I'm very sorry for your loss."

"Thank you." A knot lodged in my throat. Damn. I wanted to be fully focused on what he said and not have my mind wandering back to how this all came about, but the sadness never left me.

"First of all, family law is complicated. You do have some things working in your favor, such as the fact that they named you guardian and you immediately took the kids to live with you. Your file tells me they didn't even spend one night in social services care."

"God, no. Of course not. I spent the night with them at the house when it happened. Then I brought them over to my house. I couldn't afford to pay the mortgage for their mansion, so I rented it out."

"Right, about that. I don't like to draw conclusions, but it might be why Jim's parents are suddenly interested in having the kids."

"What do you mean?"

"Whoever has the kids also has the rights to the house."

What? "But the house belongs to the kids."

"Not until they turn eighteen. Until then, the guardian is the executor. Under certain circumstances, they could argue that it's in the children's best interest to sell the house. Again, I don't want to assume anything. This is all circumstantial. Anyway, the motives don't matter, only the facts. I've reviewed your income and your assets, and they're quite sizable." That sounded encouraging. "However," he continued, and my stomach dropped, "with two kids under your care, the judge might look unfavorably at other things."

"Such as?" I whispered.

"First, there's your income. Depending on where the kids go to school later on, that could eat a huge chunk of your paycheck."

"Then I'll just fight for a better position or take on a second job."

"Which would leave you fewer hours to spend with them."

I sighed. "Right. Which came first, the chicken or the egg?"

"The problem is that you're a single income household. If you were to lose your job, it would severely impact the children's quality of life."

"Hugo, I'll be honest. I'm going to be a single income household for years. I have zero time to date. And if I did start dating now, I couldn't drag someone I barely know into a custody fight."

"No, of course not. This would only work in your favor if it was someone you were already in a long-term relationship with or had been seeing for a while. If you were to get married to someone you barely knew, it would count against you because it would make you seem impulsive. I was hoping you'd tell me that you have a longtime boyfriend. One who's ready to propose."

"What?" I blinked rapidly, as if that would make me able to hear better.

"If you were married and your partner had a decent income, it would make your case easier."

"Unfortunately, I don't, and I can't just whip someone up on demand. Do you have any other advice on how I can strengthen my case?"

"You could take another angle. Demolish their case. Prove they'd be unfit to take care of the kids. But in my opinion, that's not a good road to take. It often ends up very messy. The kids notice that, and after all, Jim's parents are their grandparents—down the road, they'll want to think fondly of them too. They're small now, but these are the kinds of things that shatter families for decades." He sighed. "I don't have any more solutions off the top of my head for you right now. I do have to do some more due diligence. I was simply hoping you would—"

"Be ready to get engaged," I murmured. "Got it. Thanks again. This means a lot to me. Have a great day, Hugo."

"You too."

After hanging up, I didn't drive off right away. I needed to compose myself. I'd been hoping for much better news—or at least a solution besides "get married."

I couldn't believe that I wasn't enough. I had a great job and a house that I'd been paying off for seven years. I could offer the twins a fantastic life, and I loved them to the moon and back. How could that not be enough?

I still hadn't driven off when my phone screen lit up with a message from Nick a few minutes later.

Nick: Hugo told me he spoke to you but didn't give me details. Do you have time to talk? I'd love to know what's going on.

I smiled despite the fact that my heart was still heavy. How did Nick have the power to make my day better simply by checking on me?

Nick

It was five o'clock and rush hour at the gym, which was one of the reasons why I liked to be around. Obviously, since I owned multiple venues, I couldn't be everywhere at once. But this was our flagship location, so I spent most of my time here. Gabe and Maddox were here, too, by the weights station. I wanted to shoot the shit with them but waited for Allison's reply first. Instead of messaging me back, she called.

"Hi," I answered.

"Hey."

"So, how did it go? He wouldn't give me any details because he went into a meeting."

"Not good. He basically told me I should get married," Allison said.

"What the fuck?" I snapped.

"Yeah. Said it would be best if I had a long-term boyfriend who was ready to propose."

"That was his legal advice?" I was going to have a word with Hugo. I kept my voice down and moved into a corner so I didn't attract any attention to myself.

"Yes. Has to be someone I've known for a while, too, or it would look too suspicious. He said the other option would be to tear down Nora's in-laws, show they're unfit and all that."

"Fuck yes." *Yeah, so much for keeping my cool.* I looked around, but no one glanced my way.

Allison laughed. "I can't do that, Nick. They're the twins' grandparents, and even Hugo said he wouldn't recommend it because it makes family life much harder."

"Did he offer *anything* useful?"

"He said he wanted to check with me first to see if marriage was even a possibility. I guess now he'll think about other options, knowing that it's not."

"Good. Because if he doesn't come up with something useful, I'll have to look for someone else, friend or not."

"Let's just see what he comes up with," Allison said quietly, then sighed. "I need to go pick up the twins. Thanks for contacting him. He really has been helpful."

"Anytime. Is there anything else I can do? My offer to distract you isn't only for Saturday evenings." Even though I was still pissed at Hugo, I kept my voice light because she seemed to need it.

"I promised the twins that we'll have a bubble bath tonight, but thanks for the offer."

"I can do late-night phone calls, too, if needed. Just putting it out there. Any time." I accentuated that last part. I really wanted her to count on me whenever she needed a friend.

"Nick..."

"I'm at your beck and call, Allison."

She laughed again, but it was still restrained.

Damn it. Hugo's news was clearly weighing on her, and why wouldn't it? It was a serious matter.

After hanging up, I went straight to my brothers. Gabe had just finished on the treadmill. Maddox was still working on the weights, but he paused when he saw me.

"So, you stopped for him, but not for me?" Gabe teased.

Maddox quirked a brow. "Nick looks like he's about to blow for some reason."

I jerked my head back. "Is it that obvious?"

"To me," he said. "What's up?"

"I just talked to Allison. Hugo didn't have any useful advice. The only bright idea he had was for her to get married."

"Is that feasible?" Maddox asked. "Is she in a relationship?"

"No."

Gabe gave me a shit-eating grin. "You could take one for the team."

"What do you mean?" I asked.

"Marry her."

Maddox burst out laughing. So did I.

"Yeah, right," I replied.

Once he'd composed himself, Maddox said, "I mean, it would only be half crazy. Imagine Gran's face if you told her you're getting married out of the blue."

I shook my head. "This isn't helping."

"But think about it," Gabe went on. "You're making bank. The kids actually know and like you. I bet that would help the whole custody thing."

"Gabe," I groaned. "Let's stick to real solutions."

He shrugged. "I don't have any. How was your outing with her on Saturday, by the way? You didn't say a word."

"We had a lot of fun."

Gabe grinned. "Fun enough to propose?"

Oh Jesus. He wouldn't give this a rest.

But strangely enough, I could see the merit in it.

Chapter Six

Nick

My brother's words kept percolating in my mind for the whole damn week. It was a crazy idea. I couldn't understand why I simply couldn't get it out of my mind. I'd called Hugo to ask him what that was all about, and he told me that the simplest solution often worked best, but that he was still working on building a case for Allison. He insisted that starting a smear campaign against the grandparents should be the last resort. After I had time to cool off, I agreed. Kids knew when something was wrong. I knew that only too well.

I hadn't been shell-shocked when the news came out that Dad had another family. On some level, I always intuited that something wasn't right: his comings and goings only on the weekend, the fact that he knew stuff about children our age, such as which stickers were on trend, which TV series, and so on. I never truly understood how Mom couldn't tell and believed my father's lies that he wouldn't marry her because his parents wouldn't approve. How had she not gotten wind that he was married?

Then again, I shouldn't judge too harshly. Mom hadn't had all the tools we have today. You couldn't look up someone's life with a few clicks. And Dad had been careful. There had never been a mention of his other family in any newspapers. I'd never know how he managed to keep a tight lid on that, especially when his wife was at the helm of Whitley Publishing. It was bizarre, but that information had never been public. It was as if neither we nor they existed... until we were front-page news. Once the scandal broke out, he ran away.

I'd made my peace with all of this a long time ago, though. I wasn't quite sure why I was now reminiscing about everything again. Probably because of this whole custody thing. But right now I had plenty of things to do. I planned to open five more branches of Whitley Fitness this year throughout the country. We had enough in Boston, but there were plenty of areas in the US that I wasn't covering yet.

I was tempted to put the marriage option on the table for Allison, but it was insane. A marriage of convenience, I supposed. No one could know the extent of what we would be doing because if it ever got out that it was a fake marriage, that would defeat the entire purpose.

Nah, it was a shitty idea. I'd like to help Allison out, but I didn't think I could do it. It would be too big of a lie.

When I went to bed later that night, the idea was still playing in my mind. But I couldn't share it with Allison. It was crazy.

The next morning, though, I gave in. I woke up at six on the dot, and it was the first thought that came to mind.

Fuck it. Just get it over with, Nick.

I called Allison even before I got into the shower. I had a golden rule: if an idea kept popping into my head repeatedly, it meant it needed my attention.

"Good morning. I hope I'm not calling too early," I said when she answered.

"No, I've been up for over an hour. But what's wrong? Any news from the lawyer?" She sounded frantic. Of course she would be—I was calling at the ass-crack of dawn, after all.

Jeez, Nick, way to freak her out.

"No. Not at all. Is this a bad time?"

"Yes, actually. I'm trying to bribe the twins into having breakfast so we can leave."

"Oh yeah, sorry. But after you drop them off at daycare, could we grab a coffee near your office? What I want to talk about won't take much time." This was not something I wanted to propose over the phone—no pun intended.

"Why?"

"I want to discuss some things."

"Nick, you're scaring me."

"No reason to be scared, I promise."

"Okay." She still sounded wary. "Sure, we can grab coffee. That means I can skip it now and focus on getting them fed. There's a coffee shop on the ground floor of my building. We can meet there."

"When?"

"One hour, give or take."

"Perfect," I said before hanging up.

This was crazy. Utter and total lunacy. I couldn't explain to myself why I kept obsessing over it. Those kids deserved a good home, and Allison could give them that. I saw her with them. She genuinely cared about them. I couldn't believe that their grandparents wanted to take them away from her, away from Boston. They lived in Montana in a small town. Everything would change for the twins.

As I stepped into the shower, the enormity of the situation hit me. *Am I really going to suggest to Allison that we should get married? What's gotten into me?*

And yet, even though I was in complete disbelief, I was already starting to imagine how being married to her would work. My entire body stood at attention—including my pulsing cock.

Fucking hell, I couldn't be thinking with my dick when it came to this. This wasn't about me wanting Allison—although there was no doubt about that. Saturday evening, it took all of my self-restraint not to touch her, not to flirt. Being married to her would never work. But I just had to suggest it, to put it on the table. We'd both have a good laugh and agree to never speak of it again. I was sure of it.

Allison was already at the coffee shop when I arrived. She was sitting at one of the tables, sipping coffee.

She smiled sheepishly when she noticed me. "Sorry, I got a head start on the coffee. Turns out it was a bad idea to leave my house without having a cup."

"No problem."

"It's self-service. Do you want to grab one?"

I sat down. "No, I'm good. I'll get it later."

She frowned. "Nick, you're scaring me again."

"I'll get right to it. Then you can tell me how crazy this all is, and we can put it behind us."

Her eyes widened. "I'm listening. This doesn't sound very encouraging, though."

I leaned back in the chair, studying her. She looked stunning, as usual. Her hair was falling over one shoulder. It was a sexy look on her, preppy but also hot. Because I was sitting at the very edge of the table, I had a view of her legs too. Her skirt wasn't short, but her legs were endless. And they looked amazing in those high heels.

"Nick!"

Her voice snapped me out of my thoughts.

"Right. When we spoke about what Hugo told you, I was at the gym. My brothers and I started talking about it, and they suggested, jokingly, that *we* could get married."

Her mouth fell open, her right eye ticked, and then she shook her head, wincing. "Sorry. I don't think I heard you correctly."

"Yes, you did."

"I don't get it."

"It would make sense. You need someone who'd make a good impression on paper, right? I have a solid business. More than solid, honestly, but I don't want to brag. I have assets. You've known me for a long time, so it wouldn't seem like you just picked me up off the street." I hadn't even realized I'd been thinking these points through until I said them out loud.

For a few seconds, neither of us said anything. Then Allison began to laugh.

"Oh, Nick. You truly are good at lifting my mood," she said with a smile. "This was good. It's brightening up my morning, which started by the kids having a tantrum and throwing milk on me."

"You wouldn't even know it," I said. "You look fucking perfect. And, Allison, I know it's insane, but I wasn't actually joking."

She frowned. "Nick, come on. I'm pretty sure it's not what Hugo had in mind—me just marrying someone for the sake of being married."

"I think that's exactly what he meant, but he didn't lay it out like that." Because he was a lawyer and legally that wasn't the soundest advice.

I swallowed hard. Allison looked at me as if I'd grown a second head. I was fixating on her lips, and I had to stop it because she was going to notice.

"I don't think this is going to—"

A loud beeping sound interrupted us. She glanced at her phone.

"Shoot, I have to take this. It's my assistant. She never calls me unless it's important."

"Sure, no problem."

She put her phone to her ear.

"What do you mean, they're already here waiting for me? The meeting is supposed to start in fifteen minutes." She sighed. "Okay, I'll be right up. Yep. No, I'm already here. I just grabbed a coffee." She listened and then responded, "Okay, yes. Sure."

After hanging up, she pursed her lips. "Sorry to cut this so short. Not sure why they want to start this meeting earlier."

"Don't worry."

"Do you want to drop by the house tonight?"

Did that mean she was considering it?

I flashed her a smile. "Pizza night?"

She laughed. "Why not? I always say Mondays are a special kind of hell. Everyone deserves a treat at the end of it."

I was going to file that information away in my brain.

She rose to her feet abruptly. I swear to God, I nearly groaned. Fuck my life, she was sexy. How could anyone focus around her? With her standing in front of me, I had an even better view of her legs. An image flashed into my mind of me bending her over right here on this coffee table, hiking her dress up to her waist, and making her mine.

"Nick, you okay? You seem lost in thought."

No, I'm just fucking lost in a fantasy. The way she said my name only fueled it further.

"Go ahead with your meeting, and I'll see you tonight."

She laughed, and I detected a hint of nervousness. "I'm really sorry you came all the way here and I only had, like, fifteen minutes. I swear it was supposed to be half an hour."

"That makes me feel really special," I teased, standing as well. If I had those legs right in front of my eyes for any longer, I was going to lose my composure for sure.

I watched her intently as she walked through the glass door leading to a marble lobby. I'd definitely lost my mind, but I was pretty sure she was considering my offer. After the initial shock and disbelief, I didn't think she was completely discarding the idea, at least.

My pulse quickened. I'd always followed my instincts and done things spontaneously, but this was on another level altogether. Yet I wasn't feeling sorry for sharing my thoughts with her. Not even one bit. She was ready to fight for those kids, and I wanted to help any way I could.

Another image flashed in my mind of Allison here with me and the coffee shop completely empty. This time, I took her in my arms, ordered her to wrap her legs around me, and pressed her against the nearest wall, exploring her in all the ways I wanted.

Chapter Seven

Allison

"Your projections are on point, as always," Derek said.

Derek was the CEO of the M.K. Ledger. He and the chief of marketing had been sitting in my office for the past two hours, and we'd gone through all the numbers I'd worked on every night this past week. My hard work had paid off.

Focusing on the meeting had been difficult, though, because my mind was still on what Nick had suggested. I was half convinced that I'd dreamed the entire conversation.

The chief of marketing excused himself after we finished, saying he had another meeting, but Derek lingered.

"Now, to move on to other things," Derek said. "I have a proposition for you."

"I'm listening."

Whenever he had a proposition, it was something new and exciting. I couldn't wait to sink my teeth into it.

"I'm in talks of acquiring a small company. Would you like to be in charge of the M&A process?"

That was quite a challenge. I'd be in charge of the merger and acquisition, which would be a feather in my cap and nice addition to my résumé.

"I love M&As," I replied. They were fun and challenging... and ate up a lot of time, I realized, but didn't say it out loud. *Shit.*

"Take your time and think about it. I can send you some paperwork we have. You'll need to sign a nondisclosure agreement first."

"Sure, no problem."

"I know that in the past, you would have done it without hesitation, but your situation has changed a bit."

Derek looked me straight in the eye when he said it. He'd been very understanding when I'd been a bit erratic and occasionally late the first month after the twins moved in with me. But once things settled down, we found our routine, and it ran a bit smoother. I didn't want to give him a reason to think that I couldn't do my job, though.

However, that gave me an idea.

"I will consider it, but an M&A would take a lot of my time."

"I know that."

I didn't even hesitate. I rolled back my shoulders and said, "It would be fair if that were reflected with an extra bonus."

He smiled. "Allison, one of the things I've always loved about you is that you're not afraid to ask for what you deserve. You know how to drive a hard bargain."

I smiled right back, though my heart was pounding in my chest. That would mean additional income. It wasn't something that would be recurring, of course, just for the duration of the project. But M&As could last well up to two years. Hopefully, a judge would see that as a sign that I was truly willing to do anything to give the twins a fantastic life.

Except marry Nick, huh? a voice said at the back of my mind.

Oh, man. I truly hadn't imagined that, had I?

"Send me the NDA and the paperwork, and I'll get back to you."

He nodded. "And I'll think about your request as well."

I knew I wasn't going to get him to actually agree to a bonus right now. He and I worked exceptionally well together. However, asking for a raise always felt like pulling teeth. It frustrated me to no end when he said that a raise wasn't in the budget when the company made record high profits.

After he left my office, I managed to relax, standing and stretching my legs a bit. They'd gotten stiff over the past two hours. I rotated my ankles a few times too. Even though most people took off their shoes while at their desks, I refused to do that. My feet swelled in the summer, so sometimes it was hard to get them back on.

Now that I was alone in my office and the adrenaline had worn off, I was starting to rewind this morning's conversation with Nick. It had been in the back of my mind until now, but suddenly it was front and center again.

"We could get married." His voice resounded clear in my mind.

Goodness. I needed to sit down for this.

I plopped back down into my chair, grabbed my glass of sparkling water with two slices of lemon, and took a hearty sip.

I couldn't wrap my mind around what he was saying, and it was making me jittery.

"Allison, you've got a full day of work. Time to kick ass," I told myself.

But how could I when I couldn't think about anything else?

I took out my phone and messaged him even though my inbox was close to exploding. I needed to double-check. I felt silly typing it, but I sent it before I could change my mind.

Allison: Did we meet this morning, or did I dream about it?

I put my phone down, intending to check my first email until he replied, but he did so right away.

Nick: Yes, we did.

Then he sent another one.

Nick: I know it's crazy.

Allison: Totally.

Nick: So, what do you say I grab a bottle of white wine for tonight? I feel like that conversation might need more than pizza.

That actually made me smile.

Allison: Sure.

Nick: I won't make it until after the twins are asleep, though. I've got a late meeting.

Allison: No problem.

Nick: Anything that would make a shitty Monday be less shitty?

He certainly is husband material.

Where the hell did that thought come from? It was just because of this morning's conversation, I was sure, but I'd never really had someone who cared what my favorite wine was—or anything else for that matter.

Allison: Chocolate.

Since he asked, why not give him an answer?

Nick: I'm on it.

I stared at my phone. Oh yeah, I was looking forward to tonight. Far more than I was willing to admit.

At eight o'clock on the dot that evening, the twins fell asleep. I stood in front of their door for a few minutes, watching them, until my stomach started to rumble.

They'd both had dinner, but I was holding out for pizza. I generally ate after they did anyway. It was easier logistically.

Nick was supposed to arrive in half an hour, so I had some time to refresh myself. I jumped into the shower, quickly rinsing my hair as well. After stepping out, I combed it, planning to let it air dry because it was a gorgeous evening.

Putting on a summery dress that felt much more comfortable than the suit I'd had on at the office, I sprayed on perfume for no reason at all, then decided I could do with some mascara as well. Why I needed it at eight thirty in the evening, I couldn't say, but I didn't want to analyze that too closely.

After I finished, I headed downstairs. I saw a shadow move through the window to the backyard and realized Nick was already out there. I immediately swung the door open.

"Hey," I greeted him.

"Hey." He smiled lazily. "Didn't realize you…"

"Locked the door," I finished for him. "Yeah. Sorry."

"You want us to stay outside?" he asked.

I eyed the bottle of wine and the pizzas. "Sure. I'll grab glasses and plates. Be right back."

Nick had visited frequently since my sister died, so it wasn't the first time I'd noticed how attractive he was. Hell, when Jim first introduced me to him, I'd been very taken with him. But I'd always focused on my career. Up to now, I thought of him only as a friend who was just trying to help me out because the twins were his best friend's kids.

But now?

Goodness. I sucked in a breath.

Nick's eyes were on me. My stomach somersaulted as I headed back inside the house. Grabbing two wineglasses and plates, I hurried outside. Nick was leaning against the table. He'd already opened the boxes and the bottle of wine. That's when I noticed the smaller bag.

I licked my lips. "Yum. That's my chocolate?"

"Yeah. Whatever the lady wants, the lady gets. And I'm not saying that just to beef up my case so you'll take me on as your husband." His words nearly knocked the wind out of my lungs. I let out a deep breath.

"Nick," I murmured as I stepped closer.

I found a spot on his chest to fixate on because I couldn't possibly look him in the eyes. I started to trace his arms. He was wearing a tight shirt, and if I looked very closely, I could see all those muscles.

Way to get sidetracked. Maybe looking him in the eyes *was* the safer option, so I snapped my gaze back up.

"Mm, too soon, I get it. Let's work up to that," he said with a smile.

How was he so unfazed about this?

I swallowed hard. "Sure."

"And maybe a glass of wine will help."

"I want some pizza first, though."

I devoured a slice before Nick even reached for his. He was watching me with a smile.

"What?" I inquired.

"You didn't even ask which one is yours," he taunted.

"Oh, I just assumed that this one was."

"I'm kidding, Allison. I don't have a preference. We can share."

I grinned but then quickly took another bite because I was truly hungry.

I didn't stop at the first slice either; I immediately downed another one, but my nerves weren't settling. I took a few sips of wine, too, hoping that would do the trick, but now that Nick had said the word *husband*, things felt even more real than before.

I put the glass down, unsure where to look. It was too weird not to look at him, but somehow I was even more susceptible to those gorgeous dark eyes than usual.

"Have you thought any more about what I said this morning?" Nick asked.

"Honestly, I had a full day. And every time I thought about it, it seemed even crazier than when you first suggested it." I was speaking in a low voice, although no one could overhear us.

"I know. I actually thought a whole week about it before I even brought it up." His eyes were trained on me—almost as if he was waiting for a reaction.

"Part of me can't even seriously consider it," I admitted. "It could go wrong in so many ways. But on the other hand, Bob and Sophie keep reminding me that they want custody. I don't have time to hope some magic solution comes along. Hugo said he didn't have another silver bullet solution. I mean, this wouldn't be a silver bullet, either, to be fair, but it would increase my chances a lot." My heart was thundering in my chest. "I can't believe there's an actual chance I could lose the twins, that they could be taken away from me." My voice cracked. I hadn't even brought myself to voice this fear until now.

"And they shouldn't be, Allison. They love you. They always have, and you're their cornerstone now. Any further disruption in their lives will only make things more difficult for them, and Jim's parents should realize that. I'm actually kind of surprised that they're taking this action if they're really concerned for the twins."

Nick stepped closer, cupping my face in one hand. His touch was soothing.

"I don't want you to lose them. Hell, I've grown closer to them, too, and really don't want to see them moved to God knows where. They have stability here, and together we could make it even more stable for them. But it has to be fair for you too."

Everything he was saying was so selfless, so kind. I'd always been aware that Nick was drop-dead gorgeous.

"You want me to take out the chocolate now?" he asked in a lighthearted tone. Which of course immediately distracted me.

"No. First the pizza, then the chocolate at the end so I can properly savor it."

"Duly noted." He frowned as he added, "You won't lose them, Allison. No matter what you decide, I'll do whatever it takes to make sure that doesn't happen." He didn't seem lighthearted at all right now. In fact, he sounded very determined. I hadn't heard this tone of voice from him before.

"Apparently you're even willing to marry me," I teased.

"I fucking am." He dropped his hand, taking a step back.

"I'm sorry, I still... This doesn't feel real."

I took another sip of wine and then found my voice. "How would it even work? And for how long?"

"We'd have to ask Hugo that," Nick replied in a measured tone. He took a sip from his glass as well without breaking eye contact. "As for the logistics, I think we'd have enough time to discuss those. I could move here, or we could all go to my place. It's certainly big enough. The twins could each have their own room if they wanted to. If not, they could sleep together and have a separate playroom."

Warmth traveled through me, and it wasn't from the wine. He'd actually thought about making a playroom for the twins. How cute was that?

"Maybe it would be best if we stayed here," I replied. "Less change for them. But I don't have a spare bedroom for you."

Was that a blush creeping up my cheeks? They were definitely hotter than a few seconds ago.

Nick curved his lips up into a smile. "We'll cross that bridge when we come to it." He sounded a little bit smug, almost like he had insider information.

How would it feel to have him here in my house every evening?

"I could sleep in the twins' room. But what would we tell everyone? Our friends and families? God, this is..." I set my glass down. "Yeah, it's time for chocolate now."

"But you didn't finish your pizza yet."

"I know. Still, I need sugary reinforcements."

He laughed, taking out the chocolate. Dark cocoa and raisins—perfect combo. I immediately ate four pieces, carefully chewing. Delicious.

"Right. Now I'm better equipped to think."

Nick laughed. "You're a strange creature."

I grinned at him. "I'm a very logical person. That's why I'm a CFO. But there's not a lot of logic to this. I mean, there is, but you know what I mean." My heart was thundering in my chest. "I don't think we could get around this without actually living in the same place."

"We could ask Hugo. Don't think about it too much, okay? Maybe he'll say it's okay for us to keep separate residences. Though I can't imagine that."

"I doubt that, too, but we'll see." I bit the inside of my cheek. "Let's talk with Hugo first. I mean, this would be legal, right? What if they realize it's just a marriage of convenience? Would that count against me?"

"Allison," Nick whispered. "Relax. I didn't want to cause you even more stress."

"I don't know why I'm suddenly so worked up," I confided, then started to roll back my shoulders. It wasn't helping.

I put a hand at the back of my neck, massaging it.

"It hurts there?" he asked.

"A bit. Whenever I get tense, that spot immediately becomes sore."

He brought his right hand to the back of my neck too. His touch electrified me as he pressed his fingers along the nape. I immediately dropped my own hand, and then he pressed one finger on that same spot.

"Oh," I murmured, closing my eyes. "You're so good at this."

"That's a trigger point."

I took in a deep breath. I couldn't believe how good his touch felt. I wanted more of it. I wanted it everywhere, sore spot or no. This felt...

Oh my God. My eyes flew open. *Did I moan, or do I just think I did?*

Nick took in a sharp breath.

Holy shit. I did.

I started to cough, hoping it would somehow mask the whole thing. Nick moved his chair back, dropping his hand.

Come up with something smart, Allison. Take his mind off it. Distract, distract, distract!

"How did you learn to do trigger-point massage?" I asked, trying to keep my voice blasé, as if I was genuinely interested in this and not just trying to hide that he'd turned me on by massaging the back of my neck. "I thought you just managed the clubs."

"Sometimes, when I bring in people to instruct courses for our trainers, I sit in on them too. I like to check the quality of the teachers and learn new techniques."

"Smart. Well, that really helped. Thank you."

"My pleasure." Yet again, his voice sounded different—rougher. "I have an idea. I'll call Hugo and tell him to see us first thing in the morning."

"Think he'll have time?"

"If we go really early, yes."

I bit the inside of my cheek. "That's a great idea. Otherwise, I'll drive myself crazy. Let me just check with Doreen to see if she can take the twins to daycare. She's had to do it once or twice when I had a meeting out of the office first thing in the morning."

"Perfect. Now, how about we enjoy the rest of the pizza and the chocolate—in whichever order you want," he added with a cheeky smile, "and not talk about this any longer."

"We could try, but I'm not sure."

"Then let's make a deal: whenever one of us brings up the topic—"

"Let me guess, the other one does something outrageous?" I asked.

He grinned. "You've read my mind. See? This will work out perfectly."

Chapter Eight

Nick

We were at Hugo's office at seven thirty the next morning. I'd called him after I left Allison's place, and he agreed to see us before his first client. He asked me what it was about and was shocked as hell when I told him.

He greeted us at the door. "Allison, Nick. Come on in. Allison, it's nice to finally meet you in person."

"Likewise," she said, shaking his hand. She was wearing a suit again, and my imagination was already running wild.

He invited us to sit down. I'd never actually been here before. It was in a redbrick building downtown. His office was very spacious and lawyerly looking with bookshelves everywhere.

"Coffee?" he offered. "I have an espresso machine now."

"Let's get right to it," I said. "We're short on time."

"All right, then."

As we sat down, Hugo said, "I have to say, I was shocked when Nick told me what this was about."

"So, you think it's a bad idea?" Allison asked.

I looked at her intently. She was fiddling her thumbs and had moved forward to the very edge of the seat.

"No, I just wasn't expecting it. When I gave you my advice, I was sincerely hoping that you were already in a relationship. That would have been an easy solution. A lazy one, but lazy solutions are usually the best. Everything else carries too much risk."

Allison looked at me, and I nodded. "You take the lead with the questions," I told her.

"Fire away with anything that's on your mind. Don't hold back," Hugo said. "I'm here to listen to all your worries and tell you if they're legitimate or not."

"Could this backfire in any way? Like if anyone discovered it wasn't for real?" she asked.

He shrugged. "Like any other marriage, it will either work out or it won't. More than half of marriages end up in divorce anyway. If that were to happen after the dust settled in the custody battle, no one could blame you, and it wouldn't negatively impact your keeping the kids." He hesitated. "The grandparents could then make a case against you. But in my experience, once a judge grants custody to someone, they're unlikely to revoke it."

"That leads me to my next question," Allison said. "How long would we have to do this for?"

Hugo placed his hands over the table. "Hard to say. Depends how long the custody battle takes. Could be a few months, could be a year, maybe two. But I can have the divorce papers drafted up and ready to go, so the minute you get custody, we can set the divorce in motion."

She looked at her knees. "And we have to live together?"

I glanced at Hugo, waiting for his reaction.

He nodded once. "It would be for the best. It's hard to make a case of stability if you two live in separate homes. It could work, but I wouldn't advise it."

I turned to face her. "Allison, we can solve that. It's not an insurmountable obstacle."

"What else do you want to know?" Hugo asked.

Allison laughed, looking at the floor. "Sorry. I just can't shake the feeling that it isn't real that we're here, asking these things." She glanced at me. "That Nick would even want this."

Hugo stared at me, and I knew what he was thinking. Why the actual fuck *was* I considering this? We'd been friends for a long time but weren't close enough for him to ask. I could tell when I set up this meeting last night that he'd been wanting to, and that he still did now too.

"For what it's worth," he said, "I think people get married for worse reasons. It's commendable that you two want to make sure that the kids end up with someone who has their best interest at heart. I suggest you two sign a prenup so that there are no issues afterward. The divorce would then simply be a formality."

"All right," Allison murmured. "So, you think this could work? That I would for sure keep custody?"

"It would definitely work in your favor. You'd have a household with two incomes, plus a stable relationship. It's good that you've known Nick for a while. We still have time to decide how we play this for the court. For example, should we say that you two have been together since you first met?"

"That would be at Nora and Jim's wedding," I replied.

Allison shook her head. "That won't work. That was seven years ago, and we only saw each other a few times at birthday parties until they passed away. And I'm sure each of us has dated other people in between."

"Then we could use that as your starting point. You two bonded after the catastrophe and so on." Hugo spoke in a very matter-of-fact tone. Allison winced. I didn't like it either. "Of course, that was only four months ago. But we live in an age where things happen very fast. The situation is unique and could spur a romantic relationship."

Allison finally looked at him. "You're certain there are no drawbacks? That there's no other way I could keep custody?"

"There's always a possibility that you could win in court against your sister's in-laws. I wouldn't discard that. But we'd need to smear them good. It could get nasty," Hugo admitted.

"So we're back to attacking them," she said, sounding distraught.

I hated the stress this was placing on her. The more we discussed the marriage option, the more I could see ways I could help her and make her life a bit easier. And let's face it, it was no hardship on me. I'd live with a beautiful woman and hang out with the two best kids in the world. I could do this for a while.

"Custody battles can be very dirty," Hugo replied. "That's why I don't advise to actually go into battle." He checked his watch. "Okay, I've got to get going. I'm sorry, but I need to jump onto a Zoom meeting."

"Yes, of course," Allison said. "Thank you so much for seeing us this early."

The second we stepped out of the building, Allison sighed, putting a hand to her temple.

"Coffee?" I asked her.

Even though her head was tilted forward, I saw her lips curl up in a smile. It felt like a personal victory.

"Not a bad idea. I skipped it again at home."

"When do you have to be at work?"

"I have a bit of time."

I kept a hand on her back as I led her to the Starbucks down the block.

Even though it was early, it was already warm out. I didn't know why I bothered with suits in summer. They looked good, but I got too damn hot in them.

I took off my jacket and pushed my sleeves to my elbows. I caught Allison watching me. When she noticed me looking at her, she immediately glanced away. I felt victorious again for no apparent reason.

Starbucks was all but empty, so after we got our drinks, I suggested, "Want to sit in here?"

"Sure, let's go to one of those. They look cozy," she said, pointing to the couches.

She sat down on the one farthest from the door, and I lowered myself right next to her. The couch was big, but I wanted this closeness. In Hugo's office, I barely resisted the urge to pull my chair right next to hers.

"It was good that we went to see him. That he put you at ease."

Allison shrugged. "Some things are clearer, but that doesn't mean I'm more at ease."

I nodded. "I know what you mean."

"You do? You seem so blasé about all this. Like you're not even the slightest bit worried about anything."

"It's a gamble. It's definitely crazy. But is it worth it? I think so. And another one of my rules is if something is worth it, I go ahead with it. No matter how complicated or hard things may be down the road."

"That's a fantastic outlook on life. I'm the same, actually, but this is just so... you know, out there that..." She crossed her legs, sipping her coffee. Her skirt rode up a few inches.

I closed my eyes, looking away. The images in my mind had a life of their own. *What the hell is going on?* I opened my eyes, grabbing my cup from the table in front of us and sipping from it.

When I first met Allison at Jim's wedding, I thought she was hot. But I also knew she deserved someone who wanted to have a relationship and the whole nine yards.

Fate sure was funny. Who knew that years later, I'd be carrying her over the threshold into a house with a readymade family to be a husband and dad?

Whoa. That thought made me take a deep breath. Fake or not, suddenly things got real.

"What would we tell our parents or our friends?" she asked, drawing me away from my thoughts.

Good question.

"Whatever we're comfortable with. If we tell them the truth, no one will judge, at least not on my side. Then again, they can't slip up and expose our ruse or this will all go to hell. I'll need to think on that. What about your parents?"

"My parents are very kind," she said with affection in her tone. "These past few months have been extremely hard on them."

"I can imagine. Losing your child must be awful," I said, realizing how much her entire family had been through these last months.

Allison winced. "Let's not talk about that or I'll become really emotional."

"Sure. What else is on your mind?"

"He advised us to live together."

"We'll do what makes the most sense. I can sleep on the couch for as long as it takes. I don't care."

"Nick, my couch is tiny. Your head and feet won't fit on it at the same time."

I leaned in closer, narrowing my eyes. "We'll buy a new couch."

She laughed. "Right, I didn't think about that. Guess we could have a pull-out and take turns sleeping on it. And—" She stopped abruptly and stared at her cup.

"What's on your mind?"

As she took another sip of coffee, I noticed that her cheeks were tinted pink. What was she blushing about?

The mere possibility that her thoughts were as out of control as mine only fueled me more. I was so attracted to this woman that I couldn't think straight. How the hell did I think I could live with her?

"During this time... would we be celibate?" she asked hesitantly. "Or would we have separate lives?"

"Fuck," I exclaimed.

She laughed. "Finally, you're panicking about something. I thought I was the only weird one."

I burst out laughing. "I didn't think about that. We'll play it by ear, I guess."

She raised a brow. "How could we play something like that by ear? It's important."

"Either of those two solutions sucks," I told her openly. "So maybe we could come up with something else."

"Like what?"

"No idea. Hence playing it by ear." The more I thought about it, the more I found those options completely unacceptable. The thought of Allison going on a date with some guy was unthinkable. But being celibate was simply not possible. Slowly, I was starting to realize, there were no other options.

"I can feel you panicking," Allison said, nudging me with her shoulder. She miscalculated the angle, though, because I definitely felt her breast brushing my chest. Her breath caught, and when she gasped lightly, her eyes snapped up.

Swallowing hard, I tilted my head, looking directly at her. She was so damn close, I could smell the coffee on her lips. Those perfect and inviting lips.

"We'll work it out." My voice was so rough, I almost didn't understand what I was saying myself. "The important thing is that the kids stay with you."

"Oh, what will we tell the kids?" she whispered.

Her chest was still rising up and down in labored breaths. Clearly the nearness was affecting her, and that just pumped my ego.

I was such a bastard. I was telling this woman that she could count on me, that I was willing to marry her so she could get custody of the twins, yet at the same time, I was fantasizing about making her mine and enjoyed the way my touch rattled her.

"This will confuse them," Allison added.

"Yeah, there's no way around that. Us living together and telling people that we're married, yet at the same time sort of living separate lives, is fucked up. As a kid who's been in a fucked-up family situation, that doesn't sit right by me."

Her eyes softened. "They'd love having you at the house. They constantly ask when you're coming over. I know having you as a dad, or at least a father figure, will be really easy for them to adjust to. Are you ready for that?"

"Fuck yes! I care about them a lot. And even after the divorce, I'd still be around—I'd make sure of it. I'll spoil them to the moon and back," I promised.

"That makes two of us. Before, spoiling them was my job, since I'm their aunt. But I can't seem to get out of the habit."

"So what? I think you can spoil kids and make sure they have a good head on their shoulders at the same time."

"True." Seemed like she needed more convincing.

"That's what my grandparents always did. Granted, we were older when we actually met them, so it was a different situation, but they balanced that very well."

There was a pause, and then Allison asked, "How do you think your grandparents would take this?" She moved a bit farther away from me—another sign that my nearness affected her.

"They're usually very supportive, but they don't condone deception."

She scoffed. "What a good word to describe this."

"I have no doubt that they'd be supportive, no matter their opinion. But lying to them would be hard."

"It's good that you can count on your family's support."

I blew out a heavy breath. "It wasn't always like this. For the longest time, there were two separate groups: my brothers and me and our half brothers. Two of them preferred to pretend we didn't exist, and I don't blame them. They were older when everything started. They had a front-row seat to the whole thing and what it did to their mother."

"Oh," Allison whispered. "Did she ever recover? Is she okay now?"

"Unfortunately, she got sick and passed away shortly after."

She winced. "That's terrible. Poor boys."

"Exactly."

"I'm almost afraid to ask... but how is your mom?"

I grinned. "She's living her best life, actually. She's traveling the world, doing odd jobs, mostly teaching yoga and Pilates. My brothers and I do take care of her financially, but she insists on having at least some income of her own."

"You're good sons."

"We try to be. She deserves the world. Things were difficult for her even before things came to light. Actually, I think they might have been even more difficult before because she was struggling to keep up with all our expenses."

"What do you mean? Your father wasn't contributing?"

I shook my head. "Only minimally. He gave her a bullshit story about his father, our grandfather, controlling the finances of the company and him being on a very strict leash. So she worked two jobs." Her own parents had cut off contact with her because they didn't approve of her having children without being married.

"But your father is a *Whitley*." The way she said our last name made me feel funny. There were pluses and minuses to the legacy for sure.

"Yeah," I said through gritted teeth. "Unfortunately. Thankfully, he lives in Australia now. We don't deal much with him. You know, when you first mentioned that you're willing to go to any lengths to get custody of the kids, I started thinking about my own parents. The whole situation. How my father lost interest in all his sons after the scandal. How he just up and left."

"Oh, Nick."

I had no idea why I'd even brought this up. She didn't need to know. It had been a long time ago.

"So, you grew up without him?" she asked.

"Yes. In retrospect, it was probably better. Things were tense with everyone even with him out of the picture. But as a kid, it felt terrible. Like we weren't wanted, didn't matter, and no one was in our corner."

Her shoulders dropped. "That's a really terrible thing to do to your kid."

"We'll make sure the twins never feel that way," I said, deciding to stop bringing up negative stuff. What was up with that? I rarely spoke about the past. It just made no sense. It was part of the past, and it wasn't affecting the present in any way.

Allison smiled from ear to ear. "This is batshit crazy. We can't think through every scenario and foresee everything that can go wrong. But for the first time since I got their email about trying to get custody, I'm feeling hopeful. And I should tell them that we're..."

"Engaged." The word felt completely foreign. "You should definitely tell them." I shifted on the couch so I could lean closer. I put a hand on the backrest, bringing my mouth almost to her ear. "I promise you, Allison, we've got this."

"You're awfully sure of yourself!" She was back to teasing me, which was a good sign. She'd been so tense in Hugo's office that I wasn't certain that she'd relax at all today.

I flashed her a quick grin. "Always. It's the secret to my success."

"What is?"

"Blindly believing in my ability to achieve something. It's served me very well, and I'm sure we can apply the same strategy here."

"Nick, this isn't a business project."

"Nah, it's far more than that. But we've got this, Allison," I repeated. "You and me. We've got this."

Chapter Nine

Allison

I was in a daze for the next few days. Even though Nick and I had agreed to move forward with our outlandish idea, I felt stuck. But on Tuesday morning, I found the courage and emailed Jim's parents. It took me well over half an hour to draft it, and I ended up deleting half of it. In the end, my email was short and sweet.

Hi. I've been so busy, as you can imagine, so I didn't have time to reply to your previous email. I think we should discuss it. By the way, I have news. I just got engaged.

That was it. I didn't want to give them any details. They'd ask later for sure, but for now, this would do.

I pressed Send before I could waste even more time drafting the email. It was going to be a shit show anyway.

Afterward, I stared at the screen for a few seconds, then decided to inform Nick that I'd officially told someone.

Allison: I did it. I told Jim's parents that I'm engaged.
Nick: That's great. It'll all work out. You'll see.

His positivity was endearing. I didn't share it yet, but I was grateful that at least one of us was taking this in stride.

I started to reply to him, but before I managed to type anything, my inbox pinged.

Holy shit. Jim's parents had already responded.

What do you mean, engaged? We never even knew you had a boyfriend. We're coming to Boston this weekend and want to meet him.

As the words sank in, breathing became a bit more difficult. I put a hand on my chest, trying to calm down. I was used to a high-pressure environment. In fact, I thrived on it. It was one of the reasons why I'd chosen finance. But this was something else entirely.

You're a damn CFO, Allison. You've managed situations of crisis. You can deal with Jim's parents coming for a weekend to meet your so-called fiancé.

What had I been thinking? This was a terrible idea. I didn't even know if Nick had time on the weekend. Maybe he already had plans.

I was just about to tell them that they couldn't expect everyone to change their schedule according to their whims but then paused, remembering what Hugo told us. It was better not to fight. I decided to double-check with Nick first.

Allison: They already replied that they want to come this weekend to meet you. Are you available? I'll tell them to fuck off otherwise.

Typing that felt fantastic.

Nick: I'll make time. Don't worry.

Just like that? This man was something else.

Nick: Just let me know when and where and I'll be there.

It was starting to sink in that this was real. I tried to figure how it would work out. Nick would be introducing himself as my fiancé, and then what? I'd probably have to explain how it happened in the first place.

I was already starting to get overwhelmed, but I was determined not to lose my nerve, so I emailed them back.

Sure. We'll set something up. Maybe a lunch or dinner. Next time, I would appreciate a little bit of a heads-up if you plan a visit to Boston. It's a stroke of luck that we're available this weekend.

There. That didn't sound too bad.

After sending it, I finally focused on work. I'd signed the NDA last week, and Derek had sent me all the prep files to look over. Usually, I wouldn't even hesitate and would tell him I was ready to sink my teeth into this. But right now I had a lot to consider, such as how much extra time this would take and if the remuneration was fair. Derek still hadn't said anything in regard to that.

At lunch, my mind slid right back to Bob and Sophie's visit. Nick and I had to figure out some details, so I texted him again.

Allison: We need to talk before the weekend. They'll want to know details.

Nick: We'll find a plausible story. But I don't have time to meet up this week in person, sorry. I'm traveling, visiting possible new locations.

I pouted. *What? I'm not going to see him this week?*

Jesus, Allison. Where'd that come from? Of course the man is busy.

Nick: But we can talk on the phone.

Allison: Deal. Let's do that. I want us to be prepared by the weekend.

Nick: Then call me after the twins go to bed.

Allison: I'll probably call this evening at 8:30.

Nick: It's a date.

My pulse sped up, and my mouth was suddenly dry, as were my lips. *Allison, that's just a figure of speech.*

I had to get myself under control because things were only going to get more difficult from now on. I couldn't heat up every time he touched me or looked at me in a way I assumed was flirty. Because until now, he hadn't *actually* flirted with me. I was certain it was all in my head.

I breezed through the rest of my activities for the day, energized, knowing that I was going to talk to Nick tonight. Date or not, just knowing that I was going to hear his voice made me feel better.

Unfortunately, later that evening, it took longer than usual to get the twins to bed. I ended up not calling Nick until nine o'clock, settling into my favorite corner of the couch as my phone rang.

"Good evening," Nick answered.

"Sorry I'm late."

"Don't worry." I heard the clatter of cutlery in the background.

"Are you eating now?"

"Yes. I ordered room service."

I frowned. "Nick, I feel guilty now. You didn't go out to eat because we'd planned this call."

"Nah. Whenever I'm traveling, I prefer room service in the evenings."

"Are you sure you want to do this tonight?"

"Yes. I already have a few ideas."

"Do tell, because I'm a numbers person. My imagination is limited." We both laughed at that, but he'd soon find out how true that was.

"We'll tell them that we met a few times over the years at Jim and Nora's various events, like barbeques and such. We don't need to go into too much detail. They just have to understand that we knew each other from before the funeral."

"That sounds good."

"And then... well, forgive me for being so crass, but I think this will shock them into not asking too many details. I can say that when we started to hang out more after that, I couldn't resist making a move on you because you're so damn hot."

I laughed. "That isn't crass."

"That's the toned-down version. The original one was 'you're so hot that I kept fantasizing about taking you to bed the first time I came to your house,' but I think that's too much information."

My heart nearly jumped out of my chest. That sounded almost real. Like it hadn't been made up. My entire body was burning. I swallowed hard, regaining my wits slowly.

"Too much for elderly ears for sure."

He chuckled. "Thought so. We can say that we started spending more time together. I kept coming to the house, one thing led to another, and we now know that we can't live without each other."

"That sounds surprisingly simple. And you've known the kids for a while, so it's not as though you're some strange man coming into their home."

"Exactly. I don't think we need to complicate it more than that."

"The simpler our story, the easier it is to remember. Should we decide on...?" I couldn't bring myself to say it.

"What?" Nick inquired.

I hoped he would get the hint, but clearly he didn't. "You know, D-day."

"I didn't think about that."

"And about what kind of ceremony we want."

"Fuck, I didn't think about that at all."

"I can work out some details. I'm guessing both of us would want to just get it over with at city hall, right?"

"What an enthusiastic way to put it," Nick teased.

I sighed. "I'm sorry. I know that sounded very terse."

"No, I'm joking. Yeah, city hall sounds good. Are you going to tell your parents?"

"Of course. I can't keep something like this from them. Do you want to keep it from yours? I couldn't imagine that working out."

"Nah, there are no secrets in my family. And as I said, they'll be supportive. Allison, don't fret about city hall right now. It depends when they have free slots. For now, it's all about meeting Bob and Sophie, right?"

"That's right. I always like to think two steps ahead, but I should start to accept that that's not really possible here."

"That's my girl."

I liked the sound of that so much. *My girl.*

"I'm sure I'll make a mistake or two, but this is not about having the perfect story," he continued. "Even if it were real, enough people would question why we're hurrying. Let's roll with the punches."

"I'm trying. God, I'm tense."

"The same spot as last time?"

"Yeah."

"Pity I'm not there to relieve the pressure."

I swallowed hard.

"But soon I will be." His tone was teasing but also sinful. I pressed my thighs together as heat flooded my body. I was a goner.

"I'm going to take a hot bath. That usually relaxes all of my tense points."

"That's right, you like hot baths."

"Why do you say it like that?" I asked.

"I figure that knowing some things about you won't hurt."

"Oh, right. You think that'll come up in conversation?"

"No, but see, for me to actually come up with stories, it helps if I have something to base them on."

"Makes sense."

"Well, I'll leave you to enjoy your dinner. I'm going to relax."

"When are you back?" I asked as I got up from the couch.

"Thursday night. We could meet up Friday if you want, so we can prepare a bit more."

"Actually, I think they want to meet Friday evening."

"It's going to be all good," he assured me.

"You're awfully sure of yourself."

"I told you, it's the way I go through life."

"Usually, I'm not this uncertain and nervous. Even though I've done deals with hundreds of millions of dollars involved."

"This is different, Allison," Nick said quietly. "It's about the kids. Different stakes are at hand."

"Exactly..."

"But don't worry. We'll be very convincing as a couple in front of Bob and Sophie."

His tone had changed slightly, and goose bumps broke out on my skin.

What exactly did Nick have in mind?

Chapter Ten
Allison

Friday came around much faster than I wanted. Bob and Sophie were coming to dinner at the house. They'd scoffed when I told them that we were eating at six o'clock, but I didn't back down. I wanted to make sure I had plenty of time for the twins to get to bed, and I wasn't going to change their schedule just because their grandparents didn't like to eat early.

Nick arrived at five thirty with takeout. I'd had a hellish day at work and had zero motivation to cook. He brought Italian because the twins loved spaghetti with meatballs. From the second he arrived, I was on pins and needles.

I was in the yard, keeping an eye on the twins. I'd already put plates and cutlery on the table. Nick came up behind me, putting both hands on my waist.

"You're nervous," he whispered in my ear.

"Very." Feeling his body close to mine seemed to take that edge off. Of course, it also put me on edge in an entirely different way, so I wasn't sure if it was too productive. But I preferred being on fire because of a gorgeous man rather than full of anxiety because of Bob and Sophie.

"We've got this. Trust me." He kept saying that, but somehow, I didn't believe it. "By the way, I've got something for you."

He shoved one hand into his pocket, bringing out a gorgeous ring. My jaw dropped. It was a large rectangular diamond.

"You're going to need this, fiancée."

"Nick! This must have cost a fortune. Can you take it back... later?"

"Don't you worry about any of that."

"But I—"

"We're here. How do we get in?" Bob's voice came from the front yard.

"Quick, put it on," I whispered, and Nick immediately slid the ring on. It was a strange feeling to see an engagement ring on my finger and know it wasn't real.

Clearing my throat, I yelled, "The gate's open. Just walk through and then unlock the baby gate, and you can come straight into the backyard." The yard went around the house, but I'd wanted to separate the front from the back. That way, the twins could roam around freely when we were out here and wouldn't disappear from my sight.

This is it. Showtime.

Bob and Sophie came into view a few seconds later. The twins stopped chasing each other, glancing at the newcomers, but there was no flicker of recognition on their faces. I explained to them that their grandparents were visiting, but... yeah. I didn't blame the poor kids. The last time they'd seen them had been at the funeral, and they hadn't held the twins or tried to comfort them even once. It made my blood boil that they now thought they should take them when they were practically strangers. After the accident, I'd commuted with the kids from my sister's house before I brought them to my place permanently. Fortunately, they'd adjusted quite well.

"Bob, Sophie, you know Nick."

The two of them looked like they were about to go to the opera or something. Bob was wearing a suit, and Sophie had on an elegant gown. Yes, practically a floor-length dress.

"We've met a few times when Jim and I were in college," Nick reminded them.

"Yes, Nick *Whitley*," Bob said appreciatively.

I barely held back a snort. Of course he was impressed by the Whitley name. Bob was a bit of a snob, from what Nora had told me.

"Are we keeping you from an event?" Nick asked.

"What do you mean?" Sophie replied.

Nick pointed at their clothing before I could warn him that they probably dressed like that thinking they'd have the upper hand. It was all a psychological game was my guess.

"Oh, no. We just like to be put together," Sophie said.

Nick whistled. "Babe, we're severely underdressed. Then again, this is just eating Italian in the backyard." He put an arm around my shoulders. The contact warmed me immediately.

Sophie kept looking between us.

"Annie, Jack," I called the twins. "Come here, you two." Turning to Bob and Sophie, I said, "You'll need something more comfortable if you want to play around with these two. Want me to bring you something to change into?"

"Goodness, no. I was hoping the nanny could take care of them while we talk."

I frowned. "The nanny?"

"Yes. Who's taking care of them?"

"I am."

Sophie snorted. "Don't be ridiculous. The full-time nanny."

"There is no full-time nanny," Nick said in a cutting voice. Sophie flinched.

"They go to daycare in the morning, and I spend the evening and weekends with them," I explained.

Sophie cocked a brow. "Really? You think a daycare is better than a nanny?"

So, this is how it's going to go, huh? I wanted to follow Hugo's advice and keep things calm, not be argumentative. Even though I was tempted to do just that... with a baseball bat if possible. *Keep things simple.*

"They enjoy their daycare. It's good for their development. Interaction with other kids is healthy for them, and they're learning new skills. It's far better than staying cooped up in here all day."

"Hmm," Sophie said. "You could at least have someone look after them in the evenings. What are we supposed to do now? How should we talk?"

"We'll manage. Don't you worry," I said dryly. "We can say anything we want in front of them." I almost chuckled at my last comment, knowing that wasn't what Sophie meant at all.

Annie and Jack approached us shyly. Jack held his hands up for Nick to take him in his arms. It was endearing how much these two liked him. Without hesitating, Nick bent at the waist and lifted Jack.

Be still my heart. They were so cute that I wanted to take a picture of them right now.

"Kids, do you want to say hi to your grandparents?" I encouraged.

Annie didn't say anything for a few beats. Then she said, "Hi."

"Hi," Bob replied. Sophie just nodded.

"Jack doesn't talk much yet."

"But he talks to you, right? They both do?" Sophie asked.

"Of course." I stroked Annie's hair and patted Jack's cheek so they could feel my love for them. "But they're shy when they meet new people."

"We're not new," Sophie said briskly. "We're their grandparents."

I truly couldn't believe any judge would give them custody, but whatever.

Taking a deep breath, I decided to change topics. "I hope you like spaghetti and meatballs."

"We should have met at a restaurant," Sophie said. "Just the four of us."

Clearly it was time to set some boundaries. I rolled my shoulders back and said, "No, Sophie. You informed me a few days ago that you wanted to visit. You're lucky we had time."

"We could still go to a restaurant. Where we'll be served some proper food."

This woman! It wasn't as though I hadn't met them before. Nora used to tell me horror stories of how they could be toward her, but after all that happened, you'd think they'd be a little kinder. Obviously not.

I guess a zebra really can't change its stripes.

"No, Sophie, we'll eat here. I told you that the twins' bedtime routine starts at seven. There's no time to get to a restaurant, be served, and get back home by then."

"Well, that's why you should have planned ahead for our visit," Sophie pressed on.

"This is outrageous," Bob said, and that pissed me off.

Annie went right to her chair, and I helped her into it. Jack was still in Nick's arms.

"It's really not. You came here uninvited. So, you'll have dinner with us or go by yourselves to a restaurant, and we can plan another time to meet in advance when it works for everyone involved." My tone was final.

Sophie opened her mouth, but Nick interrupted her. "I suggest we start dinner. We won't be able to entertain you for long. Allison already told you that, but we'd appreciate more of a heads-up."

Sophie grunted but didn't say anything.

Oh, so she's only mouthy with me, huh? That's interesting.

Nick lowered Jack into his chair before he came over and put an arm around my shoulders. "Need me to get anything from the kitchen, babe?" he whispered in my ear, loud enough for everyone to hear. The skin on my whole body simmered when he called me babe. Why did I like it so much?

I shook my head. "We've got everything we need. Thank you."

Bob and Sophie looked absolutely ridiculous in their outfits as they sat on my chairs and tried to eat spaghetti without splashing themselves with sauce. As a result, they took a long-ass time to actually eat. We didn't manage to make much conversation because Annie and Jack both needed my assistance with their food. Even so, they made a mess of themselves and of my shirt, of course. I looked like I'd been in a crime scene.

Nick laughed. "Want to trade spots so you can eat?" he asked when we were halfway through the meal.

Looking down, I realized I'd barely touched my plate. I smiled at him because I knew it was a genuine question, not for Bob and Sophie's sake.

"I'm good. I'll eat once these two are in bed."

"Then why didn't you tell us to come afterward?" Sophie said, sounding exasperated.

I swallowed hard, looking straight at her. "Considering the reason you contacted me in the first place, I thought you wanted to spend time with them." I didn't want to say *custody* in front of the kids or even insinuate that she might want to take them away because they'd understand that, and it would stress them out.

Sophie pressed her lips together. Bob gave her a sharp look.

The rest of the evening went by awkwardly. No one was saying anything, but that was probably because Annie and Jack were making enough noise on their own. I was used to it, and to some extent, so was Nick. Bob and Sophie looked as if they wanted to bolt out of here.

That also gave me a little hope. Maybe after tonight, they'd abandon their stupid idea altogether. Then maybe Nick and I wouldn't have to go through with the marriage.

"I'm going to get these two to bed," I said at seven. "And then I'll come right back down. It shouldn't take me long." I threw Nick an apologetic glance. He gave me a half smirk, and I knew exactly what it meant: *"I've got this."*

And I was certain he did.

The twins were actually excited for their bedtime routine, which rarely happened. They usually liked to stay up for as long as possible. It wasn't even eight by the time they were both in their beds.

"We love you," Annie said, and my heart grew twice its size in a split second. I was sitting at the edge of her bed. Jack got out of his and came to us as well, lying down next to his sister. They both cuddled me.

"I love you both so much," I said and leaned forward, kissing Jack's cheek, then Annie's before sitting up again.

It was so strange that Sophie had no interest in joining me when I offered for her to help put her grandchildren to bed. It was obvious they weren't your typical grandparents.

"To the moon?" Annie asked because I often told them that.

"Yes. To the moon and back."

"So, if you love us to the sun and back, it's more?"

"That's right. I love you to the sun and back," I corrected, tapping her little nose with my finger, and she giggled.

Annie yawned, and so did Jack. They were usually less tired on Fridays, but this time they went out like a light before I even left the room. I'd been afraid that Sophie was going to say something to upset them while we were having dinner. I could finally relax. Sort of.

Now it was time to face the music.

I rolled my shoulders as I went down the staircase. I stopped on the top step to glance at the ring Nick purchased and admired it. It was beautiful. If this were a real engagement, I would have been thrilled with this ring. But it wasn't, and I needed to keep that in mind. One day, with someone else, it would be, but not today.

As I hit the bottom steps, I caught wind of the conversation.

"The fitness branch is quite popular," Bob was saying.

"And you plan to grow it even more?" Sophie asked.

"Exactly. I want to open five more locations throughout the country," Nick replied.

"And you have shares in the other companies belonging to Whitley Industries?" Bob inquired.

I stepped out and said, "I'm back. The twins are asleep."

The mood changed instantly. Bob looked at Sophie, clearly giving her the lead. She narrowed her eyes as I sat next to Nick.

"Come on, babe, sit on my lap. We don't have to keep the PDA to a minimum now that the kids are in bed." He gave Bob and Sophie a lazy smile. "You don't mind, do you?"

Sophie bristled. She looked very much like she did mind. So I did exactly what Nick suggested and sat on his lap instead.

I immediately realized it wasn't the best idea. Especially when Nick put an arm around my waist and pulled me even closer to him. My back was flat against his chest. Could he tell that my body temperature was going up? That my pulse was racing like mad? I had to get used to this. I needed to put a wall between us, but right now, I couldn't.

"How long has this been going on?" Sophie asked. "Because we didn't hear a word from Jim and Nora about it."

"Ah, well," Nick said, sounding thoroughly relaxed, "they wouldn't have had much to say about us because we barely knew each other."

Chapter Eleven

Allison

"We only saw each other sporadically, at the occasional birthday," I said, playing off Nick.

"It was only after the funeral," he continued, "that we started growing closer."

"That's not such a long time ago. Certainly not enough to get married," Bob said sternly.

"Not really any of your business," Nick said.

Ha! I loved that he was using that bossy tone.

Both looked as if Nick had slapped them.

"So when is this... this marriage going to happen?" Sophie said, and I cringed. We should have discussed this more.

"We'll see," Nick replied. "Depends on when city hall has time."

"Well, we definitely want to be there," she continued, and I narrowed my eyes.

"It's going to be close friends and family, Sophie." Then I rolled my shoulders back. "I'm sorry to say, but you and Bob are neither of that to me."

"We are the twins' family," Bob said through gritted teeth.

Yeah, and there was no way past that. In case they won custody, which would totally destroy me, I wanted to be able to visit the little ones. I couldn't just throw Bob and Sophie out without thinking about the repercussions even though I truly wanted to.

"We'll let you know when we have more details," I assured them.

"And where will you two live?" Sophie went on.

"I'll move in here with Allison and the kids."

"In this tiny house?"

"It's in a fantastic neighborhood," I said. "And it's a decent size."

"The twins don't even have their own bedrooms," Sophie retorted.

Nick chuckled. "Sophie, I bunked with my brothers until we were much older. It's going to be a while before they need their own rooms. If we need more space, I have a six-bedroom penthouse in Back Bay."

He said that nonchalantly, but Bob's eyes bulged. They might not be from Boston, but they knew property prices around here.

"We don't want to relocate them again because they're comfortable here and they've already been through a lot," I informed them.

"So, you're going to live in two separate places?" Sophie asked. Boy, she was sly.

"No, Sophie. As I just said, I'll move in with Allison. I am, however, looking at renting out my home in the interim until we decide whether we want to sell it or move into something bigger. It's not that big of a deal to me. Home is where my wife and kids are."

And I swooned. This was exactly what I would want in a husband. Nick would definitely make his real wife very happy one day.

"You could have just moved into the mansion with the kids," Sophie said.

I cringed. "There is no way I could have covered that mortgage."

Bob smiled triumphantly.

I glanced over at Sophie, who looked like she had shit under her nose and couldn't stand the smell anymore. Neither of them was bringing up the custody issue, but I wasn't going to force it. What could we talk about anyway? I was afraid that if the subject did come up, I'd lose my cool.

Nick had one hand on my waist and started stroking my arm with the other one. The gesture seemed almost absentminded, a reflex. And I loved it.

"Sophie, I think it's time for us to go," Bob finally suggested.

Relief flooded me. This hadn't been as bad as I'd thought. I'd imagined that they'd stay here for hours and confront me about taking the kids. But I should have known better. Nora always said that Bob and Sophie rarely communicated face-to-face. They liked to hit you over the head with "advice" via phone calls and text messages once they were back home.

As the two rose to their feet, Nick moved me around on his knees so I was sitting sideways.

"Will you look at that, babe? We'll have the rest of the evening for ourselves." He wiggled his eyebrows, and I felt my face flush.

A devilish smile appeared on his face. He was up to something, but what?

Just then, he kissed me. Heat spread through me like wildfire. I kissed him right back because I desperately needed it. His mouth was hot, and the kiss was completely shameless, Nick swirling his tongue seductively around my mouth. I couldn't get enough, and then he pulled me even closer so my ass was right across his cock. I nearly moaned.

Is that a zipper or a hard-on? Hell, there was no way to confuse the two. It was definitely the latter. Knowing I did that to him fueled me even more.

The sound of someone clearing their throat broke through our make-out session. I realized Bob and Sophie were still here.

Oh, shit.

Two things dawned on me right then.

One, the PDA had been for their benefit.

Two, I'd completely forgotten that. I'd practically climbed him because I'd wanted to.

I turned around, smiling at them.

Sophie was looking at my mouth with utter dismay. I figured it meant my skin was red from Nick's kissing. Was it odd that I was proud of it?

"Sorry, we lost our heads," Nick said. "Newly engaged and all. I'm sure you can understand."

He was barely holding back laughter, and I wasn't far from bursting into guffaws myself. I was willing to bet half my savings that Bob and Sophie hadn't so much as kissed in decades.

"We'll be going," Sophie said curtly. "It was nice seeing you again, Nick. We look forward to the wedding invitation."

That sounded ominous.

Neither of us bothered to walk them to the front. They could see themselves out.

I only went after them a few seconds later to close the safety gate for the kids so I wouldn't forget to do it in the morning.

While I secured the gate, I became deeply aware that I was now alone with Nick. My body was still humming from that kiss. We hadn't discussed how things like this would work. How often would we have to do that?

I didn't want to overthink all of that now, though. I was still a bit in a daze as I walked back to him.

He was sitting in the same spot, smiling lazily.

"That went well, didn't it?" He sounded smug and full of himself.

I grinned. "All in all, I think it was a success."

"I wanted to throw them out a few times but managed to restrain myself."

"Funny, I had that urge too."

I felt so much more at ease now. I walked right up to him and then realized I couldn't sit back on his lap. Stopping myself just as I was about to, I abruptly turned to the table as if that had been my destination the whole time. Only there wasn't anything for me to do because Nick had actually cleared the table while I was up with the twins.

He rose to his feet, and the side of his thigh brushed my ass. I straightened up instantly as a current of heat went through me. I was in huge trouble.

"I loved their faces after we kissed," he whispered.

I turned around and smiled. "You were very convincing."

"Of course. I can't half-ass a kiss. Not when the stakes are that high."

His comment disappointed me. What was up with that?

"Right," I said.

Nick tilted my chin up, holding it with two fingers. The contact singed me. "All good, Allison. Are you worried?"

"I'm wondering if there's any chance that they'll change their minds so we won't have to go through with this. They barely interacted with the twins."

His eyes instantly changed. They went cold as he dropped his hand. "Don't remind me. I'll have a word with Hugo. I truly can't believe anyone would hand those two custody. I can't believe they even want it."

"Maybe they will change their minds. Maybe it was just a whim, and now that they've seen the twins in action, they've realized how much work it is. Of course, I'm sure she's planning on hiring help. I mean, she didn't even want to help put them to bed!"

Nick looked at me intensely, then nodded. "I was going to tell my family about our decision this weekend, but I can certainly hold off until we have more news from Bob and Sophie."

My disappointment only grew. Why? Because I didn't have to fake being married to Nick? I couldn't understand what was happening to me.

"Thanks a lot for tonight. Everything was amazing: the spaghetti, the way you handled them."

"The kiss?" he suggested.

"Nick!"

"Come on. We have to talk about it. It'll be weird if we don't."

I swallowed hard, laughing nervously. I felt like it was weird already, but clearly I was the only one.

"I didn't mean to blindside you," he continued. "I didn't even plan it. I just thought it would add a nice touch, you know?"

I nodded.

"And we need to talk about the other thing."

"What thing?" I was genuinely confused as I snapped my gaze up to him.

His eyes were playful as he tilted his head. "Don't tell me you didn't feel it. That would be a complete blow to my ego."

I gasped, covering my mouth with my hand. "Nick."

"In my defense, it was just my body's reaction."

I shook my head. "You really don't have to explain yourself."

Could he not see that I was already blushing like mad? Who talked about these things out loud? I sure didn't.

"I'd like to say that if we have to fake more kisses, I'll keep it under control, but I don't like to make false promises."

I laughed nervously. "I'm not sure what to say."

"I just wanted to bring it up to clear the air."

I ran a hand through my hair, licking my lips. I wanted to fan myself even though the evening wasn't even that hot. I wasn't sure this had cleared the air at all, but obviously Nick was built differently than me.

I yawned. "Thanks for bringing dinner too."

His eyes sparked once again. "You didn't pay attention, did you?"

"To what?"

"I brought something extra just for you. I put it in the fridge."

"What is it?"

"Chocolate. I figured you might need the reinforcement tonight."

Oh my goodness, I could truly kiss this man.

No! There would be no more kissing. In fact, if things went the way I hoped and Bob and Sophie gave up, there would be no kissing Nick Whitley ever again.

But I didn't like that thought at all either.

"I'll get it, and we can share."

"Actually," Nick said, "I need to go."

"Oh."

Why did I keep getting more disappointed as the evening went by? What did I expect? That he'd stay the entire night with me? The man had been traveling all week. He probably wanted to go home and relax. Or he wanted to go out on the town and have fun.

It was on the tip of my tongue to ask him what his plans were for the rest of the evening, but it was none of my business.

"Let me know if Bob and Sophie say something, okay?"

"Sure. They probably won't reply anytime soon, though. Have fun tonight," I added, hoping he'd give me a hint regarding what he was up to.

"I definitely will."

Well, what does that mean? Is he going on a date?

No, I couldn't think about that. My whole body rejected the idea. My stomach sank, and my heart felt heavy. Would it be like this when we had to move in together as well? I couldn't imagine feeling like crap every time he wanted to do something on his own.

Don't get ahead of yourself, Allison. Most likely you can forget this whole crazy idea because moving in together probably won't be necessary at all.

"Good night, Allison." He tilted forward, and for a split second, I was certain he was going to kiss me again. My entire body geared up for it. Then he brought his lips to my cheek. It burned where he kissed me. He scratched my skin lightly with his five-o'clock shadow, and when I shuddered, I hoped to God he didn't notice it.

After he straightened up, my cheek was still on fire. "You, too, Nick."

I watched him walk away and sighed. Damn, he even had a sexy walk and a sexier backside. Under the porch light, I caught the glimmer of the diamond he'd given me. *Temporarily, Allison—get it together.*

Wow, there were no two ways about it. Nick Whitley was an absolutely gorgeous man—who might or might not become my fake husband.

Chapter Twelve
Nick

On Saturday morning, I woke up later than usual. It had been a long week, and yesterday I caught up with a college friend who was in town for the day, and we stayed out until late into the night. I was glad I caught him as he was passing through.

My family was having a picnic today at Maddox and Gabe's hotel, forty minutes outside the city, if the weather held. If not, we'd eat indoors at their gourmet restaurant.

As I got out of bed, my thoughts went back to last evening at Allison's. Bob and Sophie were exactly as unpleasant as I remembered them. The whole thing had been difficult to get through, but kissing Allison had been such a damn highlight. I'd go through an entire dinner with Bob and Sophie again if it meant I got to kiss her. I'd been looking forward to the moment when I'd have an opportunity to do it again. I was sure one would rise occasionally. After all, it came with the description of fake fiancé.

After getting out of the shower, I checked my phone to see if everyone was already on the way. First, I saw a message from Allison, then realized she'd sent me a picture. No, a screenshot of an email.

Hi, Allison. It was good to see you and Nick yesterday. Don't think that changes our plans to file for custody. I look forward to your wedding.

Allison: ...

Indeed, there was nothing else to add.

Fucking Bob and Sophie. I didn't understand what their game was. I distinctly remembered Jim telling me that his parents weren't very involved in the twins' lives, that they'd rather do anything else other than take care of Annie and Jack. But their motives didn't matter. People did shitty things all the time. I'd learned a long time ago not to waste time guessing why someone did what they did.

I texted her back quickly.

Nick: Then we'll go ahead with the plan.

Allison: Looks like it.

Nick: I'll tell the family today.

I dressed in jeans and a polo shirt before leaving the penthouse. Getting used to a smaller space would be a challenge. Allison's house was cozy, but it'd been years since I'd lived in anything smaller than four bedrooms. I only needed one, but I liked the flexibility of having a home office and spare rooms. I even had one with a pool table. But I could give up the pool table and everything else to make sure that Annie and Jack wouldn't be carted off to the middle of fucking nowhere by their grandparents.

I'd have to seriously think about what to do with this place in the interim. I didn't want to sell it. And I didn't really like the idea of renting it out and having someone else live here either.

Just then, a genius idea came to mind: I'd put it up for rent but ask for a very high price so no one actually took it.

To make things work, I'd probably need to live with Allison and the kids for at least a year, maybe two.

Wow. Two years. Was I ready to put my life on hold like that?

I had to be.

I arrived in Essex right on time. The parking lot of the hotel was full, so it was impossible to see who else from the family was here.

Gabe and Maddox had done a fantastic job with the space. When they first told me they'd applied to the city to open a hotel, I'd been wary because both of them had separate businesses too. But they made it work. They'd initially planned to open it somewhere else, but then we got wind that Dad wanted to snatch up this property, and there was no way in hell we wanted him back anywhere near Boston. Fortunately, my brothers decided to buy it first. It had driven Dad right back to Australia, where he was also working in the hotel industry. He'd stayed there ever since, and I, for one, hoped we'd heard the last of him.

I headed straight to the huge backyard that went around the building. They had an outdoor area for guests too. The picnic was in the section that had previously been an adventure park that belonged to Maddox's fiancée, Cami. She'd been against selling the business to him in the beginning. I thought my brother would fail to convince her, but eventually he did—and then some.

Quite a few members of the family had already arrived. The picnic was very informal. They'd brought out wooden benches and tables I'd never seen around the hotel perimeter before.

Cami waved at me. "Welcome."

"Good morning. Hey, nice spot," I said.

"Only the best for the family," Maddox replied.

Gabe was holding our nephew, Ben, in his arms. I swear, sometimes I couldn't believe how fast he was growing up.

"Was the drive okay?" I asked my grandparents, kissing Gran's cheek.

"Of course," Grandad replied in a stern voice. "It's only forty minutes. We're not dead yet."

I exchanged a glance with Maddox, but he didn't say anything. You never knew what mood the grandparents had woken up in. Sometimes they owned up to their age, and sometimes they didn't.

I greeted everyone else after. Spencer and Penny had to be around somewhere, too, since Ben was. Maddox, Gabe, Colton, and Jake were here with their respective better halves.

Jake was holding his daughter in one arm. I had to give it to him, he never put that girl down. Then again, I never liked putting Annie and Jack down either whenever I was with them. I was looking forward to spending more time together as a family, even if the reason and logistics around it were complicated.

"Are we supposed to get food from inside?" I asked.

"The staff will bring out baskets so it looks like a real picnic," Gabe explained.

"Besides," Maddox added, "it's a very convenient way of carrying stuff. We'll eat from paper plates."

"It was such a great idea to have a picnic," Cami said. She was sitting on one of the benches, eyes closed and enjoying the rays of sunshine on her face.

"I knew you'd like it, fiancée," Maddox said and bent at the waist, kissing her forehead.

"When are you going to put a ring on that, Maddox?" Gran asked, which made my brother laugh.

"I already did, Gran, but we're both busy with other things. We want to give our wedding a lot of consideration."

I never thought I'd catch an opening so soon, but here went nothing. Besides, my brother would thank me for taking the attention off them. Gran was getting bored now that her matchmaking had been too successful and had started nagging everyone about their wedding dates.

"Speaking of fiancées, I have one."

The entire group was so silent that it was almost eerie.

"I'm sorry, what?" Gran asked.

Gabe groaned.

"Dude," Maddox said, "you didn't."

Of course he'd already figured out what happened.

"We were joking, Nick," Gabe went on.

"Yeah, dude. Come on! You aren't serious?" Maddox blinked.

"What's going on?" Granddad asked. "Not that we're not happy, Nick."

"Of course," Gran said, "but this is a bit unusual. Who is the young lady? We've never even met her, have we? Except Maddox and Gabe, apparently."

I shook my head. "It's not what you think. I'm just trying to help out Allison."

Everyone started talking at the same time. It was impossible to hear anyone specifically.

"I can't answer all your questions at once," I said, fighting laughter.

"You find this amusing?" Maddox asked.

"Yes, actually. If you calm down, I'll explain."

The chatter instantly stopped.

"So, all of you know I lost my best friend, Jim, months ago. He and his wife, Nora, passed away in a car accident. Their twins were not in the car with them. Nora's sister, Allison, has them now."

"We know that," Gran said impatiently. "Skip to the part where you *want* to marry her."

Hmmm. The way she accentuated *want* troubled me. Hopefully she'd understand.

"I have a very good reason, Gran. Jim's parents have threatened to sue for custody. I spoke with Hugo. As you know, he's the best in the field. He said they could win with her being a single mom and all. But it would help her case immensely if she were married."

"Good to know society is still misogynistic," Leo exclaimed. "And why did these two know about this and I didn't?"

"We actually didn't know about it," Gabe said. "We just... It doesn't matter."

My brother sounded completely stunned. I'd only been able to stun Gabe on three occasions in my life, this being the third. It was quite an accomplishment.

"Nick mentioned that Hugo told Allison that the judge would look favorably on a two-person household," Gabe continued.

"And we *jokingly*," Maddox emphasized, glaring at me, "said that he could be the one to marry her."

"Dude, what the hell?" Gabe asked.

I shrugged. "It makes sense. She can't marry some random person she met two days ago. At least she's known me for a while."

"Honey," Gran said in a very careful tone. She was sitting farthest from me on the wooden bench. "Do you think it's prudent? Marrying someone is more than just signing a piece of paper."

"That's actually exactly what it's going to be. We'll go to city hall, sign the papers, and that's it. It's all for the sake of custody."

"You're simplifying this too much." That came from Colton. "Have you gone over this with Hugo? Are there ways in which it can backfire? What if Jim's parents find out this isn't real?"

I nodded. "Hugo assured us that the law can't punish you for marrying the wrong person. Even if we divorce down on the road, it's nothing unusual."

"Even if?" Cade asked, an eyebrow raised.

I'd wondered when he'd start talking. He'd probably been in shock. Now I was in for a treat.

"So, in this grand plan of yours, is there an outcome that *doesn't* involve you divorcing?" he continued.

"Well, I was just saying, for the sake of explanation." *Shit.*

He flashed me a knowing smile. "Right. That's Allison, the hot chick you told me about?" he asked Gabe and Maddox.

This time, I was the one at a loss for words. I hadn't realized my brothers had had conversations about me behind my back.

Gran wasn't saying much. In fact, half the family still seemed to be mute.

I cleared my throat. "Well, now you all know. I mean, Spencer and Penny don't, but—"

"What don't we know?" Penny asked from behind me.

I looked over my shoulder. She and Spencer were walking hand in hand from the direction of the hotel.

"Our brother is getting married to Allison to help her gain custody of the twins," Maddox informed them.

Spencer's eyes bulged. Penny's mouth hung open. She looked at Spencer and then whispered, "I don't know how to react."

He narrowed his eyes. "Why? I mean, there's got to be another way to do this, right? People fight for custody all the time."

"True, but Hugo told us it's best not to gear up for a fight. I mean, Sophie and Bob *are* the twins' grandparents, after all."

"So it's better to go ahead with this charade?" Gran asked. The disapproval on her face threw me a bit.

"Gran," I said carefully, "I'm not sharing this with the family to ask for anyone's permission or blessing. I'd be grateful if you could support my decision, but we're going to do it anyway."

Gran closed her eyes, pressing her lips together. "You will always have my support, Nick."

"We just want to make sure that this isn't something that can bite you in the ass," Jake said.

"It won't," I assured them. "One important thing, though: no one except the family can know that this isn't real, just in case Bob and

Sophie do start digging around. I'll tell everyone that I fell for Allison madly and we decided on a whim to get married. I'm impulsive anyway, so that fits me. Bob and Sophie might attend the event at city hall. If they do, then we'll double down on making sure they believe us."

"Fair enough," Maddox said.

"Now, why don't we check why that food isn't coming. In the meantime," I said, looking straight at Ben, "how about chasing your Uncle Nick out to that big tree right there?"

Ben grinned. "I'll be the first one here." He broke into a run, laughing the whole time.

I ran behind him close enough that in case he stumbled or something, I could quickly reach him.

He reached the huge tree first. Seconds later, I said, "Ha, would you look at that, buddy. You won."

"I love this tree so much!"

It was definitely impressive and had been on the property forever. It was one of the reasons Cami had been so against the sale. She was attached to these old trees, and Maddox initially planned to cut them down.

"Come on, let's go back."

"What's a fiancée, Uncle Nick?" he asked me.

"It's the person you're going to marry."

He nodded. "Like Mom and Dad are?"

"Exactly." It was endearing that he called Penny "Mom." In a flash, I imagined Annie and Jack calling me "Dad."

Jesus, how did I get there? That could never happen. One thing was certain: I'd never want them to forget Jim and Nora. And I was only temporarily in the picture as a father figure. Thinking that bothered me in ways I hadn't expected.

"So now you'll have someone who'll come with you every time?"

I smiled. "Yeah, and you know who else? Two little kids."

"What? There will be more kids? But wait, don't they have to be small first? How small are they?"

"They're a bit younger than you."

He frowned. "I don't understand."

As we reached the group, I said, "I'll find a way to explain it to you, buddy. I promise."

The staff had brought the baskets while we were gone. They'd served an assortment of finger foods. While everyone was filling their plates, Maddox and Gabe came up to me, and I realized by their expressions that they wanted to continue talking about my announcement. I nodded toward the forest so we could step away from the family.

"Dude, sorry about earlier. You just caught us by surprise. Obviously, you'll always have our support," Maddox said. "But you could get yourself, not to mention Allison, into a shitload of trouble if people found out what it really was."

"Yeah, you have to convince a lot of people. And just so we're clear," Gabe added, "we think it's a batshit-crazy idea. But you have our support."

I nodded. "Thanks. That means a lot."

"So, how are you to going to do this? You're still going to live at the penthouse, right? She'll move there with the kids?"

"I'll move into her house."

"The one with two bedrooms?" Maddox asked. He didn't look concerned anymore. In fact, he was giving me a mocking smile that soon turned into a shit-eating grin. "Dude, you're so toast."

I scoffed. "I'm a grown-ass man. Allison is a grown-ass woman. We'll make do. I'll sleep on a pull-out couch if I have to."

Gabe started to laugh. "Yeah, that's going to happen. You're going to live in that small house with a smoking-hot woman, but you'll sleep on the pull-out couch."

"It's none of your business," I warned.

"No, it's not. You're right. It's just fun to meddle. I'm starting to understand why Gran likes it so much," Maddox said.

"So, your plan is to just stay completely celibate for however long this takes?" Gabe asked.

"That's between Allison and me," I said, though the question had been on my mind *a lot*.

"Then we wish you luck," Gabe said. "And by the way, we have some news about Dad."

I groaned. "He's up to trouble again?"

"He's trying to open a restaurant business in Sydney... and using the Whitley name to do it," Maddox explained.

"What the hell? People will think it's part of the company."

"We think that's exactly what he wants. Then again, it is his name." Gabe sounded conflicted.

I decided to be honest with them. "You know what? I have enough on my plate. I can't worry about Dad too."

"We'll keep an eye on him. Let's return to the group," Maddox suggested, and I nodded.

Everyone must have been talking about me while we were gone, because the whispering stopped as soon as we reached the table. That made me laugh.

"You know, you don't have to gossip behind my back," I told them.

"Oh, we plan to do it in front of you too," Meredith said. Cade's wife was just as feisty as he was. And she'd slowly adopted every new girlfriend/fiancée over the years. Which was why I wasn't surprised when she said, "I want to meet Allison. We all do. We need to give her a proper welcome to the family."

Her words struck a chord. This was bizarre. I wanted Allison to feel at ease with all of us Whitleys, but this was nothing more than a charade, after all.

"I'll talk to her and set something up," I assured her.

Meredith tilted her head. "Good. Because we have some questions for both of you about the city hall thing. But we'll give you time to organize yourselves first."

"How magnanimous of you," I taunted.

"Oh, it is," she said. "It really is."

I spent the entire day with my family and didn't check my phone once. We'd moved on from the topic of my impending marriage to other things, thankfully. I only checked my messages after I left Essex.

Allison had texted a few hours ago.

Allison: How did it go? What did your family say?

I grinned as I replied.

Nick: As expected. They all pointed out how batshit crazy this is. But we have their support. And they might show up at city hall too. Gran refuses to miss a wedding.

Allison: But this isn't real!

Nick: Doesn't seem to matter. Might legitimize it more. I'll start all the formalities and let you know how it's going.

Allison: Thanks a lot!

This was happening. Allison and I were getting married—and I was looking forward to it.

Chapter Thirteen

Allison

Nick: I'm taking care of everything related to the marriage license. I should have everything ready this week.

What a way to begin my day. I hadn't even started sipping my coffee, yet my heart was already in overdrive. Then again, the past two weeks had been slightly insane. I felt like I was going through the motions. Every day seemed to blur into the next one. Even for a simple marriage, there were still a ton of things that needed to be taken care of.

Allison: Thanks for organizing this.

He called me the next second.

"Good morning."

I chuckled. "How do you sound so chipper?"

"I've already had enough caffeine that I could run a marathon. Listen, Frances, my assistant, says that city hall needs us to choose which room we want to have the ceremony in."

I blinked. "I thought it was going to be based on how many guests there are."

"Yeah, about that."

I found myself smiling for no reason. "You couldn't talk your family out of joining."

"Honestly, I didn't even try. Whitleys love weddings."

"Even a fake one?" I double-checked. "They know it's fake, right?"

"Yep. Even that. I think my gran figures this is the only time she'll see me get married and doesn't want to miss it."

That was sad.

"Maybe it's a good thing. Especially since they know what's going on."

"Great. The family is excited to welcome you into our midst."

I felt like a feather, as if I were weightless. "That's incredibly sweet."

"I think they've planned to do that ever since we lost Jim and Nora, but now even more so."

"I'm touched, Nick." I really was. That his family would support a virtual stranger warmed me all over. "Is anyone else coming from your side?"

"No. Yours?"

"Not sure. I told my parents, but they're too frail to travel." I bit the inside of my cheek. "I've told two of my friends about the wedding—not the truth, of course—but honestly, I'm not even sure I want them there. It's weird, you know? All of them sort of went radio silent once I started caring for the twins anyway."

I'd become very discernible with my friendships after losing Nora. Two people who I'd thought were my dearest, best friends had texted me a few times to coax me into going out clubbing. I told them that it wasn't really possible for the foreseeable future but asked them to come over for a movie night. They told me that was boring. So much for that.

I had other friends, of course—I'd been living in Boston for close to six years now—but I didn't want them involved at this stage of my life.

"Sophie and Bob will want to come. My plan is to drop them an email about three days before just to annoy them."

Nick laughed. "You're smart. I love that."

"I feel like we're in a movie or something. Like none of it is real. You?" I had to know that I wasn't alone feeling this way.

"The more I have to deal with city hall, the more real it becomes for me too. By the way, we need to talk about something else. I think I should move into your place before we actually sign any papers."

"Oh, oh, of course. I didn't even think about it."

Just like that, I felt as if I'd been doused in a tub full of warm water. It was strangely hot between my thighs.

"Wait, I actually have to order a pull-out couch first. This one is... tiny."

"I can just bring the one I have at the penthouse," he offered.

"It turns into a bed? I thought you had a lot of bedrooms."

"I do, but this one actually has a bed function, and I've just never used it. It's a comfortable couch, so I'm assuming it'll be a comfortable bed."

"Will it fit in my living room?"

There was a pause. "I have no idea."

I laughed. "Are you bringing any other furniture?"

"Nah. Makes no sense. You've got everything we need. "

"Except space," I replied.

"There's plenty of space. You know what? I'll sleep on the couch you have now. If it's uncomfortable, I'll bring the one from the penthouse."

"All right."

This isn't real. This isn't real. I couldn't shake off that feeling.

"So, right. You're taking care of the marriage license. What should I take care of? Are we missing anything?"

"Allison, you're tense."

I laughed. "That obvious, huh?"

"Your voice is different."

I slumped my shoulders. "It feels like this is happening too fast."

"We can postpone it."

"No. Bob and Sophie keep reminding me that they want custody. And frankly, I don't think I could get used to what we're planning anyway. I've resigned myself to the fact that I'll be in knots for the foreseeable future."

He tsked. "That won't do. As your future husband, I can't allow that."

Butterflies roamed in my stomach. My heart skipped a beat and then seemed to grow in size.

My husband. Was it insane that I liked the sound of it even though I knew it wasn't real?

"And what do you plan to do about it, future husband?" I teased.

"I won't allow you to spend the next weeks stressing out."

"I don't think you can help it."

"I disagree."

"Of course."

"The first thing that comes to mind is, of course, distracting you. Can you book Doreen for Friday or Saturday evening?"

My stomach somersaulted yet again. The sensation was already overwhelming me. "Sure."

"That's a good start."

I was thrilled at the thought of spending time alone with Nick again. But was it smart?

Last time, I couldn't stop ogling him. My body went into overdrive just because I was sitting next to him on a swing. Now more than ever, I should try to put some distance between us, because I'd soon be living with this man. Up until now, staring at him when he came to visit was harmless. He was hot as sin, and I was single, after all. But we had separate lives besides the two days a week when he dropped by. This was different. We were going to live together.

But did I come up with an excuse and turn him down? I did not. Instead, I said, "I'll let you know when Doreen has time."

"Perfect. If she has time Friday *and* Saturday, that would be great."

"We'll stay out late on Friday? Because then I should probably tell her to spend the night here."

"Even better. Tell her that."

"Okay." My body was aching in all sorts of intimate places.

How long has it been since I've been with a man?

Too long.

"Gives me plenty of time to help you relax," he added mischievously.

"You need two days for that?"

"Yes. I take my fake fiancé duties very seriously."

"I'm liking the sound of that. Thanks, Nick." I yawned.

"Early night?" he asked me.

"Yeah, that's my glamorous life right now."

"It's going to be *our* glamorous life soon enough."

I swallowed hard. How on earth were we actually going to manage living together?

It was on the tip of my tongue to cancel any plans for the weekend. But ultimately, I didn't.

"I can't wait to see you on Friday."

"Me either."

Chapter Fourteen
Nick

I always prided myself in taking things as they came and simply doing what needed to be done. I liked to foresee things, of course. Predictions were helpful; preparation even more so. But I'd completely failed to foresee that Mom would get wind of my impending marriage.

"How come my son is getting married and I didn't hear it from him?" she said instead of hello.

Usually, she waited for my call so that I wasn't in a meeting or anything similar. Then again, it was seven thirty in the morning. She knew I didn't have any meetings scheduled this early. I was surprised she was awake, though. She was in Asia right now. I'd completely lost track of time zones.

"Who blabbed?" I asked as I threw my clothes for the day on the bed.

"It doesn't matter. You thought I wouldn't find out?"

"Mom, I was planning to tell you."

"When? I need to organize myself and buy tickets."

I stilled in the act of pulling a tie from the tie rack. "You want to come?"

"Nick! Of course!" It was the first time I'd heard her warning tone in years.

"Whoever blabbed told you *why* this is happening, right?"

"Yes. I got all the information."

"And you still want to come?" I double-checked.

"Yes. It's going to be a very nice moment, and I want to be there."

"But there's nothing to celebrate," I reiterated.

"I disagree. My son is taking this huge step to make sure that his best friend's kids are cared for."

Her words disarmed me completely.

"You don't need to worry about plane tickets. I'll buy them."

"Nonsense. I love that my sons take care of me, but I'm making a good income with my yoga and Pilates classes. And my cost of living is really low here in Bali." She spent most of her time there these days, though she moved from one island to another in Indonesia.

"The ticket is on me," I insisted. "It's going to cost a lot because it's such short notice. No reason for you to break the bank. How long do you want to stay?"

"Depends when it is. I've got some retreats planned."

"Mom, really, you don't have to come—" I began, but she interrupted me.

"I wouldn't miss it for the world. I'd rather cancel a retreat. Besides, I miss you boys." After a pause, she added, "Unless…"

"Unless what?" I asked.

"Unless you think it would make things awkward with your half brothers."

I sucked in a deep breath. No matter how much time passed, this would always be a difficult topic. My brothers and I were all closer now than ever before, but I wasn't sure how they felt about Mom. It had to be awkward for sure. Gabe was the only one who'd met her, and he'd been perfectly polite to her, but that didn't mean the others would react the same way.

"I'm sure it'll work out." I'd never allow Mom to feel unwanted, no matter what everyone else was feeling.

"Then I look forward to it. Do we have a dress code?"

"It's just a city hall ceremony."

"Oh."

I laughed. "Disappointed that you're flying over here just for that?"

"No party?"

"No. We're just going to have an early dinner at a nice restaurant afterward."

"Well, it's the company that matters. Now, tell me about Allison. I don't think I've ever heard anything about her."

I gave up on the idea of dressing while talking and instead went out to the terrace overlooking Boston. I'd miss this view, but it was more than worth giving up. Besides, it was only for a short time. Who knew? If this stretched on for too long, maybe we would all move in here. I was certain the twins would enjoy having a playroom. The realtor who sold me this place told me it was perfect to raise a family. I'd scoffed at the notion back then, but now I could see the benefits.

Fucking hell, I'm going to have a family. The marriage might be fake, but the responsibility wasn't. And I wanted to care for the twins for real. I wanted them to have the best.

And I wanted the same for Allison.

"Allison is great. She's a CFO and works hard as hell. She immediately took the twins in after the accident."

"But how is she as a person?"

"I don't know her very well."

"Oh, I don't think that's true." As usual, Mom cut through the bullshit.

"I've really only gotten to hang out with her over the past few months. She's a very warm person, very dedicated."

"And attractive, I hear."

"Leo blabbed, didn't he?" I asked.

"Yes. He might have also mentioned that you've noticed how hot she is."

I closed my eyes tightly and then opened them again. I didn't want to be short with my mom; however, I *was* going to be short with Leo later. I didn't need this type of commentary floating around. Things were going to be difficult and confusing enough as they were without his help.

"That's irrelevant, Mom."

"I respect that."

"For the time being, we're going to share a space and our lives. Then, once the dust settles on the custody battle, we'll go our separate ways."

"Yes, yes. I've got the gist," Mom said. I could tell she was fighting laughter. "I'm certain it'll go according to plan."

I couldn't resist. "Are you mocking me?"

"Oh, Nick, I know you. You're going to live with a gorgeous woman, and somehow you think that—"

"Mom, this is not helpful," I said respectfully.

"Oh, okay. I'm sorry. I didn't mean to interfere. Well, I can't wait to see you and your brothers. And meet Allison, of course, and the twins."

"You'll like Allison."

"I have no doubt. If you like her, she must be really special."

"She is." I headed back inside the penthouse. "I've got to go, Mom. I need to start my day."

"Of course. Nick, I'm very proud of you."

"Thanks, Mom. That means a lot to me."

After hanging up, I threw on my suit and headed out. I didn't often wear one, but today I was heading to an important meeting, and clothing mattered. Suits and ties always give an extra edge.

The meeting was in the opposite direction from where my offices were but not far from Allison's building. I couldn't wait until the weekend, but I could help her relax even before that.

I knew exactly what would help, so I texted Frances on the way. Allison said she liked hot tubs, and I'd just come up with something even better.

I mentally searched for anyone I could ask about how Allison used to spend her free time, but I had zero contact with her friends. My only liaison with her had been Nora, and we'd never really spoken about her sister. Whenever I went to their home, we mostly grilled and had a good time. And after the twins came, it had become harder to actually have a conversation because they were both chasing them nearly all the time.

No, I didn't know too much about Allison. But I'd have plenty of opportunities to find out.

For now, I had a surprise in store for her.

Allison

There were days when I was happy to keep my heels on the entire day. And there were others when I wanted to change into flip-flops the second I sat at my desk. This was one of the latter.

Derek had sent me the information regarding the bonus I'd get if I took on the M&A case. It wasn't nearly enough to make up for the extra time I'd spend working on it. So, I was faced with actually turning down a project for the first time in my entire career. I was certain it would send Derek the signal that I wasn't quite the worker bee that I'd been in the past.

But maybe that was for the best. Before, I never cared much about setting boundaries because work had always been first, but now it wasn't anymore. Annie and Jack were my highest priority.

As I prepared a short and to-the-point email to Derek, I felt a sense of relief. A small part of me was still a bit afraid that I was setting myself up for difficult times in the future, but I wasn't going to let that fear drag me down. I was a damn good CFO. If I wasn't wanted here anymore, I could always get a new job. I'd climbed to the top of my field in record time. No one was going to take that achievement away from me.

After sending the email, I checked my phone and noticed I had a message from Nick.

Nick: I have a surprise for you.

He'd sent me a link to a website for The Relaxing Oasis. There was a slider with pictures of a Turkish bath, steam and sauna, and even small hot pools. I was already starting to relax just looking at the pictures. I could practically feel my muscles loosening. Then I looked at what else he'd sent.

Nick: What would you say about spending an evening there? I'll stay with the twins.

Oh, this man.

Nick: I'll buy vouchers, so you don't have to worry about anything. My treat, of course.

I grinned from ear to ear. I liked Nick Whitley as a person. It wasn't just that I thought he was hot as hell and I was way too attracted to him—he was genuinely a fantastic guy.

Allison: Not your treat at all. I can take care of myself.

Nick: I know, but it was my idea.

Hmm. Knowing him, he wasn't going to let go of this too easily. I had no idea what made me write the next message, but I only realized what I'd done after I sent it.

Allison: Fine. It can be your treat, but on one condition. You join me on Thursday. I'll ask Doreen if she can watch the twins.

Nick: Deal.

Oh goodness. I'd have to wear a bikini in front of Nick. And he'd wear swim trunks, or a towel. I had a hard time keeping my wits about me when he was fully clothed. What was I thinking asking him to join me in a tight space where we'd be very scantily dressed?

Was this insane? Yes. Was I toeing a fine line? Also yes.

Did I have any regrets about asking him that?

Hell no.

Chapter Fifteen

Allison

The rest of the week went by easier, as I had an evening at The Relaxation Oasis to look forward to. And Derek had been very understanding, though the way he'd phrased his email made me think that this was going to count against me at some point.

Allison, of course I understand that your circumstances have changed. I'll find another solution.

But honestly, I didn't really care.

On Thursday, I arrived at The Relaxation Oasis right at six o'clock. It was in an inconspicuous redbrick building. Considering the location, it probably used to be a warehouse.

"Punctual as usual," a voice said to my right.

I startled. "Oh, sorry. I didn't hear you."

Nick was wearing jeans and a polo shirt, and he looked far too sexy.

Oh, heavens. I was already on edge, and he hadn't even taken his clothes off yet.

"Ready to go in?" he asked, running a hand through his hair.

I liked that he wore it slightly longer so it fell into his eyes depending on how he rearranged it with his fingers.

"Yep. Have you been here before?"

"No, never."

"How did you find it?" I inquired as he opened the door for me. The vibes were relaxing from the entrance, with soothing music, jasmine incense, and dim lights. Decorative votives lit up the edges of the floor.

"I remembered that you like warm baths and asked Frances to find me something like this."

I whipped my head toward him, my mouth open in shock. "You actually asked someone to do research about this?"

"Yes. Why are you so surprised?"

"Because you're a very spur-of-the-moment kind of person."

He winked at me. "Doesn't mean I don't like to do my research. Well, I sort of delegated the research, but..."

"Po-tay-to, po-tah-to," I finished for him.

"Exactly," he laughed as we reached the reception desk, where a young brunette was smiling at us.

"Mr. Whitley, welcome. And you must be..."

"I'm Allison." I liked the service. They already knew we were coming.

"Your time slot begins right now, and it will end in two hours."

Nick narrowed his eyes. "I'd like to extend it for the whole evening."

"I'm afraid that's not possible."

"Two hours is more than enough," I answered, wondering what she meant about our "slot."

"I'd give you keys to the changing rooms, but since it'll be just the two of you for the entire duration, that's not necessary."

I blinked several times. "Just the two of us?"

"Yes. Mr. Whitley booked the whole place."

My mouth fell open as I turned to look at him. That grin. Oh, it was smug and so damn sexy. I was already overheating, and we hadn't even reached the sauna yet.

The woman led us from the main area, then pointed to the left and said, "Men's changing room is upstairs, and the women's is on the other side. You can also change in the same space. It doesn't matter in this case." She smiled at Nick as if he'd hung the moon—and, well, he kind of did.

"Anything else you need, we're right here at your service." She turned to me with a brilliant smile. "Your fiancé is a very generous man."

I was too stunned to reply, so I just smiled and nodded.

Once she was gone, I looked at Nick. His grin was smugger than before, if that was even possible.

"Cat got your tongue?" he asked playfully.

"No, you did." I only realized how that sounded after the words were out, of course. *Oh goodness.* This evening was off to an interesting start. "Nick, I can't believe... This is too much."

"One thing you have to learn, Allison, is that things with me are always on a grand scale. Life is too short to do any less."

Wasn't that the truth?

"Thanks. This is more than I could have ever imagined."

"I figured you'd relax even more if there were no people around."

"You're right. I'm going to change. Oh, I didn't even ask. Their steam and bath sauna, are they clothed ones? Can I use it with a bikini, or do I have to be...?" I couldn't bring myself to say the word *naked*, which was just downright silly. We were thirtysomething-year-old adults, not teenagers.

"Clothing," Nick said, and his voice didn't sound so nonchalant either anymore.

"Great. See you soon!"

It was an eerie feeling to be completely alone in a changing room. I didn't bother going into any of the cubicles, just dropped my clothes on the large counter in front of the mirror and put on my bikini. It didn't cover much, but I was proud of my body even though lately I wasn't able to work out as much as in the past. The twins kept me busy and moving, though, and that helped a lot.

The guilt of being away from them gnawed at my insides again, and I chastised myself.

Allison, you're with them every night. Just relax tonight.
Yeah, but you booked Doreen again for Friday and for Saturday.
Stop it, Allison. Just enjoy it.

So I did. I pulled my hair up, tying it with an elastic band, then headed out of the changing room—and nearly swallowed my tongue.

Nick looked absolutely delicious in swim trunks. My God, those abs. How were they even possible? When I was at the gym, I'd seen a lot of men training, but Nick looked sculpted. That eight-pack and the V lines disappearing into his trunks... holy shit. Not to mention his arms. They were strong, almost to the point of bulky, but they worked on him because he was so damn tall and big.

"Are you listening?" His tone implied that he'd asked me something before and was waiting for my reply. But ogling Nick Whitley was a full-body effort. My ears hadn't been functioning at all.

"Hmm?" I asked.

He grinned. "What do you want to do first?"

"Let's go in one of those small tubs. No, wait, the steam room." I laughed. "I can't decide. Do you have any preference?"

"The tub sounds good."

I nodded. "I never quite like going into a tub after I've been in a steam room or a sauna. I feel that no matter how much I shower, I can't get the sweat off myself." I spoke very quickly, which only happened when I was nervous, but I hoped he wouldn't pick up on it.

I walked in front of him because that made ogling him more difficult. I was certain that if I kept doing it, he'd catch on eventually.

We both used the showers next to the pool. The water was pleasantly warm, which instantly relaxed me. I hated when the shower next to even a heated pool was freezing cold. What was the point of it? To give me hypothermia?

Afterward, I walked down the pool steps carefully. The water was perfect. The bottom of the pool was dark blue with iridescent lights to look like the sky, and the overhead lights throughout the area were dimmed. I had to give it to Nick—it was peaceful to know that there were no other people here. No conversations going on, no one else moving through the water or flipping magazines while lying on the sunbeds.

There was a huge moonlit window in the ceiling, and I leaned back to admire the view.

"This is amazing," I said.

"Yeah, it really is."

I looked at Nick. He was looking at me, not at the pool.

I swallowed hard. Had tonight been a mistake? No. I was simply on edge. Nick was doing a very nice thing. That was all.

"Thanks for this."

"My pleasure. And just so you know, there's more to come."

"Oh?" I said as he walked closer to me.

Oh, no, no. He couldn't just flash his perfectly sculpted torso in front of my eyes. Did he want to make me weak in the knees? Was that his endgame? Because I could see myself heading straight to Puddleville.

"Nothing," Nick said. "I've already said too much."

I lowered myself into the water, swimming backward to give myself something to do. But the tub was small, so there wasn't much swimming. I wondered why they'd put so many sunbeds around it. There was no way that you could fit more than ten people in here, and even then you'd be crammed next to one another like sardines.

"Are you relaxing?" he asked.

"Yes," I replied truthfully, then glanced at him again. He'd joined me in the water. That was good, safe. I mean, his eyes were also very, very ogle worthy, but I'd at least gotten used to them. But those muscles? Hell no.

"You've had a rough week," he concluded.

"I've had rougher, but it's been intense. I keep wondering if I decided the right thing in one aspect."

"Want to share it with me?"

I was surprised. I'd never actually had someone to talk about work with. Whenever I'd gone on dates, and even when I'd had boyfriends, we rarely chatted about each other's jobs.

"My boss asked if I wanted to take on an extra project, an M&A."

Nick frowned. "An M&A? Merger and acquisition, right? That's a whole lot of work."

"Yes, I know. In the past I've always volunteered for projects like that. But now with the twins... "

"Allison," Nick said. "I'll be around from now on, so if that's something you want to do, then you should do it."

Oh my goodness. Had the water suddenly gotten even hotter? Because I was hyperventilating.

Nope. I was actually melting.

"I can't believe you just said that."

"I'm serious."

I shook my head. "I'm not sure what to say."

"We're a team, Allison. Never forget that."

"Oh."

Nick frowned, coming closer to me. Which made the advantage of not seeing his abs completely disappear. I was right back on edge.

"Why are you surprised?" he asked.

"Because until now, I'd never thought about it."

"Me marrying you didn't give you the hint?" He curled up a corner of his mouth.

"You're right. I just... I don't know. I figured that you'd like to help, but not as a team. I've never been a team with anyone."

"Neither have I. I hope I'm not going to blow this. But we'll figure it out somehow. I'm very confident in our chances."

"That's because you're always confident." I playfully swatted his shoulder—except I somehow ended up with my palm on his chest. It was even harder than I'd imagined. I was downright desperate to check if his abs were the same way too.

I heard a very low groan and immediately moved my hand.

"That's true." He cleared his throat. I took a step back in the water but didn't make it far because we were at the edge. "So, hit me. What's the issue with the project?"

"For the first time ever, I asked how much more I'd get paid. Usually, I just say yes and hope they throw a bonus my way. The money the company's offering is simply not enough for the number of hours I'd have to put in, so I turned it down. And I feel surprisingly good about it."

Nick grinned. "That's good. You should know your worth and ask to be paid for it."

I nodded. "I think so too."

"For future reference, if you want to take on a project, we'll work out a system."

"But you've got a lot on your plate too. You want to open new branches."

"I'll manage."

For the first time, I realized that his confidence made me relax. I didn't have to be on edge all the time, thinking about all the things that could go wrong.

"What do you say about swimming for a bit?" I suggested.

"You go ahead. This thing is so small, I'd reach the end in three strokes."

I rolled my eyes as I floated backward. "I didn't mean actual swimming, just moving around a bit."

"That's fine. I like watching you."

We both fell silent as I kept moving backward. The only sound was that of water moving. I then turned back, swimming in the other direction. Like this, I couldn't see him at all. *Phew, that's better.*

I relaxed until I hit a solid wall of muscle and immediately straightened up. I accidentally brushed him with my forearm as I turned around, then with my palm. Those abs truly felt amazing.

"Damn, Allison."

I jumped back. "I'm so sorry, Nick. I didn't realize you were here."

"I moved. I should have given you a heads-up." His voice was a bit rougher than before.

He smiled lazily as I took a few more steps back, putting one arm at the edge of the pool and then the other one, as if he was trying to show off his biceps.

Wait a second. His smile had turned into a smirk. He *was* doing it on purpose.

Oh shit! That meant he'd realized the effect he had on me.

I was in deep.

Chapter Sixteen

Allison

"I'm going to go to the steam room," I announced.

"Sure. Want to go alone, or do you want me to join you?"

Oh, yes. Please join me and rip off my tiny bikini. Drop your boxers and let's do it.

There was no way I could say no. And truth be told, I did want to be around Nick. I liked talking to him. I liked *him*. But I wanted to stop being so attracted to him. It was going to make things more complicated.

"Sure. I'd feel weird in there all by myself."

"All right, then."

After another quick shower, we headed to the steam room. It smelled amazing, like lemongrass. The steam was already very thick.

I sat on one bench, Nick on the other. There was enough distance between us that I felt as if I was practically alone, but knowing he was there also gave me some comfort.

I quickly discovered another perk: it had lots and lots of marvelous steam, which meant eye contact wasn't always possible. I could stare at this fine specimen of a man to my heart's content. *Oh yeah.*

He was sitting with one foot up on the bench, slightly lopsided, resting on one palm. Even his calves were nothing but muscles. He was truly the most handsome man I'd ever met.

When I tore my gaze away to check if the steam was still covering our eye contact, I swallowed hard. It definitely wasn't. Nick's smirk told me that he'd watched me for a while.

"By all means, take your fill, Allison."

"Hmm?"

"Would you like me to move closer to you so you have a better view?"

What was I supposed to do now, play it cool or deny everything? No, there was no point denying it. I'd been far too obvious.

"Nick…," I whispered.

"We can pretend it's not happening."

"Oh, look at your smirk. You totally don't want to let it go."

"No, sorry. I'm enjoying it too much. You were really smart about it, waiting for the steam."

I gasped. "Sorry you caught on."

Nick laughed, and his entire chest shook. That only highlighted his abs even more. *Oh, yum.*

"I only caught on because I was doing the same."

My entire body tightened. He'd been checking me out. How on earth did I not realize that?

"It's not the first time I've done it either," he continued as if he'd read my mind.

"Wh-What?" I stammered. "I didn't notice before."

"Then I'm stealthier than I gave myself credit for."

For a few seconds, neither of us said anything. Finally, I murmured, "Nick, I don't know if that's a good idea."

He got up and moved onto the bench beside me. "Of course it's not a good idea. We're going to live together."

I cleared my throat. "We are, and that means we should stop this."

He leaned in closer. "Allison, considering what we've both been doing, I don't think that's in the cards any longer."

I couldn't argue with that. He was absolutely right. "I'm not sure where to go from here."

His nearness was making this more difficult, yet I didn't want to move away. In fact, all I craved was to move even closer, to have skin-on-skin contact.

"How did we get into this situation?"

"I don't know," Nick admitted. With shock, I realized it was the first time he wasn't reassuring me. No "We'll play it by ear. We've got this!" Which told me just how much self-restraint he had to be exercising at this very moment as well.

I gave in first, only moving a smidge but enough for our shoulders to touch. I thought I'd be happy with that slight contact. But it seemed to create a chain reaction in my body, and I instantly craved much more.

I took a deep breath, steeling myself, and then exhaled slowly.

"Fuck," Nick whispered. "Damn it, this is hard." His voice was very low and very rough, as if he had to make an effort to get the words out at all.

I closed my eyes, hoping that not seeing him would make it easier to pull back, but everything inside me told me to lean in farther. Then I felt the air shift and opened my eyes.

Nick had pulled away. Only a few inches, but the small distance was enough to break the spell. I shook my head and straightened up, turning away from him. We were both silent, but I could hear his labored breathing.

Chancing a glance, I saw he was gripping the edge of the bench with his fingers. He was hanging by a thread!

"Allison..."

The way he said my name made me want to climb onto his lap. When he didn't add anything, I prompted in a whisper, "Yes?"

"You should go ahead and shower first."

I blinked, trying to make sense of what he was saying. What did he mean, shower first? There were like a million showers here and just two of us.

Oh! He needed me to go because he couldn't control himself otherwise.

"Yes, of course." I got up from the bench and tried to put the towel around me but dropped it accidentally.

"Jesus," Nick groaned.

Energy zipped through me. I didn't even have the guts to turn and look at him; I simply bent down to gather my towel, and he groaned again. I didn't realize why until I noticed my bikini had shifted, so I'd been flashing him the crack of my ass.

Darting out of the steam room without a second glance, I took in a deep breath and then exhaled, but I couldn't manage to calm down. There were a set of three showers right next to the steam room, but I headed to the changing rooms instead. They had shower gels and shampoos, and I planned to use both and then rub myself with body cream. I was going to make Nick wait a million years so we could *both* cool off.

While I washed my hair and soaped up, I glanced at my ring, which reminded me how fake this all was. How on earth were we going to go through with all this? In that steam room, a wall came between us. It was undeniable. Were we going to be able to pretend nothing happened? Should we?

I'd always been very decisive in my life. I'd known early on what I wanted to major in. Then, once I started my career, I knew I wanted to be a CFO. When the tragedy happened, I didn't even hesitate to take the twins. I never second-guessed myself; I set on a course and didn't look back.

But right now, I was at a loss. Usually, I'd call Nora and ask for her advice. God, I missed my sister so much. She was the only one I'd routinely ask if she thought I was doing the right thing. I could probably talk to my parents about this, but I didn't want to worry them for no reason. They were still grieving too; it wasn't fair to burden them with this.

As I stepped out of the shower, I figured I'd follow Nick's lead. If he pretended nothing happened, I was going to do the same. I wasn't sure how, but I was determined to figure it out.

I towel-dried my hair thoroughly before dressing and getting out of the changing room. Nick was already sitting by the reception desk in a leather armchair with a huge glass of orange juice. He immediately got up and flashed me one of those devastatingly charming smiles, and I felt my panties catch on fire. I didn't even manage to smile back. I was still trying to put myself together, but clearly, he was better at this than me.

"Want something to drink?" he offered. "Orange juice is really good."

"No, thanks. I'm good. They had some lemon water inside the changing rooms."

"All right, then. Ready to go?"

I nodded.

The woman behind the reception desk stepped out.

"We are very happy to have you as guests. Did something happen to make you cut your stay short?"

I glanced at the clock. We still had half an hour left. I was at a loss for what to say.

Nick cleared his throat. "It was perfect. We just needed to leave earlier."

"Okay." The woman still looked at us suspiciously as we bid her goodbye.

Nick and I didn't speak as we walked out of the spa. Once we were on the street, he turned to me. "Allison, how are you feeling?"

I chanced a glanced up at him. Just like that, my entire body was vibrating with excitement.

"A bit confused," I whispered. *There went my plan to pretend nothing happened.*

Nick tilted his head. "Then let's have drinks and talk it out until there's no confusion left."

I instinctively knew it wasn't a good idea. I was still too susceptible to him.

"I can't tonight."

"No problem. We're seeing each other tomorrow anyway." His eyes were glinting.

Oh God, I'd forgotten. He was right, of course. Which meant I had less than twenty-four hours to figure things out.

Chapter Seventeen
Allison

The next evening, I was just as confused as the night before. Nick was picking me up. The last time he'd come to the house, I'd already been on edge, but this was something else entirely. I kept telling myself that nothing happened. We hadn't even kissed last night. But I'd wanted to—so damn badly that my body was still shaking when I remembered how much I'd craved his mouth on mine.

But Nick and I were both adults. We could work this out.

I waited for him out by the street, and he arrived just in time. I grinned as the car approached, and when he stopped in front of me, I immediately jumped in.

He frowned. "I was going to come and open the door for you."

"There's no need. But thank you."

"You think it's a good idea to go inside and say goodbye to the twins?"

"Oh no, don't. It's actually the reason I've been waiting out here in the first place. If they see you, they might not let us go at all."

I was relieved that some of the ease between us had returned. That the sexual tension wasn't as thick. Maybe there was a chance we could forget what had happened in the steam room.

"Soon enough they won't have to."

I felt his words like a warm hug.

"So, are you going to tell me what we're doing, or is it a surprise?"

He grinned. "I'm cooking for you."

"Wow, that's actually a surprise." I was stunned. "You can cook?"

"I'm not too bad at it."

My heart started to race. "So, we're going to your place?"

"Is that a problem?" He looked at me for a beat before we drove off.

"No, not at all."

"I wanted to show it to you anyway."

"Why?"

"So you can keep it in mind in case your house ends up being too cramped."

I swallowed hard. "That's very thoughtful of you, thanks."

We spoke about our respective days until we reached his building, and I relaxed a bit. It was impressive—one of the tallest buildings I'd seen along the water. His penthouse was even more impressive, though.

"Nick, this is incredible!" I was proud of being a homeowner and everything. Boston wasn't cheap, and for someone to be able to afford a house with a single income was no small feat, but this was on another scale altogether. "All this light!" The sun was just setting, and the view from the living room was gorgeous. He didn't have floor-to-ceiling windows everywhere, but there were plenty of them to take in the surroundings. "It feels like we're up in the clouds."

"I know."

"And yet you're willing to move?" I turned to him. He'd gone straight to the huge kitchen.

It was modern, like the living room. The colors were rather minimalistic—a lot of grays and blacks and white. He had a huge fridge, plus a smaller one full of wine. The kitchen island was enormous, with a granite countertop.

"I think I might have fallen in love with your kitchen."

He winked at me. "I like it too. Gives me enough space to work. I'm a disorganized cook," he said.

"Out of all the things that have happened lately, this is something I hadn't been counting on."

"What? Me cooking?"

I nodded. "Yeah."

"Why not?"

Why not indeed?

I racked my brain, trying to come up with an explanation. "Because you're such a fan of pizza, I guess. I don't know. Sorry, I just jumped to conclusions." I shook my head. "What are you making?"

"You like spaghetti carbonara?"

"Yes!"

"Perfect, then that's what I'm making. I have everything I need, and it doesn't take long."

"God, the view here is so impressive. I like that you can see the sunset."

"And you can see the sunrise from my bedroom."

I instantly blushed. Knowing that detail seemed a bit too intimate.

"What do you want to drink?" he asked as he started to chop onions and ham. "I have wine, obviously." He pointed to the wine fridge.

"I don't want any alcohol. I'll look in the fridge to see what else I can have."

"Afraid to get tipsy around me, Allison?" Nick asked playfully.

I stood in front of the fridge and looked over my shoulder at him. He was watching me; heat gripped my entire body at the sensation. "I just don't feel in the mood for it," I whispered.

His eyes darkened a bit, but he nodded. I opened the fridge and once again was stunned at the amount of food inside.

I'd simply assumed that just because my fridge had been deplorably empty before taking the twins in, his would be the same.

"Want me to give you a tour of the apartment after we eat? Or before? I can wait with the cooking."

"Let's eat first." I took out a jug of orange juice. Maybe it would be easier to resist him on a full stomach.

"This isn't going to take long."

"I can put the spaghetti in the water," I said as he was cracking eggs.

"That would help."

I filled a pot with water and put the spaghetti in it once it was boiling. It certainly didn't take Nick long to whip up the sauce.

"Easy dinner," I remarked.

"Indeed. I like cooking more elaborate stuff, but I don't really have time, and it's inefficient. But soon I won't have that problem anymore. I can cook for you and the twins."

Suddenly, he was even more attractive in my eyes.

"It smells amazing," I exclaimed a few seconds later, trying to put my mind on something else. The scent of onions mixed with that of ham and herbs.

I opened a few drawers until I found a wooden spoon and then was about to dip it into the sauce, but Nick gripped my wrist. The contact singed me. As I looked up at him, my breath quickened.

"No tasting until it's done. You'll just be disappointed."

I smiled and took a step back as he let go of me, as if I didn't just get turned on because the man touched my wrist.

I was going to make a fool of myself this evening. I just knew it.

"Then I'll wait for your approval before I dive in."

"It's only going to be ready when it's on your plate."

My shoulders slumped. "You're no fun."

He took a step toward me, tilting closer. "We both know that's not true."

Ah, this man. Why was he calling me out like that? It wasn't fair. How could he move so effortlessly between flirty and non-flirty? I couldn't keep up.

The food was ready in a matter of minutes. We ate at the small table he had in front of the kitchen island.

I took a bite and barely suppressed a moan. "This is delicious. You're a very good chef."

"Thanks. I started playing around in the kitchen as a kid, especially once my older brothers had a lot of after-school activities and they couldn't continue cooking. Mom did her best, but with working two jobs, there was only so much she could do at home."

"I still don't understand how that all went down," I admitted. "How your father was a gazillionaire, yet you were struggling."

Nick shrugged. "I keep asking myself the same, how come Mom bought his story, but you have to remember, the internet and social media weren't a thing back then. We lived in Maine, so the goings-on in another state weren't important to us. Short of going to Boston and investigating, I don't think she could have done anything else. But still..."

"And he wasn't contributing at all?"

"He was, some. Just not enough for my mom to be able to only have one job."

I frowned. "I'm sorry. That's terrible."

"It's not, actually. It instilled in us a strong motivation to work hard from very early on. But it was difficult for Mom," he said with affection in his voice. "By the way, she'll be at the wedding too."

I was stunned. "How come? She knows it's all fake, right?"

"She does but wants to join us anyway."

"Where is she exactly?"

For the rest of the meal, we spoke about what she was doing in Bali. I also kept asking pointed questions about the recipe because it truly was delicious, and it was a bit different from the carbonara I'd had at Italian restaurants in the city.

After we finished, he said, "I want to take you on a tour of the place. Sound good?"

"Yes, please. I already know I'll love it. I still don't think it's a good idea to move out of my house, though."

"I agree. The kids' stability early on is important. Besides, I wasn't suggesting that we do that right now. I just want you to take a good look at the place and remember all the possibilities."

I nodded in agreement, loving the fact that he seemed to think of the twins often. It was almost natural for Nick, and that was so important to me.

I was shocked when he told me he had six bedrooms. How on earth was he going to sleep on a pull-out couch in the living room when he was used to all this space by himself?

"So, my plan is for Leo to put it on the market. He'll list it for an astronomical price. That way, no one will actually rent it. It'll give the appearance to Jim's parents that my moving in with you is legit. What do you think?"

Nick was right. This was all for appearances, and I needed to remember that.

"That's a great idea. I'd hate for you to lose this while you're helping me out, though." It just didn't seem fair. Nick was giving up a lot. I started feeling guilty for everything he was going through for me.

"Stop that, Allison. I want to do this. To help you. Help the kids. It means a lot to me. It's not just about helping an old friend anymore. I really want to be there for the three of you, someone you can count on… always."

Oh my. I needed to get off this topic; otherwise, I was going to start thinking things I shouldn't.

"Do you have guests overnight often? Is that why you have all the extra rooms?"

"No, not at all. This is, for example, my home office." He opened a door to a large room. "Not all the bedrooms are bedrooms. I've converted a few, like this one, and the others are still empty or used for storage."

"Oh, I like your office! It drips with authority. Power." The dark wood and masculine furniture were so alpha.

"Do those things turn you—" He stopped midsentence, but I knew exactly what he'd been about to ask—*"turn you on."*

I sucked in a deep breath. He closed his eyes, his nostrils flaring. He looked as if he was trying to ground himself.

Ha! Finally, he was starting to lose control a bit.

"I just meant that your office fits you" was all I said.

The air between us changed. It became more charged. I swallowed hard as we moved on to the next room.

"This one's actually completely empty. I've been toying with the idea of having a home gym. Most of my brothers do, but it makes no sense for me. I like training at work. It would be very easy to convert this into a playroom for the twins."

How was he so effortlessly swoonworthy?

"What do you have in mind?" I asked.

"There are all sorts of towers and climbing things we could mount on the wall. My brother Spencer has something like that at his house, and my nephew loves them."

My eyes were stinging. I was going to tear up soon. Nick had always been thoughtful, but this was something else. He cared for the twins a lot!

Suddenly, I wished our fake marriage could be real.

"I think they'd love it too," I replied.

He smiled proudly, as if he'd been hoping I'd react just like that.

We moved to the next room, which consisted of a couch and a large screen. The walls were bare, which was the same pretty much throughout the apartment. I could easily see some modern art on the walls, bringing a splash of color to the rooms.

"This is a movie room? But you already have a huge-ass TV in the living room!"

"At one point, I was thinking I needed to fill up the space somehow. I don't really use it, so one of the twins could have a bedroom here, or both if they want to stay together."

Again, Annie and Jack. My heart was feeling so good about Nick, about us.

"You really gave this a lot of thought."

"I was just thinking how logistics would work if you three came here. The next room could be yours. Then there's one with a pool table that we could use in case the twins want separate bedrooms. There are also two bathrooms in the hallway."

"No en suite?"

He winked at me. "Only for the master bedroom."

"Oh, silly me." I smirked, then glanced back down the hall. "Nick, this penthouse is amazing. I bet your bedroom is enormous."

"It is."

He walked down to the very last door, and I followed him even though I wasn't sure I wanted to peek into his bedroom. It seemed far too intimate.

When he opened the door, my jaw dropped. "You know what? I could move in here, no problem."

He started to laugh.

"And you have a separate dressing room. I don't know how this could be any more perfect."

Like the living room, this was also done in gray tones. Wait, they weren't gray—they were more woodsy. I realized the difference because it gave the room a warmer feeling.

The bed was exquisite. It was huge and had a leather headboard.

Sighing, I looked up at Nick. "You will never survive sleeping on a pull-out."

"I promise I'll manage."

"When you can no longer take the couch, you can come here and spend some time at your apartment."

Nick shook his head. "That would confuse the twins."

I felt like the worst aunt in the world. Nick included the kids in all his plans, and I hadn't even thought about them.

I dipped my head. "You're right."

"I was thinking that I wouldn't bring too many clothes. I can come here a few times a week and just take what I need for the next few days. Or Frances can do it."

"That sounds like a lot of hassle," I replied.

"I really don't mind."

"Can I take a peek in your dressing room? From here it looks to die for."

The corner of his mouth quirked up. "I'll give you a tour."

I didn't understand how I'd need a *tour* until I actually stepped into the dressing room. I'd only seen a small glimpse of it from the bedroom, but it stretched in an L-shape to my left.

"Nick, this is like your own private store. I've only ever seen something like this in movies."

He had drawers down below and hanging racks on the upper levels. All the lights came on as we moved in front of each unit. He was very well organized too: suits on one side, shirts on the other. T-shirts carefully folded.

"I think the best word to describe this place is *sexy*."

I only realized I'd said it out loud when Nick turned around and replied, "That's an interesting choice of words."

I shrugged. "Just what came to mind. And it perfectly fits you."

"So, you think I'm sexy?"

The flirty tone was back. We were very close to crossing the line once again.

I had a flashback of us in the steam room. Judging by the way his eyes darkened, he was thinking along similar lines.

"Nick...," I whispered.

"Fuck!" He closed his eyes and then opened them again. They were even darker. A shiver went through me at the sight.

Without even realizing, I stepped closer, and then so did he. He tilted my head up, cupping the side of my face and threading his fingers through my hair.

I instantly got wet. I had no idea how it was possible, but I was already on edge with need. Then again, maybe it wasn't such a surprise. The tension had been building between us for some time. Last night, it had increased exponentially.

"I've been fantasizing about this for weeks," he murmured against my temple.

Every word only turned me on even more. "What exactly?"

"Touching your hair. Especially after last night." He exhaled briskly, and his breath shook. "I nearly canceled today."

I gasped lightly.

"But then I couldn't because I needed to see you."

Chapter Eighteen

Nick

I'd been so good at holding myself in check all evening. In fact, I deserved a damn medal because I was on my best behavior last night too. I'd been so close to pulling her into my lap in that steam room and kissing her. And we would never have stopped at a kiss. It would have been impossible. I wanted to do things differently today, yet here I was, hand buried in her hair, unable to stop touching her.

"Nick!"

I slowly pulled back. I wanted to kiss her temple and then get us out of the bedroom to somewhere safe. Instead, I did something else entirely.

I kissed a straight line from her temple to the corner of her mouth. She was trembling, and I couldn't stop myself any longer. I licked her upper lip and bit the lower one. She opened up without my even having to ask, and I captured her mouth. This was everything I'd needed and wanted for weeks—way before our fake marriage plans. That one kiss in front of Bob and Sophie had been great but nothing compared to this.

I wasn't holding back at all, giving her my tongue, exploring her mouth as I gripped her hair even harder. I liked that it was so thick and luscious; I could probably bury both hands in it.

I only paused the kiss enough to tilt her head up so I could move my mouth down her jaw and her neck. She was wearing another flowery dress, and all I could think of was how easy it would be to take it off her. I was already losing my mind, and we hadn't even moved in together.

When she reached for my shirt, I realized the feeling was mutual.

She wasn't pushing me away. Instead, she moved her hands under my T-shirt.

I wasn't going to let her walk out of here tonight without having her. It wasn't possible. We both desperately needed it.

She pushed her hand even farther up my chest as I deepened the kiss. She was moving her fingers in a pattern. I smiled against her mouth when I realized she was tracing my abs.

"Don't laugh at me," she said when our lips parted. "I've been dying to do this since you took me to the barbeque."

I moved my mouth to the side of her neck. I wanted to taste her everywhere at once. At the same time, I wanted to pause after every kiss to take in her reaction.

"Nick!" she exclaimed when I kissed down her clavicle and right between her breasts.

I let go of her hair and pushed my hands up her legs, hitching her dress up. I needed skin-on-skin contact, and I fucking loved the easy access.

Drawing one hand up the back of her left thigh, I cupped her buttock, groaning against her neck.

"You're not wearing panties?" I asked.

"Oh no, I am. They're just not very modest."

I moved the other hand up her inner thigh until I reached the apex. I wasn't touching her between her legs, though. Not yet.

But a fraction of a second later, I lost the fight with myself. I needed to check to see if she was wet for me. I pressed my fingers across her opening. Even through the fabric, I could tell she was very turned on.

"Oh God!"

She lifted one leg, rubbing her thigh along mine, almost as if she wanted to jump me on the spot. I turned rock hard that very second. I walked her backward and lifted her up at the nearest set of shelves. I pulled all the suits above to one side so she had space to sit there.

She gasped, looking around. "What are you doing?"

"What?"

I set her down on the carefully folded undershirts. Then I realized she wasn't going to be comfortable like this, so I lifted her by the ass again and pushed all of it onto the floor with my other hand.

"Nick, we're making a mess."

"I don't care, Allison. I so don't fucking care."

I pushed her dress up to her waist, and she leaned slightly backward. She was level with my pelvis, so I lowered myself onto my haunches to explore her legs.

"You look so damn gorgeous. I memorized every detail about you last night."

"That can't possibly be true," she murmured.

"You have a birthmark here." I tapped the back of her calf.

"That's right."

"And one here." I pointed to her right outer thigh.

She nodded. Her entire body was shaking. "You looked very carefully."

"You have no idea," I replied.

I kissed from her ankle to her knee. She pressed her thighs together, but I shook my head. "No. Keep them wide open and touch yourself over your panties."

She swallowed hard, leaning against the back of the dresser.

"Like this?" She drew her finger in a perfect line from her entrance to her clit. She'd soaked the fabric through.

"Just like that. Move it up and down slowly until you can't take it anymore."

"And then what?"

"Then I'll give you more instructions."

I kissed her thigh, watching her follow my instructions precisely. Then I moved to the other leg, but I didn't start kissing it from her ankle up because then I couldn't see her touching her pussy. I was desperate for that view.

Her breath was becoming more labored. She was starting to move her finger faster.

"No, that's too fast."

Then I noticed she was just pressing hard.

"You're cheating. Slowly and lightly, until I tell you to stop," I ordered.

"Nick." She shut her eyes firmly, straightening up, then moved her finger just the way I was telling her. The fabric was becoming more and more soaked through. She was fucking gorgeous.

"I can't...," she whispered.

"Can't what?"

"I can't take it anymore."

"Yes, you can, babe. Trust me. Just a bit more."

When her moans turned to whimpers, I knew she truly couldn't take this anymore.

"You can put your hand inside your panties. Actually, no. Move the fabric to one side. I want to see you touching yourself."

Her pussy was already red and lightly swollen when she pushed the fabric to one side.

"Can I press harder?" she panted.

"Yes. Touch yourself exactly the way you need, Allison."

"Oh God, yes." She threw her head back, moaning, and rubbed two fingers up and down in quick succession.

I immediately pushed my pants down, just enough so I could grab my cock. I watched her continue to touch her pussy frantically. She thrust two fingers inside herself at once, which meant she was ready for my cock.

I lifted her ass with both hands and brought her closer to the edge of the shelf, then froze.

"Fuck! I need to get a condom."

"N-No. Are you... I mean, are you clean? I've been on birth control since forever."

"I'm clean," I assured her. "Are you certain about this?"

"Yes, yes, please."

I didn't even have enough self-restraint to kick off my pants and boxers, letting them drop and pool around my ankles. Nor did I lower her panties—they were perfect just the way they were, pushed to one side.

I couldn't take it slow. I entered her in one move, pushing in until I was buried inside her. She must have been close to climaxing because her inner muscles were clenching like crazy.

I pulled out before slamming back in long, hard strokes and noticed her expression changing instantly. She pressed her lips and eyelids together, as if she was bracing herself.

I couldn't believe it. I was fucking her like a caveman in my dressing room, but she was comfortable. She was enjoying this.

And that was all that mattered.

I wanted to focus on her face, but her features started to blur as wave after wave of pleasure coursed through me. Being inside this woman and watching her give in to me so completely was damn amazing.

I kissed her neck, regretting that I didn't take off her dress first. But I was too far gone to do it now. I simply wanted my nose buried in her neck and my cock in her pussy.

I slammed in again and again until her inner muscles tightened even more around me. She was ready to come, and I was determined to get her there before I did. Straightening up, I stroked her clit with two fingers, not unlike the way she'd done before.

She immediately responded, bending at the waist abruptly, then straightening up again. Her right shoulder spasmed, moving backward as she gasped my name. She tightened around my cock so much so that I could barely move. I fucked her through it anyway, knowing she needed more. We both did.

I put both my palms under her thighs and tilted her up so she was at another angle. I could reach even deeper inside her like that.

"Oh my God! Niiiiiick!"

I changed the way I touched her clit from continuous moves to the occasional flick. Her dress shifted and covered my hand, but I didn't need to see what I was doing. I was letting her reactions guide me even while I was chasing my climax.

I needed to make this woman mine again. And when that happened, I was going to take off all her clothes so I could watch her beautiful, naked body. But right now, I was starting to lose myself in her.

The muscles in my thighs burned, as did those in my ass. I was pushing without giving myself a break, but we were both on the cusp, and I couldn't stop.

When her groan turned into a plea, I knew what she needed. I started circling her clit faster, and she exploded within seconds. Her entire body undulated beneath me, her pussy clenching so tight around my cock that I came too. I buckled over her, pushing in and out, in and out. I wanted us to chase every single drop of pleasure. I moved relentlessly fast and deep until we were both over the edge. Then I slowed down, but I couldn't stop moving.

"Nick," she gasped.

Regaining some of my senses, I kicked off my pants and boxers. While still inside her, I carried her out of the dressing room.

She sighed, resting her forehead against my shoulder, drawing in deep breaths. "Oh my God," she murmured.

I walked her straight to the shower. Even though I was semihard inside her again, I couldn't have her right now. I'd been a brute back there in the dressing room, and I didn't want to hurt her. Instead, I set her down in the walk-in shower and pulled out of her. She protested as I grabbed the hem of her dress and pulled it over her head, throwing it away from the shower. But then she pushed her own panties down, moving her hips playfully from left to right as she stepped out of them and then kicked them away.

"You're so beautiful," I said.

"We're doing everything backward," she murmured as she tugged at my own T-shirt, pulling it over my head.

That made me laugh. It described our situation exactly right.

She turned on the water. It came straight from above, and she yelled, "Oh, damn it. I forgot I didn't want to get my hair wet."

It was too late now, though. "Will it help if I get wet with you?" I said, stepping under the spray.

"Wasn't that your idea already?"

I smirked. "Maybe."

We cleaned up quickly, barely managing to keep our hands to ourselves, then stepped out into the large bathroom. Allison dressed at top speed, and so did I. Then I took her hand, leading her back to the living room.

"Want something to drink?" I asked.

"Sure. I'm a bit parched. I wonder why." She winked at me.

"What a coincidence. So am I. Want me to open a bottle of wine?"

She hesitated. "No, it's getting late."

I glanced at the clock. Fuck, I hadn't even realized it.

I looked at her intently. She was on the opposite side of the kitchen island, leaning forward with her forearms on the countertop.

"Allison, just putting it out there. How about texting Doreen to ask her if she could stay longer?" After a beat, I added, "Or spend the night?"

Even as I said it, I knew it was a mistake. Giving in to this was wrong. What the fuck had I been thinking?

Allison bit her lower lip, then straightened up. I hurried around to her side of the island.

"Not a good idea?" I said.

She looked up at me, her eyes full of mixed emotions. "No, I don't think it is. I'm..."

I laughed.

Her brow furrowed. "What's so funny?"

"Yesterday, we said we'd clear up any confusion today..."

"And now everything is even more confusing," she finished for me. "I don't think it's a good idea to stay longer."

"No, it's not. You're right. This is just..." I sighed heavily. "Fuck. We've just made everything more difficult. But we're adults. We'll manage."

"How do you always sound so reassuring?"

"I told you, it's my secret weapon."

For once, I wasn't convinced that we'd manage, though. Hell, I was semihard right now for no reason at all. This conversation certainly didn't warrant that reaction from my body.

"You really think so?" she asked me, and I nodded.

"Yeah. You can count on me to..." What, keep it in my pants? What the hell was I going to promise? "To do what's right."

I wasn't sure what that meant yet. But as usual, I was going to figure it out.

"Nick, you're amazing, and I... Look, if circumstances were different..."

"Allison, we both know what the circumstances are. No point torturing ourselves with what they'd be otherwise." I tilted closer to her because I needed this more than anything right now. "This was amazing. And it stays here, okay? Between these walls. Our secret."

She laughed nervously. "Wasn't going to brag about it anyway."

I was feeling a bit shitty right now, knowing what we were doing was not going to help the kids in the long run. I needed to remember the whole point of this facade; otherwise, I'd fuck it all up.

But the temptation to kiss her was almost too hard to beat, so I tilted my head away, taking a deep breath before kissing her forehead and straightening up.

How the hell was I going to live in this woman's house and not give in to my attraction to her when I still wanted her so badly?

Chapter Nineteen

Allison

I daydreamed about my evening with Nick for the entire next week. It didn't even matter where I was: at home with the twins, at work, or commuting. Images kept flashing in my mind, and I smiled like a lunatic every time. It had been a weak moment and generally a bad idea, but that didn't mean I couldn't enjoy reminiscing about it. Even though I absolutely and firmly did not intend to go down that road again.

We were doing this for the kids. The fake marriage was just that. If we confused it with a relationship and it didn't work out, how would that help the children? Though I guessed it would be no different than when we fake divorced later on.

Ugh. This whole thing was making me crazy.

Did I think it was going to be problematic that we'd be living under one roof? Yes. Did I also think it was unfortunate that I didn't have an extra bedroom? Hell yes. I mean, what if Nick liked to be comfortable when he slept and only wore boxers? I sometimes went downstairs to grab a glass of water in the night. What if in my sleepy haze, I couldn't resist those abs and just jumped him?

Those kinds of thoughts percolated in my mind a lot.

So when Nick texted me to say that his assistant had secured a date at city hall two Saturdays from now, an avalanche of feelings overwhelmed me. However, for the first time, I was certain this wasn't a mistake.

Allison: Great. Are we still supposed to go to city hall and choose a room?

Nick: Frances is taking care of everything.

Allison: I'm going to go all out for a dress. Not a traditional dress, but something very fancy. I know it's not real, but I still feel like celebrating.

Nick: You'll look stunning.

Allison: So will you. Suits look amazing on you.

Nick: By amazing, you mean sexy?

Allison: Nick!!!

Nick: Just trying to get the facts.

Allison: No, you're trying to get a rise out of me.

Nick: Is it working?

Oh, it definitely was. The impulse to flirt almost took over, but I fought it bravely and decided to switch topics.

Allison: I'll tell Bob & Sophie.

Though I planned to do it literally at the last minute on Friday so they wouldn't be tempted to come.

I spent a lot of time looking at bridal websites for my fake ceremony attire before deciding on a gorgeous dress from a local designer. He made what he described as "nontraditional" wedding dresses because they were colorful.

Mine was light pink with flowers of black lace sewn on the top. I splurged a bit on it, but I could afford it. I was so short on time that I didn't even go to pick it up myself and instead had it delivered to the house. It arrived three days before the big event. When I came home with the twins from daycare, a huge box was sitting on the doorstep.

"What's inside?" Annie asked.

"My dress for Saturday. Want to see it?"

"Yes!" she exclaimed, clapping her hands.

Jack didn't seem to understand what the excitement was about, but he dutifully followed his sister, and they both sat on the couch, watching me as I opened the box.

"It's a princess dress," Annie said, "like mine."

"Yours is more beautiful," I told her.

I'd splurged on their outfits too. They were so damn cute. Jack had a little tuxedo, and Annie had a gorgeous gold dress because that was her favorite color right now. I loved spoiling her. Both of them, really.

"Do you want me to put it on?" I asked them.

"Yes!" Annie clapped her hands again.

Jack looked confused, but he clapped as well.

Oh, my darlings. I loved them so much.

"I'll be right back."

I changed in the bathroom with the door ajar so I could still hear what they were up to. I'd sent in my measurements, and the designer promised me that the dress would fit perfectly. I was usually skeptical about these things, but I figured, why the hell not? Thankfully, it fit like a glove.

I hurried back to the couch, and Annie giggled as I approached, but then her smile fell.

"You look like Mommy, Auntie Allison."

My heart gave a mighty sigh.

"Thank you, Annie. Your mommy was very beautiful."

I sat between them. They both instantly put their heads on my lap, and I caressed their hair. It was part of our everyday cuddle routine. Suddenly, I wondered what it would look like with Nick here, considering this was going to be his bed. But I had too much to think about to worry about logistics right now. It would all work out one way or another, as Nick insisted.

"All right, it's time for dinner."

"Can you wear your dress the whole night, please?" Annie asked.

Huh. That had the potential to turn into a disaster. But I didn't have to cook. We still had plenty of leftovers from yesterday. I just had to reheat it.

"Only if you help me put on an apron," I told Annie.

She was obviously feeling very clappy today, because she jumped down from the couch and ran toward the kitchen, clapping loudly. I followed her quickly and took the apron out of the drawer where I stored towels and such. I quickly threw it over me and then lowered myself onto my knees so Annie could tie it at the back.

"I'm happy Uncle Nick is coming to live with us."

"I'm happy, too, Annie."

"He always brings pizza."

I laughed. Nick knew his way to these kids' hearts.

I wondered how Annie would respond to him being here every evening during our routine and so on. An image flashed in my mind of the four of us cuddled on the couch. I melted at the mere thought.

Don't get used to it, Allison. This is just to help you out with custody. Then it'll be you and the twins again, and Nick will go back to his life.

Of course he would. If I had a penthouse, you'd have to drag me out of it for me to leave. I'd never do that voluntarily.

We had garbanzo beans and rice for dinner. It had been one of Nora's favorites. I felt much closer to her when we had this meal, and I knew the same was true for the twins. I asked them a bit about their daycare, and suddenly Jack was very chatty. He was becoming so much more confident. I loved it. He seemed to be coming out of his shell more and more. Jack loved the new girl the daycare had hired from the morning he first saw her, and I was sure she'd made all the difference in the world to him.

After I put the twins to bed, I finally managed to take off the dress and laid it out on my comforter to admire it. It was truly gorgeous and worthy of a wedding day, fake or not.

I couldn't believe I was getting married in two days. And yet, I didn't have any wedding jitters.

On Friday evening, I was eating my words because I couldn't go to sleep at all. I tossed and turned in bed and couldn't separate one thought from another.

At about one o'clock in the morning, I realized I wasn't going to sleep at all, so I grabbed my phone. I was debating if I should spend time on social media or watch YouTube tutorials on how to wear my hair. It would have been far too complicated to ask Doreen to come tomorrow morning to watch the twins while I went to a salon, so I'd decided to do it myself. To my surprise, I had a message from Nick.

Nick: Hey, are you sleeping?

He'd sent it an hour ago, so he probably wasn't awake anymore, but I decided to reply anyway.

Allison: Wide awake.

He called me right away. Swallowing hard, I put the phone to my ear.

"Hi," I said.

"Why are you whispering? Are the twins with you?"

"Oh, no, sorry. I don't know." I sat up on the bed with my back against the headrest.

"I can't sleep," Nick said.

I laughed. "Neither can I. We're both going to be zombies tomorrow."

"I think adrenaline will kick in as soon as we arrive at city hall."

"Yeah, that is a distinct possibility."

I hadn't spoken much to him since our night together. I knew he was deliberately trying to minimize our contact—which was a good thing, considering that right now, my entire body was full of energy just because I was hearing his voice.

"Ready for tomorrow?"

"Absolutely not, but I'm going to trust a certain sexy CEO that things will work out."

"I see. So, you trust that sexy CEO a lot?"

I paused. "Yes. Shouldn't I?"

"Right now, I don't even know what to tell you."

Holy shit. Did he mean that he didn't want to do this, or was he talking about our sexy night together?

"Nick, if you don't want to get marrie—"

"I would never pull out at the last minute on something like this."

"It's not like you would jilt me at the altar or anything." I felt sad at the idea. But I knew the deal, so I shouldn't be upset.

"Allison, we're going through with it. It's just hitting me how insane this all is, that's all."

"Only now?" My voice squeaked like Annie's sometimes did.

"It started some time ago, but now it's even more real." He sighed. "So listen, I know I've been dragging my feet with moving my stuff, but I figured there's no reason to hurry. My brother Leo will drop by the house tomorrow morning with my suitcases, and you can tell him where to leave them."

"Of course. You've decided to sleep on my couch after all?"

"Yeah. And if that's too uncomfortable, we'll switch it with mine. We'll figure it out."

"Of course."

"By the way, Leo had an interesting idea. He offered to drive you."

"Really? How come?"

"I don't know. Sort of a 'giving the bride away' tradition, I guess."

I smiled in the darkness. "I love that idea. Even though this is all unconventional, why not?"

"Then Leo will be picking you up."

Silence followed his words, and then I heard him swallow audibly. What was he thinking about? My pulse quickened for no reason.

"I forgot to tell you that Bob emailed back. They're coming."

"For fuck's sake," Nick exclaimed. "I can't believe them."

"Yeah, I can't either. He had the gall to lecture me about telling them last minute too. How about taking a hint, Bob?" I asked no one in particular.

"That's frustrating, but we'll manage."

It was more than that. The Whitleys knew what was going on, and so did the two friends I'd invited. Which meant we didn't have to pretend in front of them. But with Bob and Sophie, it was another matter altogether. Nick assured me that his family knew not to give us away, as did my friends. But still, it was all unnerving. I was afraid that Bob and Sophie suspected this was a sham marriage and were trying to obtain proof. Why else would they drop so much money on tickets?

I yawned, to my surprise.

Nick clearly heard it, as he said, "You're starting to get sleepy. Good. I'll let you get back to bed."

"I'm not sure if that's a good idea. I have to be up in five hours. I might be even more tired than if I don't sleep at all." Then I yawned again. "Nah, changed my mind. I'd better get to sleep before it goes away."

"Good night, Allison."

"Good night, Nick."

After we hung up, it dawned on me that this was the last time we'd say good night on the phone. Tomorrow, it would be in my living room.

I immediately dropped into a deep sleep and started to dream about going to get water downstairs and running into a very naked Nick. It was one of the best dreams I'd had in a very long time.

Chapter Twenty

Allison

The next morning, things were a little bit crazy. The twins woke up unhappy, which sometimes happened. Only today it was problematic because we were on a schedule, and they disliked being on a schedule. Especially on Saturday mornings. I bribed them with gummy bears, and they dutifully dressed in their outfits.

At nine o'clock on the dot, the doorbell rang.

"Leo is picking us up," I told Annie and Jack. They were sitting on the staircase, looking so pretty that I wanted to cry. If only Nora could see them now... They were truly adorable.

"Who is Leo?" Jack asked. I wanted to fist-pump the air every time he said something. After his parents died, he really withdrew into himself, but after four months, we were finally making some headway. The daycare was partially to thank for that.

"Uncle Nick's brother. He's driving us."

"Okay."

I opened the door to find Leo smiling broadly. I hadn't seen him more than once or twice over the years, probably.

"Hi, Allison. Nice to see you again."

"Likewise. Those are Nick's?" I pointed to the two huge suitcases next to him.

"Exactly."

"Just leave them here by the entrance."

Leo rolled them inside, then turned to me. "Damn, you look a lot like a bride."

"What's that supposed to mean?" I raised a brow.

"Nothing. We all just assumed..."

"I like to dress up." Then I made a shushing sign and glanced at the twins. "They don't know *everything*," I whispered.

"Right." Turning to them, he said, "Uncle Nick told me that you're Annie and Jack." He pointed at Jack when he said Annie and vice versa.

"No, doofus," Annie said, and I gasped.

"Annie. We don't call people doofus."

"I didn't know it was a bad word," she replied.

It wasn't per se, but I just hadn't expected her to use it. Had she picked it up at daycare?

"All right, group, let's go."

Both twins came with their hands stretched forward, which meant that they wanted me to hold their hands. We drove in my car because I already had the car seats there.

On the way, I asked Leo, "Is the family already there?"

"Yes. Mom too. She can't wait to meet you."

"Oh." Suddenly I felt a lot of pressure. "Um... how is she? I need to know how I can impress her."

Leo gave me a shit-eating grin that looked a lot like Nick's. "You don't have to impress her, Allison. Trust me, she already loves you."

That caught me off guard. "Wait, what?"

"Because you managed to get Nick to say yes."

"I... That's not... I mean, she knows, right? Nick said she did."

"Yes, and she totally ignores it. She acts as if it's, like, a real thing." Leo sounded as miffed as I felt.

"That's bizarre," I whispered.

"I know. But Mom works in mysterious ways. Gran is kind of singing the same tune."

"So, your grandmother and your mother get along well?" I asked.

Leo glanced at me before focusing on the road. "How much do you know from Nick?"

"He told me some things, but... You know what? Forget I asked. This is only, like, the third time I've seen you. You don't have to share any personal things with me."

"You're part of the family, Allison. There are no secrets between us. I wouldn't say they're exactly friends, but they do communicate regularly. Maddox, Nick, and I were worried about Mom attending the event along with our half brothers, but so far everyone's been civil."

"I can't even imagine how difficult that situation is."

"It's hardest for Mom, so it's even more surprising that she wanted to come. But it's good to see her. She's not in Boston very often. She keeps asking us to travel to wherever she is in Asia, but we never really do. And—"

The twins started to fight then over who had more gummy bears, and I spent the rest of the route half turned around while trying to play referee—pretty unsuccessfully.

Miraculously, they stopped as soon as we pulled up in front of city hall. It took me a second to realize it was because Nick was coming to the car.

"Uncle Nick looks like me," Jack said proudly.

Will you look at that? This was the day that Jack decided to start speaking more. I loved my little boy so much.

When Nick opened my door, I practically jumped out of the car. He took a step back, looking me up and down.

"You look stunning." His voice was laced with surprise.

I turned around once on the spot. "It's an actual bridal gown, albeit a bit of an unusual one. I didn't want to show up here underdressed." He looked absolutely handsome in his suit.

He opened the door to the back, and in no time at all, we got the twins out of the car seats.

"Uncle Nick, doesn't Auntie Allison look pretty?" Annie asked.

Looking straight into her eyes, Nick said, "Yes, she does. She's the most beautiful woman in the world."

His words went right to my heart, I swear. Did he mean it? No, he was probably just saying that because he knew it would make Annie happy.

He took both of them in his arms, which was the sexiest thing ever. Carrying one kid in each arm was no small feat. They were very heavy. I could barely lift Annie, let alone Jack. We headed toward a huge group just outside city hall.

"Hi, everyone!" My stomach was suddenly somersaulting, like it was preparing for bungee jumping. I searched the crowd, but Violet and Danielle, my friends, weren't here yet.

"All right, everyone. Some of you know Allison, others don't, so let's get introductions out of the way," Nick said, putting the twins down. They were both still holding his hands, though.

"I've got this," I assured him.

Over the next few minutes, I introduced myself to everyone. It was impossible to remember who was who. I vaguely knew who Maddox was, but I'd never met the rest, and I got all of their names mixed up.

"By the way, I'm sorry we didn't get to throw you a bachelorette party," the woman named Meredith said. "Everything happened too fast."

"We're very good with celebrations," yet another woman said. I think she was Natalie. She had a cute baby in her arms who kept fussing about. I wanted to reach for the baby and hold her close.

Since the twins moved in with me, I'd started having baby fever. Before, I'd never had that in my life.

"The group is complete," Nick said. "We should go upstairs."

"Actually, Violet and Danielle aren't here yet," I said. "But they know which room we're in. They can join us upstairs whenever they arrive."

Nick opened the door, and just as we were both about to walk in, I heard Bob call, "We're here too."

I sighed. Secretly, I'd been hoping they'd missed their plane or something.

I swear I felt a current of awareness go through the group.

Panic rose in my throat. "Nick, your family—"

"I told them everything about Bob and Sophie."

It was such a weird feeling to realize that I could trust him.

Bob and Sophie looked like they were attending a movie premiere. *Oh, for God's sake.* They were a bit ridiculous. Bob was wearing a suit, but it was far too shiny for this time of day. Sophie had on a floor-length black dress. You'd think she was attending the Oscars, not a ceremony at city hall.

They made a beeline for us.

"Bob, Sophie. I see you made it in time," Nick said.

"Yes, we did our best," Bob replied dryly.

"Let's all go in," Nick urged. "Otherwise, we'll be late, and city hall works on a very tight schedule. We'll leave introductions for later."

"Don't worry," his grandma said. I remembered distinctly that her name was Jeannie Whitley. She looked at me with so much kindness that I wanted to hug her.

Nick released Annie's hand to put an arm around my waist, keeping me almost glued to him. For a split second, I was confused as to why. Then I realized that with Bob and Sophie here, we had to act like a couple. It was a good thing I'd splurged on this gorgeous dress; otherwise, they would have gotten suspicious right away.

Up close, I couldn't miss the smell of his aftershave. It went straight to my head. I even felt a little lightheaded.

Annie came to the other side of me, giving me her hand. A knot formed in my throat. We looked so much like a family.

It's not real, Allison. All this is so that the twins stay with you, but you can't expect Nick to be in the picture forever. At least not in this capacity.

The twins would be sad further down the road when Nick parted ways with us, but I couldn't think that far ahead. I needed to take it one step at a time.

Our room was on the second floor. I was stunned when I stepped out of the elevator and saw gorgeously decorated signs with our names pointing toward the room. There were balloons as well.

I looked at Nick in surprise, and he winked at me. "I told Frances to go all out."

"Why?" I whispered.

"Why not? You told me you were in the mood to celebrate. I figured you'd enjoy this."

I was about to ask what "all out" meant, but it became obvious when we stepped into the room. I assumed this was going to be a very terse city hall room. Normally, it probably was, unless it was professionally decorated by someone who clearly knew how to do weddings. There were flowers pretty much everywhere, along with balloons and even a photographer in the corner to commemorate the event.

"Nick," I murmured, "this is too much."

"Nah. It's exactly right."

Chapter Twenty-One
Allison

There was no aisle to walk down, so Nick and I simply moved forward. The officiant was sitting down at the desk. I glanced around the room, trying to take in the details. It was a mix of a simple courthouse and a wedding venue because of all the decorations. It didn't look too intimidating, but at least it wasn't as cold as I'd imagined.

"Welcome," the officiant told us. He seemed to be in his late sixties. He, too, glanced around the room, but unlike me, he didn't seem impressed by the decorations. Twice he cocked his brow and shook his head.

Nick and I exchanged a glance, and I almost burst out laughing. Poor man. He'd probably expected to come here and do a quick, no-nonsense ceremony, then promptly continue his Saturday. Well, it was probably going to be short, anyway.

"All right, is everyone here?" he inquired. "Can we start? Is there music?"

"No music," Nick said, and the man looked relieved.

I carefully avoided Nick's eyes; otherwise, I would burst out laughing. I glanced behind me and noted that the only guests who weren't here were Violet and Danielle. I wondered what happened to them.

It didn't make sense to make this poor man wait to start. He had more ceremonies to perform. And it wasn't fair to the other guests either. I noticed Bob and Sophie all the way at the back, sitting alone in a row. Their presence unnerved me. The fact that all the Whitleys were here just made my day even though I didn't know them yet. They were Nick's family, and that gave me comfort.

I turned and faced the officiant. "We can start."

"All right. I'm here to officiate the marriage of Nick Whitley and Allison Holmes. Everyone ready?"

I was truly laughing now, but the man silenced me with a stern brow.

How did we end up with the grumpiest officiant in the city? Not that I knew too many, since I hadn't actually attended a wedding at city hall before. I had no idea what to expect, but I'd assumed he'd at least ask if we wanted to take the other one to be our wedded wife and husband, respectively, only he didn't.

He robotically spoke three sentences before finishing with "You can sign here and here. Please check that your names are spelled correctly and that the date of birth is also correct."

"That's it?" Nick asked, voicing my thoughts.

The officiant looked up at me. "Yes. It says here you wanted the fast-track version."

"We do. We have kids with us," I said. "They might get impatient."

Once again, he cocked his brow like he was asking me why I was polluting him with an explanation when he didn't ask for one. This man was hilarious.

I quickly checked the name before signing. Nick did the same.

"You may exchange rings," the man said.

The wedding rings took me by complete surprise.

First, because I'd completely forgotten we'd need them.

Second, because they were absolutely gorgeous. The platinum bands had tiny stones set throughout. Nick's were a bit smaller than mine. I glanced at him, and he simply winked at me before we exchanged the rings.

"Congratulations, you are now husband and wife."

I was waiting for a "You may kiss the bride" or something, but it never came. However, that didn't stop Nick. He twirled me around to face him, smiling at me.

"Wow. This was quick, wife, and now you're mine." Before I knew it, he put a arm around my back, plastering me to him, and then pushed me backwards as his mouth came down on mine. He lowered me theatrically, and yet I never felt like I might be in danger of losing my balance. Except when he slipped his tongue past my lips.

Holy shit. How was he kissing me like this with everyone watching? I was instantly on pins and needles. Energy gripped my whole body, concentrating between my thighs.

It's just a kiss. It's just a kiss.

Only it wasn't—not after our night together. It wasn't wild or overly sexual, and when he straightened us up slowly, he continued kissing me.

When he pulled back, I realized that everyone was clapping, and I felt a pair of tiny arms wrapped around my calves. I looked down to see Annie looking up at me with a toothy grin. Jack was holding his hands up. Nick immediately lifted him into his arms, then took my hand and kissed the back of it.

The Whitleys were smiling from ear to ear. In fact, everyone was smiling except Bob and Sophie. I honestly didn't even care about them. Even though this was all fake, the enthusiasm in the room was very real. And why not be happy? The two of us were doing a fantastic thing for these little nuggets. It was definitely worth celebrating.

The photographer came over and said, "Let me snap a picture of the bride and groom alone."

Annie tightened her grip on me.

"We'll do it like this, with our kids," Nick said.

I loved that he didn't even hesitate to include the twins. And I couldn't believe he'd actually thought of a photographer. It hadn't even crossed my mind, but it was genius. Why not have keepsakes of this day? We could always snap pictures with a phone, but having a photographer made it all the more official.

I looked at him, and he must have sensed it, because he turned to watch me too. Our faces were less than an inch apart.

"Great idea to bring a photographer," I told him.

"I thought you might like it."

How would I go through the real thing one day and not compare it to this?

"All right. Who else wants to be in the picture with the bride and groom and the kids before we take group photos?" the photographer asked the attendees.

All the Whitleys started talking at the same time. They were up on their feet, making a beeline toward us. Bob and Sophie were the only ones who didn't join in.

Fantastic. I didn't want them in the picture at all.

"Abe and I should have priority," Jeannie Whitley said.

Nick grinned. "Of course, Gran. You always do."

Everyone else was younger, obviously, so that made sense.

Jeannie came over to my side, beaming. She leaned into me as the photographer instructed us to smile and said, "You're doing a wonderful thing. And people get married for far worse reasons. You might be surprised at how this turns out."

Instead of flashing the photographer a huge smile, I gave him a jaw drop. Then I smiled and hoped the photographer would delete that one and simply pick the best pictures to send to us.

Oh my goodness. Leo had hinted at something like this, but I didn't take him seriously.

Afterward, a gorgeous woman came toward us.

"Mom, you made it," Nick said.

Oh, that's right. I'd forgotten who she was amid all the introductions.

"You two make a gorgeous, gorgeous couple. And son, you look great with a kid on your hip." Nick had been holding Jack, and they truly looked like father and son.

Annie had gone from hugging my ankles to wanting to be carried, too, and I obliged.

I glanced at Nick just as he looked right at me. I knew without saying a word that he was thinking the same thing. Did everyone in the family believe this was going to last forever? Why would they even think that?

Thankfully, his brothers and their respective partners were far more laid-back.

"Thanks for making this quick," Spencer said. "Ben is already looking at these balloons like he wants to pop every single one of them."

I started to laugh. The photographer was fast and captured Nick, Spencer, Penny, and me all laughing from ear to ear.

The photo session took much longer than I'd anticipated because everyone wanted to take a picture with us, and then we had several group shots as well.

We realized it was our cue to leave when the officiant cleared his throat. "The next couple has been waiting."

Mr. Grumpy Ass was still grumping.

"We should get going," Nick said, checking his watch. "We have reservations."

I glanced around the room again. Still no Violet and Danielle. I realized we hadn't been in touch in a while, and I hadn't been going out with the group since I took in the kids, but I thought they'd like to share this moment with me. Clearly I was learning who my friends were.

Just as well. My life was changing, and the single lifestyle was definitely not in the cards anymore.

Nick and I once again walked in front of the group. The twins demanded to be put down. Then they grabbed each other's hands and walked in front of us. My heart was about to burst.

As we neared Bob and Sophie, they finally got up. They both gave us very polite and restrained smiles.

"We're going to the restaurant now?" Sophie asked.

Nick nodded. "Yes. We've got lunch reservations."

"That's awfully unusual for a wedding," she said. "No party, just restaurant reservations?"

I squared my shoulders, looking her straight in the eyes. "We wanted the daytime celebration so we didn't mess up the kids' evening routine." Which was 100 percent true.

Sophie shook her head. "You know, as I keep telling you, Allison, all that would be solved if you'd just hire a full-time nanny. But then, I suppose you can't afford it."

Nick stared at her. "Sophie, Bob, today is for celebrating. If you're just going to make snide remarks, then we're disinviting you from the luncheon."

Sophie jerked her head back. "I always wondered why my son considered you his best friend. Jim was very well-mannered and polite, and you are..."

"Blunt," Nick finished for her.

There were murmurs behind us, but I didn't want to turn around to see who said, "Who the hell is that hag?"

I was hoping Sophie didn't hear. Oooor... maybe it wouldn't hurt if she did.

Neither she nor Bob said another word. Once again, Nick put an arm around my waist, and I leaned into him.

"I love that you've got my back," I whispered to him.

"Fuck yes, I do. Especially now."

What did he mean by that?

I didn't have a chance to ask him because the next half hour was a bit crazy. There were a ton of cars parked around city hall, as everyone had driven here.

Leo wasn't chauffeuring me and the twins this time. Nick was.

"This day is perfect," I told him as I climbed into the car.

"How come?"

"It's the perfect mix of celebratory without being over the top. I was never a fan of weddings."

"What a coincidence. Neither was I. But that's mostly because everyone seemed more preoccupied in asking me when I was going to settle down and become serious."

I wiggled my eyebrows. "You know what's worse than being a bachelor?"

"What?"

"Being a single woman. People treat you like you have a disease."

"Well, not any longer," Nick said. "Wife."

"You're right, *husband*. Now I'm a married woman. Serious and all."

I was euphoric. This would be how I'd plan my real wedding, I decided. A short ceremony at city hall with a pretty dress, followed by a delicious meal with family and close friends. Speaking of which...

I turned backward, grabbing my bag from between the twins, who were fast asleep, and checked my phone. I frowned when I read the most recent message I'd received.

"What's wrong?" Nick asked.

"Violet and Danielle texted that it doesn't make any sense for them to come since it's... you know..."

"Some friends," Nick said, voicing my thoughts.

Yes, this was fake, but I still felt a bit betrayed. I truly thought that the three of us would always be friends.

"Are you okay?" he asked a few moments later. "You've gone quiet."

"It's been hard. I don't have many friends left these days," I admitted.

"You mentioned that."

"But it's worse than I thought. I'm not sure what happened. All of my friends sort of disappeared. They stopped inviting me to things. Granted, I declined all invitations because my life had changed, but I couldn't spontaneously go out for drinks and stuff like that, or have a girls' weekend. But..." I sighed and looked out the window. "I figured that eventually we were going to find a balance. I was closer to Violet and Danielle than the rest of my friends. We lived together for three years after college because we wanted to save on rent."

Nick slid his hand over mine. I startled, not because I didn't enjoy it, but because my entire body reacted to his touch. Was this because today was special, or because of our night together?

"Just putting it out there, but all the women in my family are dying to adopt you."

"Really?"

"Yes. They even wanted to throw you a bachelorette party."

"I know. Meredith said that. I wonder why they didn't."

"I said no." Nick looked bewildered. "I never realized you might want one."

"I didn't either... until now. It doesn't sound bad."

He shook his head. "The minds of women are always a mystery."

That made me laugh. "Don't feel bad about it. Sometimes I'm a mystery to myself."

"And I can't wait to uncover every single one of those mysteries," Nick said.

His voice was a bit lower, but his eyes were playful, nonseductive.

Wait, I spoke too soon. I'd seen that glint before he ravaged me in his dressing room. Yep, that definitely counted as seductive. How was I going to manage tonight and every other night living with this man until I got out of this debacle?

It didn't matter. For now, I was determined to have fun for the rest of the day. I was genuinely curious to get to know the Whitleys, and this lunch was just as good an opportunity as any.

Then realization hit me.

"With Bob and Sophie here, how are we going to play this out?"

"What do you mean?" Nick asked.

I kept my voice low because the kids were still sleeping in the back, and I didn't want to wake them up. "Won't it seem weird that I don't know your family?"

"If they voice any concerns, I'll take care of it. And besides, this all happened quickly. You barely had time to get to know everyone." He grinned. "We barely had time to know each other—except in the most essential ways, of course."

Ha, this man! Is he starting to be shameless already? First that sexy glint in his eyes, and now he was throwing innuendos at me. But I didn't have time to mull things over too much because we arrived at the restaurant a few minutes later.

It took us forever to wake the twins, but then they went from sleepy to overexcited when they realized we didn't go home. They loved adventures. I'd liked the restaurant from the pictures Nick's assistant sent me, but it was even more gorgeous in person. It was professionally decorated in the same style as city hall was, with flowers and balloons.

The photographer had tagged along, only this time he had what looked like a video camera, too, and was already filming the activity.

There was a long table set up for us in a small room with huge windows overlooking the inner courtyard. It was something out of a dream, with perfectly trimmed bonsai trees and plants with multicolored flowers everywhere.

"I'll have to send your assistant flowers or something in thanks," I told Nick as I looked around the room. "This is gorgeous!"

"Don't worry. I'll give her a raise for putting that smile on your face."

I wanted to ask why my smiling was so important to him, but how on earth could I without sounding weird?

"Definitely do that. She went above and beyond."

"Do we have a seating arrangement?" Colton asked.

Nick rolled his eyes. "No, brother," he emphasized. "It's just family, so everyone can sit wherever they want."

I personally hoped that Jeannie and Abe were going to sit nearby because I wanted to get to know them better. And of course Helen, Nick's mom. I looked around for her, but then Bob and Sophie walked right up to us.

"We're going to take the seats nearest you. We won't stay long, so we want to be able to chat while we're here," Bob said.

Chapter Twenty-Two
Nick

I wanted to throw Bob and Sophie out right now. This was supposed to be a relaxed day with the family and Allison's friends. Having these two here made everything more complicated. What the fuck did they want to talk about anyway? All their bullshit just made Allison uncomfortable.

"When is your flight?" I asked, making it clear exactly how excited I was *not* to have them here.

"At five o'clock," Sophie replied.

I almost groaned. That was a fucking eternity away.

"We'll sit here," I said, pointing to the two seats at the head of the table. "You can choose either side. Mom, Gran, Granddad, you can sit over here with the twins." I gestured to the seats I was referencing.

"I think the twins want to sit with us and Ben," Spencer said.

I turned to Allison. "That work for you, babe?"

She nodded. "Sure."

Allison's eyes lit up. I wondered why but didn't have time to dwell on it.

As we all took our seats, waiters started to circulate with drinks, asking us what we wanted. They had a mix of champagne, juices, and water. It took a while for everyone to settle down. Mom was sitting right next to me. She kept glancing down the table.

"All good?" I asked her.

She waved her hand, nodding. "Yes, yes."

"Where did you sit during the ceremony? I didn't see you."

"I was right behind your grandparents with Leo and Maddox. Everyone's been treating me really nicely," she added in a low voice, correctly guessing that that was my real question.

"That's good."

I wasn't expecting my brothers to jump with joy and ask Mom to be included in all family events from now on, but I was glad that they didn't make her feel unwelcome.

Once everyone was seated, the waiters came with the first round of finger food.

"This is unusual," Sophie said, scrunching her nose at the plate. "To have food like this served at a wedding reception."

Allison cleared her throat. "Once again, we've got kids. They need to be fed, and they like this food. It's perfect for their little stomachs."

"Ben was starving," Spencer added.

"You did the right thing, Allison." That came from Colton. "And I, for one, am extremely happy you've had the foresight to ask for the food to be brought the second we came."

I gave him a nod. My oldest half brother had been the most difficult to win over. Personally, I'd never thought it was possible. I wasn't in the habit of trying to get people who didn't like me to change their mind. But when Colton came around, he *really* came around. I was counting on him to have my back in any situation.

Sophie pursed her lips as we all started to eat. I realized that Allison was tense again, so I put my left hand between her shoulder blades. She softened against my touch. I'd keep my hand here the whole damn day if it helped. Then I nudged her leg with mine under the table and put my mouth to her ear.

"You okay?"

She nodded, smiling. I was addicted to this woman: the way she smelled, the way she did just about anything.

As we ate the appetizers, Sophie said, "I'm surprised your parents aren't here, Allison. Why on earth would they miss their only remaining daughter's wedding?"

There was a loud clank. Gran had dropped her fork. I should have warned her about Bob and Sophie, about how rude they could be.

"That's a very insensitive question," Gran said right away.

The corners of my mouth twitched. Sophie's face fell. Being scolded by a ninety-year-old was probably the height of humiliation for her.

"I didn't mean it that way," Sophie said, but by the tone of her voice, it was clear that she did.

"My parents are not in good health, and traveling is very difficult for them," Allison offered. "I thought you knew that. I know Nora mentioned it many times."

"We're going to visit them soon," I added as I brushed my wife's shoulders with my fingers, rubbing them up and down.

I quickly realized I was doing it for my benefit as much as hers. This wasn't just for Sophie and Bob's sake. I fucking needed to touch this woman. I even shifted closer on my chair. My thigh was now touching hers, and I instantly felt a change in her body. She straightened up slightly. This was insane. The more I touched her, the more I wanted her. The ceremony at city hall made everything seem real, seem possible. If I were to have a family, this would be it.

"Hmm. And none of your friends are here either," Sophie continued, addressing only Allison.

"Since it was such short notice, not everyone could make it," Allison said easily. "And as you know, we wanted to keep it small since the venue couldn't accommodate a lot of people."

Sophie narrowed her eyes. I knew Allison was close to losing her cool. Hell, I was close to doing the same. These two assholes hadn't even bothered spending one second with their grandchildren since they arrived, not at city hall nor here at the restaurant. Ben and the twins were running around the place, and my family took turns chasing after them. But Sophie and Bob hadn't made any move to suggest they wanted to be around the kids at all.

I'd instructed the photographer to also take videos of the event, figuring they could come in handy for a potential trial. We'd have solid proof that they couldn't even be bothered to be grandparents, much less the custodial guardians for the twins.

The waiters circulated with drinks and brought wine options as well. I looked around at my family, and something about this picture felt completely right. Ever since Leo had gotten engaged, I'd started to feel out of place at family gatherings. I was literally the odd man out. And while my relationship with my brothers had always been tight, there was no denying that it had changed now that they all had someone in their lives. Inevitably, we drifted apart as they spent more time at home. We didn't do brotherly outings like before. I never truly understood why, but right now, I was beginning to.

For fuck's sake, Nick. What the hell are you even talking about? You and Allison just signed a document to make things easier for her to keep custody.

Yet I couldn't shake the feeling that this was simply right.

"Are you going to have a honeymoon?" Sophie asked, continuing her inquisition.

"No," Allison replied, "there was no way I could get time off work. Maybe we'll plan something next year for the four of us to go."

I could see that happening. We'd take the kids to Disney World. The twins would love it.

Fucking hell, I was already making plans for next year.

"You'll continue to work?" Bob asked.

"Of course she will. I have a strong, independent woman next to me," I said. "CFO is no small position."

"But I don't understand. You're married now," Sophie said. She and Bob exchanged a glance. You'd think that Allison had announced she planned to be a stripper.

"There is no reason that I can't have a career *and* be married to Nick." Her voice dripped with pride.

Fuck, I loved the way that sounded. She was married to me. *Allison is married to me!*

Sophie straightened up. "No woman who cares about her family wants to work."

I saw red, and all thoughts of playing it cool flew out the window.

"Not even your sister—"

"Stop right there, Sophie," I cut her off. "Try to be civil if at all possible or else you need to leave right now."

With horror, I realized that Allison was trembling slightly. She rolled her hands into fists, grabbing the knife and the fork so tightly that I wondered if she was preparing to launch herself at Jim's parents.

"You're kicking us out?" Bob said.

"You've definitely overstayed your welcome," Gran replied.

"Yes. This is a time to celebrate," Grandad added, "and you two seem to have come here looking for a reason to pick a fight. It's not the time or place for that."

"Damn right, it's not," Bob said. He rose from the table. "Come on, Sophie. Let's go. We'll settle this in court. We will crush you—"

"Don't you dare talk to Allison like that," I said through gritted teeth as both she and I stood up. "You might not know much about the Whitleys or care about us, but we have access to the best lawyers in the state. You try to intimidate my wife and you're going to regret it."

I looked directly at Bob, and he jerked his head back at the sincerity in my gaze.

Even though they weren't from Boston, they knew exactly how powerful the Whitley name was. Until now, they probably thought they could just intimidate Allison because she was still grieving after losing her sister. Because they thought she was alone. But my woman was not fucking alone.

She's not your woman, Nick, just your wife.

That's right. My wife was not alone.

"Please leave," Allison said.

The two of them moved out of the way without another word and then left the room.

Allison released a deep breath that sounded shaky. I tilted her head to me. "Are you okay, honey?"

"That was horrible," Mom said in disgust. "I don't even know them, but they're not good people."

"They're not," Colton said.

It dawned on me now that everyone had witnessed the scene. This was exactly the kind of evidence we'd need for a trial, if it came to that. I checked to see where the photographer was; maybe he caught a few shots, or even better a video. I'd find out later. I still thought Jim's parents were bluffing.

I looked at my brothers. "You all have been suspiciously silent."

"Clearly both of you had it handled. We figured there was no reason for us to pile on too." That came from Jake, but he was looking straight at Allison now. "What my brother said is correct. The Whitley name does hold weight, and you will win in court."

Allison sighed, and her shoulders finally slumped. "Thank you. God, I'm so sorry for this."

"You know what? Maybe it's for the best," Gran said as both Allison and I sat down. "Now we can all relax and enjoy the rest of the day."

Allison's face lit up. "You're right, Jeannie. I thought those two were going to stay here right until it was time to go to the airport. I'm glad they're gone." She covered her mouth then, looking at the kids. Fortunately, they were with Ben, playing some game. It didn't even look as though they noticed their grandparents left.

"I don't know if it was smart to treat them like that," Colton offered, "after what Hugo told you about avoiding confrontation."

"They had to be dealt with," I said in a tone that brooked no argument. Then I turned to Allison, once more touching her jaw so she'd look at me. "They were antagonizing you. I won't allow anyone to do that. Ever."

"You're mine now," I wanted to say, but I stopped myself just in time. Good God, I had to get myself under control. She wasn't mine. Why did I keep forgetting?

I swallowed hard, digesting all of this.

She nodded. "Thank you."

As I let go of her face and turned around, I noticed both Mom and Gran looking at me with very wicked smiles. Then I glanced around the table. Half of them had their eyes on us. I could practically see real wedding bells ringing in my grandmother's mind. I could only hope she wouldn't say anything. Allison needed more of a heads-up about how crazy the Whitley conversations could get. I needed to prepare her, and she'd had enough craziness for today.

"Well, I, for one, think we should just enjoy this beautiful, beautiful day. It was a very nice touch to have a photographer," Mom offered.

"Yes," Gran added. "I wasn't even aware that there were going to be decorations and such." She was looking straight at me, clearly fishing for information. I was going to satisfy her curiosity, but not right now.

"Nick came up with all this. I didn't know either," Allison responded.

I was still looking at Gran. Her entire face transformed, and I knew exactly what she was thinking. She glanced at Mom, who returned her knowing smile. Those two were getting very friendly lately, but I wasn't complaining about it at all.

"Since they're gone," Meredith said loudly, "I propose a toast for two of the best people I know." She raised her glass of champagne, and everyone else followed suit, including me and Allison.

"Thank you all for being here," Allison replied, "and for making me feel so welcome and accepted despite the fact that you don't know me."

"The fact that Nick is willing to do so much," Gran said, "is very telling."

"But Nick doesn't really know me that well either."

"No, but he's got very good instincts about people." Then Gran looked straight at me. "And he's not afraid to follow them."

That wasn't subtle at all, but thankfully, she didn't insist on saying any more.

Everyone was much more relaxed for the rest of the meal. They served our dinner of steak and rice with mixed vegetables a few minutes later. We even had a makeshift wedding cake the restaurant had prepared, and we enjoyed dessert together.

It wasn't too long after that the twins and Ben were sleeping on the couches by the window. Jake's daughter was napping in her carrier. Catching up with the family was always great, and I loved that Allison was feeling at ease around them.

Chapter Twenty-Three
Nick

By the time we drove home, it was way past the twins' bedtime. It was already eight o'clock.

Allison kept glancing into the backseat at them. "I bet they'll wake up and stay up for hours once we're home."

"Allison, tomorrow is Sunday. Even if we stay up late, we'll sleep in tomorrow."

"That's right," she said, then added, "husband."

For most of my life, I'd been certain that I would never want anyone to call me that. I wasn't even sure when I decided, but it was probably around the time I found out that my dad had another family. Or maybe after, when I saw the disaster he'd left in his wake. No clue. But I didn't mind Allison calling me husband at all. Maybe because I knew it wasn't real.

When we arrived at the house, we were both silent for a few moments, neither of us making a move to get out of the car. Finally, Allison whispered, "I can't believe we've gone through with this."

"I'm feeling exactly the same. But we've come this far. Let's do this."

She quickly got out of the car. Damn, the woman was fast. I always liked opening doors for her, but she wasn't giving me the opportunity.

Allison's prediction turned out to be wrong. The twins didn't even wake up when we took them from the car seats and brought them inside. We carried them upstairs and lowered each one into bed.

"Let's just get their shoes off and that's it. Don't take their clothes off. I don't want to bother their sleep," Allison said.

As I took off Jack's shoes, I had a flash of a memory of Mom bringing the three of us home after a birthday party and telling us that we had to be in bed by eight. We were a bit older than the twins were, but not by much. I remembered Mom reading us bedtime stories... and virtually nothing like that with Dad.

The idea that Jack and Annie wouldn't know their parents saddened me. But they were going to have Allison and, at some point, her real husband.

Hell no!

The thought of her calling someone else husband didn't sit well with me *at all*. I had no idea why I had so much trouble processing it or making peace with the fact that this was a temporary thing.

We left the room, and something shifted between us.

Allison stepped away. "Leo left your suitcases downstairs. We could make space for your stuff in my dresser. And we can take your empty suitcases to the garage once you've unpacked."

I ran a hand through my hair. "Let's not deal with any of that tonight. There's no hurry. I'll just take what I need and do everything else tomorrow. Is there enough space in your bedroom to put a second dresser for my things?"

"We could do that," she replied. "I'm going to change into something more comfortable and then bring linens downstairs."

"Thanks. I'll open the pull-out."

"Perfect."

She dashed into her room faster than I'd hoped. I didn't want this day to be over yet. But after a few seconds of listening to her walk around her room and the unmistakable sound of a zipper being lowered, I decided it was better if I went downstairs. Otherwise, I was liable to bust into her room and have a real wedding night.

I headed straight for the couch, which had an easy system. It wasn't terribly big, but the mattress seemed half decent.

"This is the best I have. I hope they fit," Allison said from behind me a few moments later, her voice low so as not to wake the twins.

I straightened up and turned to look at her. *Fuck me.* She was wearing a very short dress, or was it a nightgown? No, I was sure it was a dress. Her hair was still styled, but she'd changed it, loosened it somehow. She was even sexier than she'd looked in the wedding dress.

"You can use my shower if you want to," she offered.

"Great. I'll be quick."

"And I'll make the bed now."

"It's fine, Allison. You've had a long day. I'll do it."

"Hey, we both had a long day."

"I'm taking care of this. If you want to do something, sit in that armchair and keep me company."

"You're bossing me around in my own living room?" she asked.

I tilted closer. "I thought you liked it."

She gasped. "Nick. I thought we were going to ignore that."

I took in a deep breath. I'd been alone with this woman for a hot minute and was already crossing boundaries. "You're right. We *are* going to ignore it. Forget what I said."

"Like that's easy," she said, walking backward to the armchair. As she sat down, she ran a hand through her hair. She then pulled her legs up as well, and for a split second, I thought I was having visions. As she twisted to put her legs under her, I caught a glimpse of her pussy. She wasn't wearing panties.

Come on, Nick. Think of things you hate, like cilantro. It tastes like fucking soap.

It wasn't working.

"Nick? What's wrong?" Allison asked.

I glanced down at the floor, trying to get myself under control. It was having the opposite effect. "I'll go shower."

"What happened? You just sort of went blank." She rose from the armchair, repeating the same motion. I groaned, and she covered her mouth, her eyes wide. "Oh my God. I flashed you, right?"

"Yes. Twice."

"What? I didn't hear you."

I cleared my throat. "You flashed me twice."

She wasn't just covering her mouth now but her whole face with both hands. "I'll be wearing panties from now on when I'm in the house."

Hearing her actually say that she wasn't wearing anything had the most bizarre effect on me. It was turning me on. Then again, I couldn't think of a single thing she could do right now that *wouldn't* turn me on.

I wanted to reassure her, but if I touched her—hell, even went near her—I was going to have her right there in that armchair, and it was only our first night together.

"I'll go take that shower now."

"Yeah, good thinking. Do you need me to show you up?"

"No, I'll find my way," I said before going up the stairs, taking two steps at once.

As I walked into her bedroom, I looked around. It was big. Nowhere near as big as mine, but as far as master bedrooms went, it was decent. So was the bathroom.

I took off my suit and dropped it to the floor, not caring that it was going to get crumpled. I wasn't going to wear a groom's suit again anytime soon. I turned the water ice-cold. It was brutal. My entire body felt as if someone had cut off my circulation.

It was exactly what I needed.

I'd brought my toiletry bag with me and found my shower gel, rubbing it over my body. After the initial cold shower, I turned the water to warm. Clearly this was going to be more difficult than I'd anticipated. I'd postponed thinking about logistics because it seemed like a waste of time, but maybe I'd been wrong. Then again, I hadn't expected to maul her in my dressing room either. This was all uncharted territory for me.

After I finished the shower, I put on slacks and a T-shirt and headed downstairs. Allison had changed into long pants and a T-shirt, and I exhaled in relief. *Thank fuck.* If she'd been wearing that same short dress, I wasn't sure I'd let her go upstairs without being properly kissed—or fucked.

"I had to go upstairs and swap linens because those were far too big for the couch, but these fit better."

I hadn't even realized she'd done that.

"Thanks, Allison."

"It's the least I can do after flashing you not once but twice."

She was smiling, but I knew her mannerisms well enough by now to realize that she was nervous. She stood by the kitchen counter, leaning against it, fiddling her thumbs. I walked straight to her.

"Allison, we'll get used to this," I said.

"Will we?"

I had no idea.

She sucked in a deep breath. "Nick."

Damn it. How had I ended up in her space? I glanced down, which turned out to be a big mistake because I looked straight into her cleavage. I took a step back with great difficulty and rolled my shoulders.

"It has to get easier."

She nodded. "Do you want me to make some tea or anything?" I shook my head, and she blew out a heavy breath. "I don't know how to navigate this. I mean, I know this is your space now in the evening. Are you sure you don't want to take my bedroom instead? I can camp out here."

"Allison, I'm fine on the couch, really. I'd never let you sleep there."

"But here's the thing. I'm actually a pretty bad sleeper, so sometimes during the night I get restless."

"And what do you usually do then?"

"Come down here and drink some water, eat some ice cream. Sometimes I even go out in the yard."

"You can do all of those things anyway. I sleep very deeply."

She tilted her head. "Opening doors wouldn't wake you up?"

"No, and if it does, I'll join you."

"How do you even know I'd want company?" she teased.

"Oh, so your midnight activities are secret?"

She licked her lips, and I swallowed hard. We were slipping right back into dangerous territory.

She seemed to realize that, because she said, "I'm going to go upstairs. It's been a long day. I'll try not to wake you tomorrow morning."

"As I said, all good."

"But the kids might be harder to keep quiet."

I looked her in the eye, holding her gaze. "Allison, it's all good. Promise."

She nodded once. "Okay. Good night, Nick."

I watched her retreat upstairs, and even in her long pants, my dick found her ass attractive. Oh well. We'd have to manage this somehow.

Usually, I was a late sleeper on the weekends, but honestly, adjusting to an earlier sleep schedule was going to be the least of my problems now. Resisting the urge to seduce this gorgeous woman, be it the middle of the day or the night—*that* was another story altogether.

Chapter Twenty-Four
Nick

The next morning, I woke up with a stiff neck. Then as I started to move, I realized more parts of my body were in pain, like my back and right hip. I felt like an eighty-year-old. I immediately rolled off the couch, my body creaking with every movement. There was no fucking way I could sleep on this thing again. It was a torture device.

I tilted my head to the left and the right, glancing at the clock. It was six in the morning. I blinked several times to make sure I wasn't imagining things because I hadn't woken up that early in years. Last time I was probably in high school, and Mom had to drag me out of bed. Why the hell would I wake up now?

Then I realized it was because of the fucking couch. My body was protesting too much. I debated going back to sleep, but no way would I put myself through that.

Instead, I went to make some coffee. It was a small Nespresso machine, and thankfully, Allison had the coffee capsules right next to it. I was a bit of a coffee snob and instantly decided to chat with her about bringing my professional barista machine from home, along with a better fucking couch.

Served me right. That's what I got for always flying by the seat of my pants instead of planning things meticulously. I usually reserved that side of me for business, but it wouldn't have killed me to come here and check the couch first before throwing my back out sleeping on it.

I chose the darkest brew and made myself a strong cup. After a few sips, I was looking at the day in a more optimistic manner. I could solve anything.

As I took the sheets off and turned the bed back into a couch, I could swear I heard the twins talking. I listened intently. Yep, that was Annie's voice. I hurried up the stairs and straight into their room. They were both camped on Jack's bed.

"Uncle Nick!" Annie grinned.

"You sleep here?" Jack said.

Wow, that was the most words I'd ever heard from this kid... well, since the accident.

"Yes, I am." I sat between the two of them. "What are you doing up so early?"

Annie shrugged.

"Right," I said. "Do you want to go downstairs?"

She nodded. "Is Auntie Allison there too?"

"No, she's still asleep. Let's let her rest for a bit."

"We gotta be quiet?" Annie asked, holding her little finger to her lips.

I nodded, and she moved over me until her face was straight in front of her brother's. "Jack, quiet."

Jack nodded, frowning as if he was trying to process this very important information. These two were adorable.

They got out of bed at the same time, but Annie grabbed Jack's hand. She kept making shushing sounds at him even though the poor guy wasn't saying anything. I walked behind them as we went down the stairs, which took a long time because they were tiny and the steps were huge. They didn't ask for help, though, and I was certain they could make it on their own. They just needed me to be patient.

"What do you eat in the mornings?" I asked them.

"Pancakes," Annie said without even hesitating.

Then she looked at Jack sternly. He frowned but didn't reply.

I barely bit back laughter. I was certain that they didn't have pancakes every morning, but what the hell? It was Sunday. I needed some damn pancakes too.

"Do you know where the ingredients are?" I asked.

They shook their heads in unison. No matter. The kitchen wasn't huge, so I wouldn't have an issue.

I opened all the drawers and cupboards in quick succession and easily found what I needed. Allison had premade batter mix, and she also had a waffle maker.

"How about waffles instead of pancakes?" I suggested.

"Yess, waffles! Waffles are the best!" That came from Jack.

I was stunned. Apparently, so was Annie, because she was staring at her brother with her mouth open. Then she hurried to Jack and took him in her arms.

Jesus, these two. Why didn't I video this? I was certain that Allison would have loved to see them right now.

"Okay, then! I'm starting on the waffles."

"I can help," Annie said, then immediately went to one of the two learning towers that were propped against the kitchen island.

She carefully slid onto hers and Jack on his. Those were a very cool invention because they were at the height of the kitchen island and the twins couldn't fall off. They were both looking at me expectantly.

Shit, I'm supposed to give them tasks?

"I'll give you some batter to mix."

They both nodded in unison, hanging on to my every word. As far as winging it went, I was doing a spectacular job. I found two bowls for them and put some batter mix in, along with eggs and milk, and gave them plastic spoons.

I observed them for a few seconds to make sure there was no way for them to hurt themselves. But they were great. I made a mental note to ask Allison what other things they could do in the kitchen. Clearly they loved to be involved.

The waffles were ready in no time. I found a selection of spreads and syrups in the fridge and took all of them out just as footsteps sounded from the hall.

"Good morning," Allison said as she entered the kitchen.

Her eyes were still heavy with sleep. She rubbed at one of them with a little yawn. Her hair was in complete disarray, and she was wearing the same pajamas as last night.

"It smells delicious. Oh, everyone's awake." She looked from me to the twins and then back at me. "What's going on? Why didn't anyone wake me up?"

"I was already up when I heard these two, so I decided we could start by making breakfast. We made—"

"Waffles," she finished.

"Yes," Annie exclaimed.

"They told me you always have pancakes, and then we made waffles."

Allison opened her mouth, then closed it again. She looked at me with a conspiratorial smile. I winked, silently letting her know that obviously I wasn't buying the tale of pancakes every morning.

"You want something else?" I asked her.

"No! I love waffles." She came closer, looking at the twins' workstations. "Okay. Where do you guys want to eat, outside or inside?"

"Outside!" they shouted.

"Auntie Allison, Jack talked," Annie said seriously. "Jack?"

Jack shook his head. I guess he was shy.

"He spoke a bit," I praised him.

Allison smiled from ear to ear. To my astonishment, her eyes became teary. She'd told me before the wedding that he'd been more vocal, but now it seemed that Jack was back to his old self.

"That's great, Jack. You know we love you to the moon and back, and whenever you feel comfortable talking, you do it, okay? I'm very proud of you, and I'm sure that Mommy and Daddy are too."

Now Allison was teary-eyed in earnest.

Annie was looking at me in confusion, and then she noticed Allison's tears. "Why are you sad, Auntie Allison?"

"I'm not sad at all. These are tears of happiness," Allison said quickly, but Annie reached out to give her a hug anyway. "All right, guys, take the waffles outside, please. Uncle Nick, can you go ahead with them?" She helped them down from their chairs and handed them some plates. Jack managed the waffle plate.

"Sure!" I grabbed the syrups and spreads and ushered the little ones out back.

I realized Allison wanted a moment alone, probably to compose herself. After they sat down at the table, I hurried back inside the house to check on her.

"Allison, you okay?"

She was leaning against the kitchen counter. Her eyes were a bit red.

"Yes. It truly hit me that Jim and Nora will never experience this—their firsts, you know? When they learn to tie their shoes, when they first go to school, and so on."

"I had a similar moment this morning. That's why it's so important that they have stability and have us now." She nodded, and I asked, "Are you ready to come out?" I grabbed two more plates.

"Are my eyes still red?"

"A bit."

"Then I'll wait a few more minutes. I don't want to confuse them. I want to be strong for them."

"Allison, you are strong, and they know that. Trust me."

"How would you know?" she whispered.

I set the plates back down and stood in front of her, cupping her face with both hands.

"Because they do. Kids have good instincts. Just because you get emotional doesn't mean you're not strong. Take all the time you need. I'll entertain them."

"It's okay. I'm good. I'll come outside," she said. "Let me just grab pomegranate juice. We all love it."

I took the plates, and she came out a minute later with the juice and glasses. The twins had already gobbled down their waffles by the time we sat down. They were going to ask for seconds soon. Luckily, we'd made enough to feed a small army.

Glancing around the table, I couldn't shake the feeling that we looked like a real family. I'd truly never envisioned myself as a dad, and I still didn't, but did you ever, really? As far as this morning went, I hadn't done such a bad job—except for the fact that I hadn't changed their clothes.

"After you eat, we should go and put all your clothes in the wash, okay? And dress you two in something new," Allison said, as if reading my thoughts.

"Noooo! I am a princess today," Annie protested.

Jack just shrugged.

"Fine, then," Allison gave in. "You'll be a princess for as long as you want."

As we ate the rest of the waffles, she turned and asked, "How come you woke up so early? You said you always like to sleep in on weekends."

"Not possible."

"Why not?"

I decided to fess up. "I'm bringing my own couch. I'll see how I can get that done today."

Allison gasped. "It was really that bad?"

"Absolutely awful. I don't know how I ever fooled myself into thinking it was comfortable, but it was not."

She winced. "I'm truly sorry, Nick. But don't stress about it. If we can't find a way to bring it today, I'll sleep there, or we can find a way to share the bed."

"Hell no," I exclaimed.

The twins both gasped—actually *gasped*.

I turned to them. "I'm sorry. Uncle Nick said a bad word. I usually never use it," I lied.

Annie covered Jack's ears. "Uncle Nick, no bad words."

"You're right."

She took her hands off Jack's ears and sat back down. It was adorable. She seemed like a miniature teacher.

"I won't do that again."

The look on Annie's face was so serious that I had to fight the urge to laugh.

After we finished breakfast, the twins started to yawn in unison.

"Hmm, guys, what do you say about a nap?"

To my astonishment, both of them agreed. I remembered one thing clearly from when I was a kid—I usually fought sleep like hell.

"I'll go upstairs with them and then clean up." Allison gestured to the table.

"No, I'll clean up," I said. "I made the mess, and I really don't mind."

"Oh, okay," Allison said with a huge smile. She'd been doing this all by herself for so long, and I could tell she was pleased with the help.

Once they'd gone upstairs, I immediately called Frances.

"Good morning!" I said as soon as she answered.

"Hey, Nick. What's going on?"

"Listen, I need you to organize some movers for me today."

"Absolutely. What do you need them to bring you?"

"The couch from my cinema room."

"I'm on it. I can get someone there in probably an hour."

"There's no rush. If it's not here until the evening, it's more than fine." She really was a great person to work with. "And thanks a lot for organizing everything yesterday."

"The missus liked it?" she asked.

"She absolutely loved it. You did fantastic." I'd already put in her raise with HR, so she'd see that in her next paycheck. She was a great asset to me and my team.

"Thank you! I'll have your couch delivered ASAP."

"Thanks."

Even though I wanted as few people as possible to know about our arrangement, I'd told my assistant the truth. Otherwise, conversations like this would be fucking awful.

After finishing the call, I quickly cleaned up. I'd just started the dishwasher when Allison came down the stairs.

"They went out like a light. I think they were still exhausted from yesterday." She yawned. "As am I. God, I really do need a coffee."

"Which reminds me," I said, turning around. "I'd like to bring something else here besides my couch."

"Oh?"

"My coffee machine."

Allison laughed. "That was the first thing I saw in your kitchen, and I thought, 'How is he going to survive on my poor little Nespresso machine?'"

"So, you don't mind?"

"I won't say no to barista coffee," she assured me with a wink.

Suddenly, I had the urge to move everything I needed here and never leave. *Strange...*

I took out my phone and said, "Let me just text Frances. I've already arranged with her to have my couch moved here, and the guys can pick that up too."

"That was quick. I'm impressed. So... she knows about everything?"

I nodded. "I figured it was easier. She's tight-lipped and knows how to keep a secret."

Just as I finished texting, I looked up. "I'm sorry. I didn't think about double-checking with you."

"No, that's fine. It's just a bit weird. I don't even know what we should keep secret and what we shouldn't."

"I think the only people who need to know the truth are those closest to us. Everyone else must think this is a real marriage."

Allison nodded in agreement.

I wiggled my eyebrows and walked closer to her. She backed up right into the counter. "We should definitely keep what happened in the dressing room a secret," I said.

It was high time for me to come clean—at least with myself. I couldn't stop flirting. The more I fought it, the more I seemed to be doing it.

"My God, Nick." Then she narrowed her eyes and playfully pushed me away. "Wait, so you didn't share that with anybody in your family?"

"Why in the ever-loving hell would I do that?"

She licked her lips, which only fueled my imagination more. They were plump and perfect, needing to be kissed.

"I don't know... Yesterday, it felt like everyone sort of knew more than they were letting on." She shook her head. "I don't know how to explain it."

"I do. It's a general thing in my family. Everyone thinks they know more than you do about your own life. Mom and Gran made some comments to you that were insinuating."

"Oh, you heard those? I was starting to think I'd just imagined them."

"No, you didn't. They both said it loud enough for me to hear it too. That's just their way of putting ideas into your head."

"About you and me...? Nope, I'm not going to finish that thought!"

I chuckled. "That's for the best."

She lowered her arms, and I noticed her nipples were peeking through the fabric, which had absolutely not been the case before. She looked down and immediately crossed her arms over her chest again.

"But that means that they're getting their hopes up, right? That this is something more."

"That's not my problem. Or yours. Gran's been getting her hopes up about us all getting married for years."

"But everyone else *is* married, or at least engaged."

"True, and Gran has been playing matchmaker for some time."

"Really? Oh, I've heard about meddling grandmothers. Mom used to say that her own grandma was like that, but she passed away long before Nora and I were born." She smirks. "So, Jeannie was successful, huh? Considering that all your brothers are taken."

"How do you know that they didn't just change their minds?" I challenged.

"Pfft." She waved her hand. "Because men are stubborn. Usually they don't see what they need even if it's dancing naked in front of them."

Or standing in front of them in pajamas with their hair in disarray and nipples peeking through their shirt. I was starting to get her point.

"She was successful with quite a few of my brothers," I admitted. "But not all of them needed her involvement."

"And she thinks you do?"

"I never know where I stand with Gran. But it's safe to say she was happy yesterday."

"I wonder what that means."

I gave her a half smile. "So do I."

Chapter Twenty-Five
Allison

Being married to Nick Whitley was hands down one of the highlights of my life. Was it crazy? Yes. Was it also working better than I'd expected? Yes.

Was I also in danger of jumping his bones every single evening? Hell yes.

My fear now was that I actually was going to fall for him and that I'd be hurt when we separated later on. How crazy was that?

He brought his new couch that very same day. I liked it much more than my old one. It was super comfy.

One evening, a month after the wedding, I got the dreaded email from Bob and Sophie's lawyer. They were informing me that they were taking me to court for custody.

I froze, reading the email several times. I'd been expecting it, of course. I'd actually been bracing myself for it, but seeing it in black-and-white was driving my anxiety to the max.

"Allison?" Nick said. I startled as I watched him come off the last stair. The twins were already sleeping. "What's wrong? You look tense."

In response, I simply turned the phone around. He walked to me with quick steps and glanced at it.

"We were expecting this."

"I know," I whispered. "I'm so stressed, though. What if they're successful?"

"Allison," Nick said in a gentle tone. He pushed my hair over my shoulder and then cupped my face with both hands. "We've got this. We're together in this." Hearing his words calmed my anxiety, but it started to make my pulse race for other reasons entirely. "Forward it to Hugo. He'll take care of everything."

"Will I have to face them in court?" I asked, and Nick frowned.

"He'll tell us if it's necessary."

As I forwarded the email, asking Hugo what exactly this meant and what the next steps were, Nick's phone beeped, and he answered right away.

"Hey, Spencer. Yeah, Allison's here." He took the phone away from his ear and put it on speakerphone.

"Perfect. We wanted to run an idea by the two of you. As you noticed, Ben, Jack, and Annie hit it off at the restaurant."

"Yes, they did," I said, grinning, and some of my worries melted away. "The twins are asking about Ben all the time."

"That gave us an idea," Penny said. "We'd be very happy to have them here for a sleepover, if that's something you approve of."

"Their first sleepover!" Excitement coursed through me. "Are you sure you can handle that many kids?"

"Between the two of us we can," Spencer said. "We also have a nanny who comes from time to time. We could ask her to join us, but I don't think it's necessary for a sleepover."

I was ecstatic at the idea of these two spending time with Ben. I couldn't believe that they were so willing to embrace us into their family. Hopefully, this friendship would continue after the divorce.

"I'll ask the twins tomorrow, but I think they'd love it. When would be a good time for you?"

"This weekend, starting Friday evening, maybe, and then we'd keep them through the day on Saturday as well."

"That's perfect. I'm happy to host Ben at any time too."

Spencer laughed and said to Penny, "He's already been asking about that."

"If you want to, we can have him here first."

"Let's start with the sleepover at our place," Spencer said.

"Yeah, it'll give you two time to...," Penny started excitedly, but then her words fizzled.

I frowned. "What?"

"I think everyone needs a breather now and then," Penny said, but I had the distinct impression that that wasn't what she actually meant.

I glanced at Nick, who was simply shaking his head. His eyes were full of humor.

"We'll let you know. Thanks a lot for suggesting this."

"Sure. Have a great evening," Spencer said.

After the call disconnected, I said, "That's very thoughtful of them."

"Yeah, it is."

"Why do you have that expression?" I pointed at him. "Like you think I'm missing something."

"Because you are. I think Penny's doing some of my grandmother's work."

"Meaning?" I asked in confusion.

"Remember what I told you about her matchmaking games?"

"Oh. Oh!" I exclaimed, then covered my mouth. "I wasn't... Okay."

"So, while I definitely think they're happy to have a playdate for Ben, I don't think their intentions are entirely innocent."

I swallowed hard as my entire body started vibrating all at once, everywhere. The prospect of a night alone with Nick was exciting. I didn't even want to admit it to myself, but it was.

"First let's see if the twins want to have a sleepover at all."

They said yes before I'd finished asking the question, so on Friday evening after picking them up from daycare, I took them directly to Penny and Spencer's house. It was a gorgeous place in Beacon Hill. I had a strange feeling when dropping them off and Spencer immediately took them to Ben's room, leaving me alone with Penny.

"Any plans tonight?" she asked. We were both in their kitchen, enjoying a glass of fresh orange juice.

"No, it's been a long week." I'd been obsessively checking my personal email in case Hugo wrote back. He'd replied to my questions, assuring me the chances of actually going in front of a judge were minimal. But other than that, I hadn't had any news from him. He'd also sent me and Nick a standard divorce document, which we'd use once all this was over. We both read it carefully. It already felt bittersweet to think about, which was ridiculous. It was simply a formality, and it was what we'd agreed upon, after all.

"So, you'll be staying at home."

I nodded. "Pretty much. I think I'm going to order something in."

Penny frowned before taking a sip. "Nick's not home?"

That was my first cue that she was up to something. It dawned on me that Nick hadn't been exaggerating.

"We didn't speak about what we were doing tonight. I think he's meeting a friend."

Her shoulders dropped. "Right. Of course. I truly admire you two for what you're doing. It has to be incredibly hard to live with someone who's not... your partner."

"It's not that hard. Nick and I sort of have a system for sharing a bathroom and so on." As well as pretending we weren't ogling each other. But things were going to come to a head sooner or later. I felt it in my bones.

And that wasn't the only problem. Over this past month, we'd grown incredibly close. I couldn't wait for those hours after the twins fell asleep when it was just the two of us, talking about our day, sharing our hopes and dreams. When the four of us were together, everything felt dangerously real. I was falling for Nick Whitley—there were no two ways about it.

"Then I'll let you get on with your relaxing evening. Thanks for bringing the kids over. We'll call you tomorrow and get them back to you later in the afternoon."

"Great, thank you. If anything happens or you decide it's too much, you can always call me and I'll pick them up."

"Nonsense," Penny said. "That won't be necessary. I truly love spending time with kids. Have a great evening."

After I got into my car, I started to wonder what Nick *was* doing tonight. I'd been in such a frenzy this week between work, checking emails, and preparing the twins for the sleepover that I didn't even ask. I decided to text him as I headed home.

Allison: Hey, what are your plans for the evening? Are you out already?

He replied a few seconds later.

Nick: You'll find out as soon as you come home.

Oh goodness. Does that mean he's at the house?

Excitement coursed through me as I glanced in the rearview mirror, checking my appearance. I looked like a CFO, or maybe a teacher, depending on how you looked at it. I'd had a big meeting today, so I was wearing a conservative suit. I'd even pulled my hair into a very tight bun. I typically disliked this look, but I found it helpful in meetings. It made me feel more professional if nothing else.

As I drove home, I took out the elastic band and pins at the next red light. My hair fell in nice thick waves around my shoulders.

I parked in front of the house and got out of the car, wondering what this evening would entail. This was our first night alone.

"Nick!" I called out, but there was no answer, which meant he wasn't in the backyard. I hurried up the steps, opened the front door, and stepped inside, my entire body immediately relaxing. The air smelled delicious: a mix of spices.

I toed off my shoes and didn't call Nick's name again because I could hear him. I tiptoed to the kitchen and watched for a few moments. *Holy shit.* I wanted to memorize everything about this moment. This gorgeous man was in my kitchen, wearing jeans and a button-down shirt. He'd pushed up the sleeves, as usual. I also noticed that he'd undone the top few buttons.

He must have sensed my presence, because he looked at me from the side.

"How long have you been standing there?"

"I just arrived."

"Should I pretend I didn't see you so you can get your fill?" He winked, and in the span of two seconds, my body reacted to his presence.

"What are you cooking?" I asked, coming closer.

"Chicken with white wine and rice."

"Yum. I thought I could smell the wine." I would gobble down anything, but this sounded delicious.

"It won't take long."

"I thought you were going out with a friend tonight."

Nick looked strangely at me. "I was supposed to, but I wanted to be home with you." He wiggled his eyebrows, and I swallowed hard.

What did this sexy man have in mind? He was all about keeping boundaries between us. But maybe that was because of the kids so as not to confuse them.

Then again, I was all over the place, too, when it came to him. What were we doing?

"I'll set the table," I offered.

"It's all taken care of."

"What?" I glanced at the table. "I can't believe I didn't see that."

He'd literally taken care of everything.

"How long will until it's ready?"

"Five minutes, more or less."

"I'll take a really quick shower and get out of this suit."

Nick nodded, and I thought I heard him swallow audibly. The look on his face made me wonder if he wished he could join me, but then he said, "I'll be right here."

I ran upstairs, my heart pounding at a million miles an hour. I was having dinner with Nick.

It's not a date, Allison. It's normal for you to have dinners. You've been having dinners ever since he moved in.

Except this time it was without the kids.

I could offer to repay him for making dinner. Maybe with a massage? I could start with those gorgeous muscled shoulders in the back and move to the front...

Ugh. I needed to get my mind out of the gutter.

I'd never showered so quickly in my life. I didn't want to make Nick wait or let the food get cold.

I put on my favorite perfume before throwing on a light yellow summery dress that wasn't too revealing. Although, like all my clothes, it was fitted and very feminine. Because I was stuck wearing suits all day, I enjoyed wearing dresses when I was home.

I went downstairs barefoot. Even though the custody issue was still at the back of my mind, I couldn't help but feel optimistic that things were going to work out one way or another. I had an inkling that my optimism may have something to do with the sexy man camping on the couch.

"You already served the food," I said, stunned.

"And poured the wine." He winked at me. "I want to make this a very relaxing experience for you."

It looked extremely romantic. I realized belatedly that there were flowers in a small vase. Roses.

"Nick," I whispered, stopping in front of it and touching the petals, "when did you get these?"

He came up right behind me. "Tonight." His voice had changed somewhat from a few seconds ago. It was lower. "I figured you'd enjoy them."

He was running his fingers up and down my arms. This felt so much like we were a real couple, like we were truly married and just enjoying a night together without the kids.

"Thank you. I love them."

"Dinner is served. I didn't even ask you, but I chose white wine," he said as he pulled out the chair. I sat down, and he pushed it under me.

"We're having chicken, so white wine is good. Besides, you said you cooked with it as well."

He sat in front of me. He'd put the rice in a bowl and the chicken in another one. I quickly loaded my plate, and as soon as Nick put the rest on his, I immediately dug in.

"You should be a chef," I said.

"You've only had my food a couple of times."

"I know, but everything has been exquisite."

The dish was creamy and well-seasoned but not too heavy because he'd countered the cream with white wine. I bounced my shoulders, humming. He laughed.

"What?" I asked.

"You do that when you're eating something you like. I've noticed you have a little happy dance."

He'd noticed that about me? *Oh my.* "Doesn't everyone?"

"I don't know, Allison. I don't pay as much attention to other people as I do to you."

There it was, that flirty tone and the sexy eyes. I was a goner. Nick most definitely had other plans for tonight.

"How's work?" I asked, trying to distract myself. "By the way, did you decide where you'll open the new fitness center?"

"I'm going to put that on hold for now. We've got enough going on."

My jaw dropped. "Nick, you don't have to do that."

"I know. But opening new locations requires travel, and I don't want to miss out on any time with you and the twins."

Oh my goodness. This was completely unexpected. I almost teared up. Nick was a wonderful man.

I took a few sips of wine, and soon my entire body relaxed. I then realized Nick was looking at me intently.

"What? Do I have something on my mouth?"

I stretched my legs under the table and then felt Nick trapping them with his. We both froze, but I decided not to pull back. I liked his touch. More than that, I craved it.

"Penny and Spencer were really welcoming," I said, desperately trying to cut through the tension. "Oh, by the way, Penny seemed to be very disappointed when I told her that you might not be home tonight. I think you were onto something with that matchmaking thing."

Nick laughed. "I had an interesting call with my gran too. She was asking *in detail* about my plans tonight."

"So, what did you tell her?"

"I teased her. I didn't tell her anything."

I giggled. "Nick, you're bad."

"She deserves it. Usually, I don't mind sharing stuff about my life, but I feel like everyone is trying a bit too hard. And I never understand why they keep pushing when I've always made it clear that I'm not marriage material."

His words felt like a punch to my gut. Of course he wasn't. He was only doing this so I'd get custody of the twins. Why did I keep forgetting that?

"What do you want to do after dinner?" His voice was so nonchalant, like he hadn't just dropped a bomb on me.

"How about we play a game of poker?" I asked, voicing the first thought that came to my mind.

Chapter Twenty-Six

Nick

"Poker?" I said, certain I'd heard wrong.

"Yes." She nodded vigorously. "Or I have board games."

I hadn't seen this coming. I figured she'd want us to watch a movie or something, cuddle up on the couch, *and* have some sexy times. I wanted to take us back to that night in my closet. Pretend marriage or not, that night had been real. And this past month since we signed the papers, other things started feeling real too. I was closer to Allison than I'd ever been to a woman, and to my astonishment, I wanted more of it. I wanted everything.

"Poker it is, then." Between that and board games, I'd take poker any day.

She jumped up from the table, scurrying away to the console under the TV. Something had changed these past few seconds, but I couldn't put my finger on it. She'd finally started to relax, but then she somehow withdrew again. Why?

"I found a deck of cards!"

She bent at the waist, putting her ass up in the air. I could see the shape of those round lumps perfectly.

I quickly got up to carry everything to the kitchen, not bothering to clean up. I could deal with that later.

Something in her body language was still off, and I was determined to get to the bottom of it, even if it meant playing poker. Clearly I'd said something wrong, but I couldn't figure out what for the life of me. Was she so bothered by my family trying to matchmake us?

I set our glasses down on the small coffee table in front of the couch as she approached it.

"You do know the rules of poker, yes?" Allison asked.

"Yes. I prefer a bigger round. Then again, I haven't played in years."

"Aha," she said. "Then prepare to have your ass beaten by me. I happen to be very good at poker."

"How come?" I asked.

"My friends and I played obsessively in college. I'm sure I've still got it."

"Is that so? Challenge accepted, then."

As she started to shuffle the cards, I decided to be up-front. "Allison, something's changed since dinner." She glanced up at me, and her hands stilled. "You were relaxed, and then you couldn't get away fast enough. Did I say something wrong?"

She shook her head. "No, not at all."

"But something is off."

Her shoulders drooped. "Nick, this is..." She sighed. "I don't know how to explain it without sounding silly."

"I promise not to judge."

She pressed her lips together. "I thought that once we'd lived together for a bit, things would get easier..."

"But they're not," I finished for her.

"No, not at all. Every time I think I have things under control, something happens and..." She closed her eyes. "I realize I really don't, that I'm still not sure how to best handle this. I figured poker would be a very safe way to spend the rest of the evening. There's no way to turn it into an innuendo."

"W*eeeee*ll..." There was strip poker, after all.

Allison looked at me, jerking her head back and then shaking it. "Nick, you know what? I don't even want to know."

"I wasn't going to say anything."

She went back to shuffling, then looked up at me and sighed. "No, I do want to know."

"You just said the opposite."

"I know, but otherwise I'll think about it for the rest of the evening. How would you make this into something dirty?"

"I could suggest we play *naked* poker."

She blinked rapidly. "You mean strip poker?"

"Exactly that. I just jumped to the naked part."

She turned red faster than I thought possible.

"See, we were both far better off if I'd kept this to myself. Like, every time you lose, I'll imagine what clothing item you could take off." I tilted forward slightly. "I don't imagine you have too much on."

I knew I'd gone too far the second she exhaled sharply. But I'd lasted *weeks* without openly making a move on her, hadn't I? Being alone with her tonight changed things.

"Nick...," she whispered, then stopped. When she spoke again, her voice was more confident. "You know, I'd chastise you for even putting that idea in my mind, but I'm not a liar. That was the first thing that popped into my head when you said naked poker. Because if one of us would end up naked, it would be you. That's how much I trust my skills."

Yes! She was flirting back. I had no idea why I was celebrating when we'd both agreed to keep things platonic, but I was victorious.

I was so close to her. It would take almost no effort at all to lean over and kiss her. Her lips looked delicious, and they were beckoning me.

I drew in a deep breath, glancing down between us at the cards. She'd mixed them so well by now that there was no need to keep doing it, but she'd started to move her hands again. I caught both of them, setting the cards to the side and then holding her palms up, resting my thumbs on them. That was when I realized that there was a light tremor in her body.

"Allison, I know what we agreed on back at the penthouse. I remember every word. Actually, I remember every fucking second."

"So do I." Her voice was barely audible, like she wouldn't even admit that to herself.

"But I don't know how to do this," I continued. "I want you so damn much that I can't even think straight. I came here with the intention of helping you relax, and now I'm flirting with you."

"I was wondering about that."

"I promise you, I'm not doing it on purpose. I'm not an asshole. There's something about you, us, that draws it out of me."

"I feel it too. So, where does that leave us?"

"Playing naked poker."

She grinned. "I wouldn't mind seeing some of those sexy muscles."

That was all it took for any sort of self-restraint to simply melt away. Just like back at the penthouse, I couldn't think past the fact that I needed this woman right now with every fiber of my being.

So instead of making a counter proposal, I kissed her. Fuck, I'd missed this, her sexy mouth. She tasted like white wine.

She groaned, instantly opening up. Her tongue met mine with fervor, and I knew we weren't going to honor our agreement. Not tonight. It was impossible, not when kissing her felt so damn good.

I pulled her onto my lap, and a whooshing sound filled the air.

"The cards!"

"Fucking forget about them," I growled. I sure as hell couldn't think about anything else but how much I needed her.

I pushed my hands under her dress. Her skin was smooth and inviting, and I wanted her completely naked.

When she groaned against my mouth, I moved farther down to her neck. Last time, I hadn't been able to even see her properly, but this time I was going to do things differently. Even though I was once again so desperate that I was very close to shoving her panties to one side and thrusting into her right away.

I ran my hands over her torso. There didn't seem to be a zipper, so I simply yanked the dress over her head. Then I pressed down on her shoulders so she was lying back at an angle.

She was wearing a simple white bra and panties, but she looked sexier than ever.

"You're so damn beautiful. I didn't get to have a good look at you last time."

"No," she said, her eyelids hooded, "you were too busy devouring me, and I didn't mind one bit."

"I want to do things differently this time, Allison."

I saw a glass of wine out of the corner of my eye, and that gave me an idea. I reached for it and told her, "Lean back as much as you can."

She licked her lips and lowered herself carefully. I poured a bit of white wine in her navel, and she gasped. Realizing I didn't have the access I wanted like this, I quickly moved her to the couch so I was still sitting between her legs. The wine I'd poured was dripping down her skin. Her panties dampened. She moaned again, which told me that the area was already sensitive. I kissed back up to her navel.

"Nick!" She arched her back, rolling her hips back and forth.

I reached under her back, undoing the clasp of her bra. Her breasts were gorgeous. Leaning in, I pulled one into my mouth, sucking at her nipple until she was no longer whispering my name but crying it out.

Her heels pressed against my ass, and I realized she'd lifted her legs and trapped me between them.

"I just want to make sure you stay here," she said with a coy smile.

"Don't worry, Allison. I'm not going anywhere."

I rested on my knees, hovering above her as I worked both of her breasts with my hands, especially teasing her nipples.

I congratulated myself for bringing the couch here because it was fucking perfect for this. Then I grabbed the glass of wine, taking a sip before lowering myself to her breasts and sucking a nipple into my mouth. She turned absolutely wild. My mouth was cold, but then it slowly warmed back up, and the change of temperature was wreaking havoc on her senses. Hell, it was wreaking havoc on mine.

I felt her nails dig into my back. A few seconds later, I realized she was trying to get my shirt off. I hadn't taken my clothes off last time either, but I wasn't going to make the same mistake twice. I wanted her to be able to touch me all that she wanted.

I didn't want to stop exploring her body, but it was the most efficient way to get naked, so I pulled away from her.

"Nick!" she protested. She made to grab my arm, but I quickly moved out of the way.

"Just taking off my clothes, Allison. Just for you."

"Oooh, I get my own personal stripper," she said, then turned onto her side, propping her head on her palm and looking at me hungrily.

I started by undoing the buttons of my shirt.

"You're doing this slowly on purpose to tease me," she pouted.

"Obviously," I admitted.

"That's not fair. Why do you wear an undershirt? It's making the whole striptease idea seem lame."

"Don't worry, that'll come off too." Losing patience with the last buttons, I just reached back, grabbed the fabric between my shoulder blades, and pulled it over my head. I did the same with the undershirt.

"Oh yeah. Now that's what I'm talking about."

When I finally tossed them away, I noticed she was in a sitting position. Her face was level with my abs.

"Do you know how much I've been dreaming about these?" she whispered. She put both forefingers underneath my nipples and traced a crisscross pattern all over my abs while I worked my belt.

As soon as I undid it, she lowered my zipper, tugging at it very aggressively. I grinned, pushing down my pants. She immediately helped me yank down the boxers, too, then looked up at me. My cock was already erect, practically in her face. With our gazes locked, she licked once from the bottom to the tip. I groaned, moving my hips forward on impulse. Then she repeated the motion, never breaking eye contact.

"You're so damn sexy." My voice was so broken that I was surprised she heard anything. But then her eyes turned darker, and I knew she had. "I love every single one of your curves, your breasts, your waist... your ass. I've fantasized about that so many times."

She gasped, then lowered her mouth.

"Touch yourself, Allison. I know you need it, and I can't reach you like this."

Her eyes were completely wide now. I knew she'd touched herself the moment it happened because her lips clamped even tighter around my cock. She closed her eyes and whimpered, and the vibrations traveled all through my body. I pushed forward on instinct, deeper inside her mouth, and she took me in all the way.

I couldn't see her properly, but I didn't miss the way her arm moved. It was frantic. She was dying to come just like this, with my cock in her mouth and her hand in her panties. I nearly exploded at the thought.

"That's it, gorgeous." I wrapped her hair around one hand, pulling it at the back of her head. I wanted to see the curve of her neck while she slid her mouth down on my cock. Her hums intensified, and every single one of them went straight through me.

I couldn't believe how on edge she was. Then again, she wasn't the only one. These past few weeks had been excruciating, knowing that only a flight of stairs and a door separated us.

I knew exactly when she started to come because she stopped moving her head. The sound she made was animalistic, guttural. It shook her entire body. It was such a damn privilege feeling this woman's climax course through me. I didn't move at all, just watched her come down from the high and open her eyes slowly, then her mouth. She smiled after pulling back.

"I want to taste your pussy, beautiful. Right now."

"Yes, please." Her eyes darkened.

I pushed her back on the couch and took off her panties. They were completely soaked. I tossed them on the floor and positioned myself so I had access to her pussy and she could suck my cock as much as she wanted. I opened her thighs wide and, without giving her any warning, licked her clit. Then I moved farther down her slit. The pleasure was surreal. Somehow tasting her pussy while she had my cock in her mouth made everything even more intense. We were giving each other pleasure and exploring.

I teased her clit again and again, following the cues of her body. This was what she needed, so I was going to oblige. Only it was becoming increasingly more difficult to focus. The way she moved her mouth on me brought me closer to climax every damn time.

When I knew I wasn't going to be able to hold back much longer, I pulled out. "I want to be inside of you." I hovered with my mouth over her pussy.

"I need it, too, Nick," she whispered. "So damn badly."

I slapped her pussy twice as I straightened up. She cried out so loud that for a split second, I thought she came. Fuck no, the only time she was allowed to come was on my cock.

I grabbed both her ankles, putting them on my shoulders. Her mouth was red. I liked watching her like this, completely vulnerable. I traced the contour of her lips with my thumb. "I fucking love that you're so red."

She licked her lips. "Please, please push inside."

I went in all at once until I was completely buried in her pussy.

"Nick!" she groaned and grabbed her breasts with both hands.

"You feel so damn perfect. You *are* perfect, Allison." I pulled back, looking between us, loving the sight of my cock pistoning in and out of her.

She lowered one hand between her thighs to her clit, and I watched her for a few moments. It turned me on that she pleasured herself without any shame. But then another instinct took over, and I moved her hand away.

"Your pussy is mine tonight. I'm the only one who can touch it."

She instantly lifted her arms above her head. I liked this position because it made the bouncing movement of her breasts on every thrust even more obvious. I touched her clit in the same way I did with my tongue earlier. The combined sensations from stimulating her G-spot and her clit was wreaking havoc on her.

"Please... I want to come. Make me come, please."

"That's what I'm here for, beautiful. I'll work you up so damn good that when you come, you won't even remember what your name is."

She gasped, pinching her eyes shut. And then her pussy started to pulse around my cock. I changed the rhythm of my thrusts, tilting my pelvis at another angle, making sure I got that G-spot good. I knew I did when her gorgeous face started to twist. The pleasure was almost torture because it was more but not enough.

Then my own climax slammed into me. I didn't feel the buildup, not in the way I'd done back when I'd been buried inside her in the closet.

I cried out her name, circling her clit even quicker. Even through the orgasm, I felt her pussy clamp tighter around my cock. She put her palms on her face, moving them upward and tugging at her hair as she cried out until sweat broke out on her temples.

I didn't stop even for a brief second, giving her all I had. I only pulled out once we were both completely done and could barely breathe.

We only stayed downstairs for a few more seconds before heading to the bathroom to clean up. Afterward, we came back to the living room. I liked watching Allison walk naked through the house. Her body was so fucking perfect.

When we were in front of the couch again, I stopped right behind her, fondling both her ass cheeks.

"Your ass is perfection."

She grinned, turning around. "So you keep saying."

She grabbed her dress and quickly pulled it over her head.

I frowned. "Why did you do that? I enjoy seeing you naked."

She shrugged. "I don't know. It felt just a bit weird."

I wriggled my eyebrows. "You mind if I'm naked?"

She tilted her head to one side. "No. But just so you know, I might jump your bones again just to get my dirty desires out of the way."

I threw my head back, laughing. "My plan is extremely similar to yours. In fact," I said, circling her nipple through the fabric until it peeked through, "I could say that you stole my idea."

I did put my boxers on, though, before we both sat on the couch. Then I pulled her onto my lap again.

"This escalated quickly," she whispered.

"It gives me the perfect opportunity to do this." I put my hand on her lower back, tilting her forward so she was hovering over me and her ass was slightly lifted. "Now I can finally tell you what I want while we talk."

"Oh, I see. That's your idea of doing two things at once, huh?"

"Exactly. Life's too short to procrastinate."

"Nick, I'm not sure what to say."

I frowned, then took both my hands from under her dress and touched her cheeks with the backs of my fingers.

"One thing's clear," I started.

She raised a brow. "Do tell, because everything's clear as mud for me."

"We can't continue the way we have up until now, pretending that we're not attracted to each other."

She straightened up. "That was probably a silly plan, wasn't it? It was going to come to a head sooner rather than later. Though I have to admit, I didn't think it was going to be this fast. Then again, I didn't think we'd have the opportunity to have the house to ourselves either." She blushed and covered her mouth.

"What just went through your pretty mind?"

"That Penny might be a genius. The timing was impeccable."

Her words took me by surprise. Then I realized she was right. "Yeah, we Whitleys are known for our impeccable timing. It's interesting."

Her brow furrowed. "Why do you sound so unhappy about it?"

"I just hadn't realized that my family could read me so well. They could probably tell from the wedding that all I wanted was to be alone with you."

She bit the inside of her cheek.

"Tell me what's on your mind, Allison. I promise I'm good either way."

She frowned. "That's just it. I'm not sure. Before… we said we'd have separate lives."

I didn't fucking want a separate life. I wanted to build a life with her.

"Fuck no. That's off the table."

The corners of her mouth lifted. Clearly she liked what she was hearing.

"And staying away from each other also doesn't seem to work out."

I liked where this was going. From the very beginning, she'd been far more cautious than I had been, and I didn't want her to feel like she had to do something just because I wanted it. Not my style.

She was mine to protect and take care of. I felt more possessive of her than I'd ever been with anyone in my whole damn life. From the day of the accident, I felt the need to be right there with her.

"And anyway, you did say that you're not marriage material. So—" She smiled, tilting her head. "—how about we're married with benefits?"

That made me laugh. I liked that she took everything with humor.

"Married with benefits. I love that. But I don't think it's enough."

All my life, I didn't think I could be a good husband. I could be an excellent fake one, but what if I could be a really good boyfriend?

"Oh?" she said.

"What you and I have is real, Allison."

She nodded. "Very."

"You're mine. And I'm yours. How does that sound?"

"Like a dream," she whispered. "I love it."

Then she grabbed her glass of wine and took a sip.

"That's warm already. I can take out another bottle."

She lowered her glass, looking at me from under her eyelids. I realized she was trying to bat her eyelashes seductively. "Yes, let's do that. And why don't we go upstairs to the bedroom?"

"Hell yes."

She laughed. "I take that as a sign that you'd also like to spend the whole night there?"

"Well, the new couch is comfortable, but I won't say no to a bed."

"Then consider that another benefit of our marriage."

Chapter Twenty-Seven

Nick

In the morning, I woke up to the sound of the hairdryer. I'd enjoyed last night more than I could have imagined, and I was ready for another fantastic day at Allison's side. I was getting used to this, and I didn't mind.

I jumped out of bed and went to the bathroom. She startled when I came in, then turned off the dryer.

"Let me just put the hairdryer away. I hate using it, but I don't want to go out with wet hair today."

"Don't stop on my account. I'm happy just stand here and watch you. Now that I don't have to do it when you're not looking."

She looked at me in the mirror, then glanced over her shoulder as if she needed actual eye-to-eye contact. "Good morning to you too. I see you woke up on your flirty side."

"Allison, a word of warning," I said, stepping up behind her. She turned her head forward so we were once again looking at each other in the mirror. "Any day I wake up naked in your bed, I won't be able to keep my hands or eyes off you."

"Duly noted."

I kissed her shoulder, putting a hand on her belly. If I could, I'd keep this woman just like this.

"What are you thinking? You have that sort of caveman expression."

"That I'd like to keep you indoors and naked all the time."

She laughed. "That's going to be a bit hard. I have to go to work from time to time."

"Here's an idea." I moved to her other shoulder, kissing it too. "You can come work with me. I'm always looking for a good CFO."

"What about your current one?"

"I'll just find him another place in Whitley Industries. I can insist on you sharing an office with me."

"And let me guess. You'd keep me naked all the time?"

"Fuck yes!" I tugged at her earlobe.

"Did you come up with this just now?"

"Yes. The idea is fully formed in my mind. I'm ready to put it into action whenever you are. Josh won't care." My CFO was great and probably wouldn't be too keen on the idea, but a guy had to keep his options open for his woman.

She flashed me a grin. "You know what? Next time some client or my boss gives me a hard time, that's all I'll think about: 'I could be naked in Nick's office right now.'"

"Exactly. Do keep that in mind."

She yawned as she started to brush her hair.

"Do you have plans for today?" she asked.

"Are you kidding? I knew I had a whole day with you."

"You're full of plans, aren't you, husband?"

"You have no idea."

Her skin sprouted goose bumps at my words. I kissed her shoulder again before taking a step back.

"Let's have a strong coffee, and then I'll tell you all about the rest of my plan."

"I think I know what it is," she whispered before starting the hairdryer again.

"Well, not exactly."

She'd probably guessed parts of it, but it was more elaborate than that.

I showered and changed into fresh clothes before going downstairs. On the way, I checked my messages. I had one from Leo, informing me that my penthouse still had zero interest, which was what I'd intended, of course. He'd thought my idea was crazy when I first told him that I wanted to charge an astronomical rent for it so no one would bite, but he agreed to help. So far, the plan was working.

By the time Allison joined me, I was already on my second coffee. I held out a freshly made one for her.

"So... what are we doing today?" she asked as she took the mug.

"How about going on a cruise?"

Her eyes bulged. "Wow. When you said plan..."

"You just thought I meant taking you to bed, huh?" I smirked.

"Uh, yes," she admitted, hiding her sheepish smile behind the coffee cup.

"Don't worry. That is definitely on the agenda," I replied with as much seriousness as I could muster.

"Don't we need to buy tickets or something?"

"That's already taken care of," I assured her.

She lowered her cup. "Nick, that's very thoughtful. I was going to suggest we eat breakfast at home, but now I'm too excited. When's the cruise?"

"We still have time. It starts at ten." It was only nine o'clock. Funny enough, after waking up at six thirty every morning for the twins, my internal clock had already shifted.

"I'm sure we can find something to eat on the ship or maybe in the harbor. Am I dressed appropriately for that?"

She turned around once. Her yellow dress was short, and it flounced around her.

"Your dress might get caught by the wind."

"You're afraid someone might see my sexy parts."

I growled. "No one can see those. They're all for me. *Just* for me."

Allison pressed her lips together as her pupils dilated a bit. "Only yours, Nick."

"I'll just cover you with my body if there's wind."

She laughed. "That won't attract attention at all."

Allison

I'd never been to this part of the harbor. Then again, there were lots of parts of Boston that I hadn't been to.

"Your smile is amazing," Nick remarked as we stood in line.

I put one hand over my mouth to hide it. "I think it's a bit too obvious."

"What do you mean, obvious?"

I made a come-here motion, and he lowered his ear to my mouth. "That it says I got laid last night, and it was amazing." Nick burst out laughing. I hadn't seen that coming. "Well, now that *will* give us away."

I started to sip from my smoothie we'd bought from the nearby cart. Nick had just gotten a bagel, and he'd already devoured it. His laughter made me laugh too.

"Nick, people are starting to look at us," I admonished.

He cleared his throat, but it took several tries for him to stop. "Let them watch us, then. What's wrong with us being happy?"

Nothing, I realized. Absolutely nothing.

His eyes were playful. God, was this really happening? Last night, I had so many worries, and now I had zero. I felt as if a weight had been lifted off my shoulders. Things were as confusing as ever, but I was looking forward to spending this "marriage with benefits" with Nick. Why hadn't we thought about it from the beginning? It made so much more sense.

"How long is the cruise?" I asked.

"Just an hour."

"That's not so bad. That means we'll still make it in time to pick up the twins."

Nick took my free hand in his. "I've timed everything. I don't want you to worry about anything. I'm picking up all the slack today."

"That, husband, is one of the sexiest things you've said to me."

He jerked his head back in surprise.

"Okay, maybe not, but it's right there in the top five or something."

"Fuck me," he said. The lady next to us actually jumped. "Sorry, ma'am," Nick apologized before focusing on me. On a whisper, he added, "I must do better, then."

"No, trust me. This is a good thing. You being... I don't know. Forget it."

At the office, I didn't have issues stating my ideas, but when it came to Nick, I found myself at a loss for words far too often.

When our ferry finally arrived, I was absolutely giddy to get on. The line moved slowly, as the person taking the tickets was very thorough about all the details. Were there people faking tickets to get onto a ferry? That seemed strange, but you'd sure think so the way she was scrutinizing them.

A few minutes later, we were inside and found comfortable seats on a bench in the middle. I would have preferred to sit in the front, but this would do. The seats were comfy, and there was a menu pinned to the backrest of the bench in front of us. I immediately inspected it. They didn't have much, so it was good I had a smoothie.

As the boat moved out of the harbor, I looked around with a huge grin on my face. I hadn't been so happy in months. I turned to tell Nick this and found him looking at me.

"What's wrong? Do I have something on my face? Smoothie?" I asked.

"No. Why?"

"You're looking at me so intently."

"I want to memorize everything about you today."

"It's just that..." I bit my lip once again, at a loss as to how to explain myself. "I haven't been this happy in a long while. Honestly, I'm not sure if I've *ever* been this happy. Especially not on a date."

He grinned. "I like that."

"The thing is that losing Nora sort of split my life into before and after." My voice shook. "I never thought I could feel fully happy again. Or at least not without also feeling guilty because my sister isn't here anymore."

Nick moved a strand of hair behind my ear. He seemed to like doing that a lot.

"But today, I feel completely happy and not guilty at all." I glanced at him. "Is that a good thing?"

"Yes, it is. Allison, I didn't know you felt that way."

"I can't help it," I whispered. "I'm sorry. I know we agreed not to talk about sad things."

He shook his head. "I want you to always tell me what's on your mind. There's no reason to keep things from me."

Well, well, my fake husband was turning out to be the best boyfriend I'd ever had.

"Mourning those we love is a way of showing them affection after they're gone. But don't feel guilty for feeling happy. Nora loved you deeply, and I'm sure that all she would have wanted was for you to be happy."

"I know that. My sister was a gentle soul. But, Nick, there's something else. Something in *me* shifted since last night."

That made him grin again. "I always like claiming credit, so I'll add that to my list of wins."

"Yes, please do." It was as if he'd unlocked something inside me. Nick had set free my ability to feel joy again. I could feel myself getting back to being the old me. Or maybe this was simply the new version of me. I'd been trying all along to get back to who I was before, but maybe that shouldn't have been the goal in the first place.

"You're lost in thought," he whispered.

"I was just thinking that all these months, I felt stuck. And I think it's because I always assumed that things had to get back to normal. That I should be my old self: single, no kids, no big responsibilities except the mortgage and my job. I figured that once enough time had passed, I'd find my groove again and be able to see my friends more often, do things the way we used to. Now I realize that's not what this is about. I'm accepting my new normal. I don't want to call myself a mom, because that would feel disrespectful to my sister, but I *am* an aunt and guardian."

Nick brought his mouth to my ear. "Don't forget that you're also an amazing fake wife."

I grinned. "That too. I should probably add it to my résumé, improve my street cred and all that."

Nick laughed in my ear. It tickled me, so I started to giggle, which earned us stares from the rest of the passengers.

Whoops. I realized then that there had been a tour guide audio going on all this time. The voice was telling us what we were seeing along the edge of the water. I hadn't paid attention to even one word, but I couldn't care less. It was still part of the experience, watching Boston from the water.

"Allison, for all intents and purposes, you are the twins' mother."

His words wrapped around my heart tightly. I had no idea why it meant so much to me.

"You're not dishonoring your sister's memory. It's what she'd hope you'd do. I just wanted to get that out of the way."

"You're very good with words," I whispered. "But now I think we should be silent, or everyone will throw us overboard."

We weren't loud, but a few passengers were giving us the evil eye. I didn't want to be that annoying person who talked during an entire tour. Well... I didn't want to be that person *anymore*. Clearly I'd been exactly that until now.

Nick seemed to be thinking along the same lines, because he didn't say anything else either, just leaned back against the wooden bench and put an arm around my shoulders.

I leaned against him, then decided I wanted a bit more contact, so I shifted so that half my back was plastered against his chest. Then I became greedy and put a hand on his thigh. There was no way I could feel up his abs without making a spectacle of us, but this was very under the radar. Then I moved so one ass cheek was basically resting against his thigh. Nick groaned, and I felt hot air against my ear.

"Allison, if you keep moving like that, I'm going to take you in the back of the ferry. And I really don't want to have you in some dingy toilet."

Holy shit. Maybe the others didn't get wind of what I was doing, but obviously poor Nick had felt all of that.

I moved so I could glance up at him. "Sorry, I wasn't doing it on purpose."

"Yes, you were." He was smiling.

I smiled right back. "Okay, maybe I was. I just didn't think it would have this effect."

He kissed me then, exploring me with his tongue. It was a very slow kiss, and I loved it immensely. It reminded me of the one at city hall. He interlaced our hands, too, and squeezed my fingers tightly with his. This moment felt more intimate than what we'd experienced at the house yesterday or back in his closet. I had no idea how long we kissed, but I didn't want it to end.

When we finally paused to breathe, he was looking at me with a smile, and his eyelids were hooded. Good to know that I wasn't the only one who was turned on. How was I always in this state around Nick? Would that change over time? I didn't think so. In fact, I suspected that the more of Nick I got, the more I'd want. Which was dangerous because this had an expiration date.

Then an even more horrifying thought came to mind: what if the custody battle went on forever, and eventually Nick and I just didn't work together anymore? I couldn't imagine anything more horrendous than living with someone who didn't want me. I'd done it once in college. I was stupid enough to give up my dorm room to move in with my then-boyfriend. When we split up, I was in the unfortunate position of having to live with him while I was apartment hunting.

But this was completely different. I knew Nick would be decent about it. Would it still suck? Sure, especially for the twins.

Oh God, the twins. I hadn't even thought about how all this would affect them.

All the worries I'd pushed out of my mind this morning were slamming back in. But then Nick pulled me closer to him, and all my worries melted away—placing those dirty thoughts in my head again.

Mental note: being close and feeling his muscles definitely drove all the rational thoughts from my mind.

We were silent for the rest of the cruise, simply taking in our surroundings and listening to the guide. I didn't end up ordering anything; I was surprisingly full from my smoothie.

Once we stepped off the boat, I checked the clock. "We should probably go pick up the twins."

Nick nodded. "I'll text Spencer so he knows we're coming."

When we reached the car, he opened the door for me. He'd insisted on putting two car seats in his own car as well so we'd always be able to have the kids with us.

It didn't take long for us to arrive at his brother's house. The second I got out, I heard laughter. I recognized Annie's voice immediately, which meant they were outside.

There was no way to get into the yard from the front, though, so we rang the bell anyway. The door swung open the next second. To my surprise, I came face-to-face with Jeannie Whitley.

"Gran!" Nick exclaimed. Her eyes fell on the arm he had around my shoulders. "I didn't know you'd be here. Spencer didn't say."

"Abe and I dropped by this morning. We wanted the chance to see the little ones again."

My heart was so happy right now. They were truly taking their grandparenting' role to a whole new level.

"Come on in," she said. "Everyone's out in the back."

We followed Jeannie through the house. It was madness outside. Spencer and Penny were both chasing the kids around, and they were all running in different directions. Three kids, two adults—they were totally outnumbered.

The second the twins noticed us, they stopped running. Instead, they came barreling toward us, but they didn't jump into my arms. They jumped into Nick's! My sexy, strong man was getting all the love.

"Will you look at that?" I teased. "You're becoming their favorite."

Jeannie was staring at Nick with a triumphant smile. Then she and Penny exchanged a glance.

Nick had been right about everything; I could feel it in my bones. These two had a matchmaking thing going on.

"How were they?" I asked Penny.

"Perfect. They had a lot of fun. They went to bed on time with no fuss."

"Then we found them playing an hour later," Spencer said.

I laughed. "They do that sometimes at home as well."

"But they slept through the night."

"Thanks so much for having them. Ben, you're welcome at our place anytime, okay?"

Ben jumped up and down. "Yes, yes, yes! I have new friends. I like having new friends. When can I go, Dad?" he asked Spencer, who mussed up his son's hair. They looked a lot alike.

"We'll figure it out."

"Jeannie, we should ask everyone over to our house," Abe suggested. "We haven't had a get-together at our place in some time."

Spencer cocked a brow. "We were there like—"

"Two months ago," Jeannie replied in a tone that made it clear she'd counted *exactly*.

"Gran, we can all meet somewhere else. You don't have to go through all the trouble," Nick said.

"Oh, nonsense, you boys. I'd like to have all of you at the house." She looked at me too. "Especially the children."

Even though she was well past ninety, she crouched easily, putting her knees on the grass, and held her arms out. Ben gave her a hug.

"You two come here," she told the twins.

They immediately asked Nick to put them down and ran to Jeannie. Lately, they were very accepting of other people. I wondered if they would get used to living with Bob and Sophie if it came to that.

"Would you like to come to my house?" Jeannie asked them.

"Yes!" all three said in unison, and I couldn't help but laugh. Clearly Ben was leading the small group.

Then Jeannie let them go and quickly rose to her feet. My parents couldn't do that even though they were in their late sixties. The woman was truly fit. She beamed at us again. She was mischievous. Or possibly knowing. Maybe a mix of the two.

"How was your evening?" Penny asked. Spencer cleared his throat, giving her what I could only describe as a warning look, and she shrugged. I realized Jeannie was hanging on to Nick's every word.

"Just had dinner at home," Nick said.

"Both of you?" Penny raised a brow. Spencer cleared his throat.

"Yes."

"I thought you were meeting your friend," Jeannie added.

This was fascinating. I wasn't mad in the slightest. It was unusual but fun.

"No, I postponed that. I was tired," Nick replied.

"I bet it was nice having the house to yourself for once," Jeannie said. "By the way, I'm very happy to have the twins as well as Ben at the house anytime for a sleepover."

"Three kids, Gran?" Spencer asked. "We'll see."

After a bit more chatting, I gently nudged Nick. "We should get going," I said.

After saying our goodbyes, we headed to the car. By the time Nick and I secured the twins in their car seats, they were already asleep.

He closed the doors quietly and then was by my side, hand on the handle.

"What was that back there?" I asked.

"You picked up on it?"

"That Penny and Gran are plotting?"

"Strong word, but sure, why not?"

I giggled. "They seemed to be up to something. You think they suspect anything?"

"As a general rule, everyone's constantly under suspicion in my family."

"Oh, that sounds ominous."

He nodded. "It can be, but there's one thing I can tell you for sure."

"What?" I inquired.

"Whenever Gran asks us to her house, they'll do their very best to figure us out."

Chapter Twenty-Eight
Nick

Gran's invitation came much faster than expected. She asked us all to her place the following weekend.

On Saturday, we arrived early, but even so, I'd spotted enough cars to know that at least half the family was already here. The twins were excited when we told them we were going to see my grandparents. The second I opened the door to the house, they barreled inside.

"Guys, you don't know where to go. Wait a bit," Allison called after them.

But she needn't have to because Gran came out into the hallway, and the twins hugged her legs tightly.

"Welcome!" she exclaimed.

Allison and I had decided to tease the family today. We weren't going to hide that we were together, but we weren't going to make it easy for them either.

"Allison, darling, welcome to our home," Gran added.

"It's so cozy," Allison said.

As Gran led us inside, she asked me, "Did you live here at all?"

"No, I didn't. My half brothers moved in with them after their mother passed away. We lived in Maine with Mom until college."

"Got it. So... are we still on with our original plan?" she asked, wiggling her eyebrows.

"We're on. But it might come back to bite us."

She jerked her head back. "What do you mean? How?"

"I can never say how or when, but it's a definite possibility with the family."

"Hmm. So, no PDA?"

I tilted closer. "If we can help it."

She bit her lower lip. "That's just the thing. I don't think I can."

"I don't think I can either." My voice was more of a growl. I cupped the side of her neck with one hand, putting my thumb just behind her ear. She tilted her head into it. "Or I could just kiss you right now and everyone would know."

Her eyes widened a bit as she licked her lower lip. "How would they know? No one's here."

"Trust me. Another rule in this house: if we do something they want to see, someone will see it through walls."

We started to laugh.

As if on cue, we heard footsteps. I let her go and winked at her. Over these past few weeks, she'd changed a lot. She was relaxed and smiled more. And yeah, I was taking all the credit for that.

Penny and Meredith appeared in the entrance hall.

"Hurry, you two," Meredith said, looking intently at us as if she was trying to decipher something. "Otherwise, the first tray of finger foods will be gone, and I don't think the catering company brought any more quiches. They're to die for."

"Today's a catering company day again?" I asked as Allison and I walked toward the living room. I almost touched her lower back but stopped myself just in time.

"Yes," Meredith replied. "Everyone had a very full week, so we didn't have time to coordinate cooking among ourselves."

"Why's that?" Allison asked.

"It took us a long while to convince Gran to stop cooking for so many people. So now at gatherings, she uses a catering company, or each of us cooks something and we bring it by. More of a potluck type of get-together."

"That's smart."

Half the family was already in the living room. Jake, Natalie, and their daughter, Meredith, Cade, Penny, Spencer, and Ben. The twins were all over Ben already. I was happy that the little guy wasn't jealous that there were two more kids in the family.

Colton and Zoey were here too. The two of them stopped talking when they saw us. Colton actually flashed me a grin, which almost made me do a double take. Our oldest half brother wasn't usually one to grin or be very humorous, but things had changed since he'd met Zoey, and the family had grown closer.

I realized that it wasn't just Colton and Zoey who were looking at us, though. Everyone else was too. What had Gran done, spread the word to everyone?

Of course, that was precisely what she'd done. Why would that even surprise me?

"Hello, you two," Jake said.

"Hi." Allison sounded a bit shy. It was hard for me to remember that she'd only met the whole family once.

"This is the very official welcome to the family. Don't know if Nick filled you in."

"He didn't!" She playfully swatted my shoulder.

I flashed her a warning look. Touching was dangerous. That was the thing with Allison: I could never touch or kiss her even just a little bit. It was all or nothing.

"Yeah, it actually is," I replied. "Jake's right. When my grandparents ask you over, it means you're a Whitley now."

Before all of this, the thought of me showing up here with a woman had been unthinkable. I was fully aware that this had happened under odd circumstances, but I wouldn't have it any other way. I wanted Allison here with me for all the other times that Gran asked us over. I wanted her to celebrate Christmases and birthdays with my family.

I wanted her and the twins in my life forever.

The recognition completely shocked me. That wasn't what we were doing at all. We were staying together until she got custody, and that was it. But when I thought of someone taking my place, that didn't sit well with me either. Not at all.

I could be a good boyfriend. But what if I could be a good husband too?

"So, what was that about a quiche?" I inquired.

"We saved you some," Natalie said. "I had to fight for it."

I started to laugh.

"They're really delicious, with ham and parmigiano and a lot of other things," she went on.

She pointed to a plate on the huge dinner table. Even though my grandparents had gotten progressively longer tables over the years, we'd come to the point where we couldn't fit enough chairs around it, so we took turns eating.

As Allison and I both reached for a quiche, I put my hand on her back. It was instinctive; I needed to be connected with her one way or another. I didn't realize I was doing it until I heard Natalie whisper something behind me. I didn't catch much, but the words *cozy* and *close* filtered through to us.

I caught Allison's eye, and she chuckled. Oh, what the hell. I was certain that by the time the day ended, everyone would know. And why shouldn't they? I was opening myself up for conversations that I wasn't ready for, but I'd just roll with it.

"All right. The rest of the clan is here too," Spencer exclaimed.

Allison and I turned in unison to see Gabe, Leo, and Maddox arrive with their partners.

"That was the last quiche, wasn't it?" Gabe said, pointing at me.

"Yes," I replied proudly.

"It pays to be early," Jake teased.

Allison's stomach rumbled.

"Damn it, I should have given you mine," I told her.

There was an audible gasp, but I couldn't tell from whom. Yeah, I was on a slippery slope and didn't even know it.

"There's plenty of food in the kitchen," Gran said. "The catering team is prepping the next round, so you can go and have your pick."

"All right, I'll go see what they have," Allison said.

"I'm coming with you," I assured her.

I figured she and I should settle on some rules if we planned to go through with teasing the family. Or we could just throw that plan in the garbage.

Yeah, I liked that much better. We'd already blown it anyway.

When we entered the kitchen, the catering team had just finished their preparations and were moving around the kitchen with efficiency.

"Let's steal something and go into the backyard," I said.

We grabbed two plates and some grilled cheese sandwiches, then went outside. We ate them much quicker than I thought we would and set the plates on the swing they'd installed for Ben.

"So," she said, looking at me with a mischievous smile, "you asked me out here for a reason, huh?"

"Yes. I have a problem," I admitted. "I can't keep my hands off you."

She grinned and immediately laced her arms around my neck. "I figured that. Just didn't know what to make of it."

I growled. "I don't think our plan was smart."

"I'm starting to think you're right. So, what else do you want to do?"

"Well, what I want to do right now is kiss you. I didn't get my fill of you this morning. That's why I can't keep my hands off you."

Rising onto her toes, she brought her mouth to my ear. I grabbed her hips firmly so she wouldn't lose her balance. "Nah, I think the opposite is true. The more you touch me, the more you want me."

I didn't argue with that because she had a point, and I needed that sassy mouth too much to waste precious time talking. I kissed her just the way I'd wanted to all day. Her lips were soft and so damn delicious. I could spend the rest of my life kissing this woman, and it wouldn't be enough. I didn't have words to describe what being with her did to me. It was transformative in a way that surpassed my comprehension.

I was so lost in exploring her mouth that I didn't even hear the door open. But I did hear the voice filtering through.

"Oh, okay. I guess we found them."

I instantly straightened up, and so did Allison. We both glanced toward the house. Swear to God, the entire family had come out to the backyard.

Maddox grinned. "That's one way to make a statement."

I started to laugh. Allison was blushing.

"No. We decided to come out here and eat. There's not enough space in the living room," I said.

"Well, well!" Gran exclaimed, smiling from ear to ear.

The only ones missing from the group were Penny, Spencer, Ben, and the twins.

"I'm very happy for you two kids," Gran said.

Allison covered her mouth with her hand. The ring I'd given her popped at me, reminding me that we were married and this could be real. We just had to make it that way. But right now, I sensed Allison was feeling cornered.

I stepped next to her and put my arm around her shoulders. "Right. I have a request of everyone. No questions today."

Half the group started to talk at the same time.

Maddox shook his head. "Dude, making a statement like that is only going to make matters worse."

I ran a hand through my hair, taking in everyone's curious expressions. He probably had a point. Fuck, why did I think this was a good idea? I should have explained what was happening a few weeks ago, at least to my brothers. Told them that Allison and I weren't just platonic roommates anymore.

"Don't put Allison on the spot, please."

"I hate to point this out," Leo said, "but you kind of did. What the hell, man? Should have found a dark corner of the house or something."

That had the effect of breaking the ice, so to speak. Allison started to laugh. At least she was relaxing a bit. Leo and I began laughing too. The rest of the family was just murmuring, but I knew they weren't going to push. We were all close and nosy, but we respected one another's boundaries.

Once everyone settled down, Granddad said, "Let's change topics. No one needs us to meddle." He was looking sternly at Gran, who, to my astonishment, nodded.

"Of course, of course," she said.

But as everyone dispersed around the garden, Gran made a beeline for us.

"I will only say one thing on the topic. I know that you two started this for noble reasons, but I was certain there was something between the two of you long before you walked down that aisle."

"Really?" Allison asked.

"Don't encourage her," I warned.

"Nick, I'm speaking from my heart," Gran admonished. "The way Nick worried about you and wanted to make things easier for you, dear, it spoke volumes. And then at the wedding, you two... Well, there was something, and it was very obvious to me. I think for some of the others in the family too. I'm glad you two saw it as well."

With that, Gran turned around and headed to the porch, where the catering team had already brought out food.

Allison was completely silent, and that kind of put me on edge.

"Allison? What are you thinking?" I asked.

She glanced up at me. "Your gran is adorable. But her spin on this is very... romantic."

Shit. Does she not feel the same way I do? Figures that I'd fall for someone who doesn't reciprocate.

"Don't worry about her, okay?"

"I just don't want to get her hopes up."

Damn. Maybe all I'd get was a marriage with benefits after all...

"Let's go enjoy the food. Don't worry about getting anyone's hopes up. If they do, it's entirely their fault."

"And yours, mister, for kissing me right here in this yard."

I growled, leaning closer. Now that everyone had seen us, I didn't really care what else they saw. And besides, I'd already used up all my self-restraint for the day.

"Nick! The food is here." She took a step back before adding, "I'm going to bring out Annie and Jack."

There was no need for that because Spencer came out with them and Ben. Penny was right behind them. Gran immediately went to her and whispered something in her ear. Her eyes went comically wide as she glanced at me. I tilted my head, shaking it, and she smiled sheepishly.

Why was everyone getting their hopes up? They were acting as if we'd just announced that we were inviting them to a real wedding.

Penny immediately pulled Allison to one side.

I said loudly for everyone to hear, "Allison, if you need rescuing from Penny or anyone else, just holler and I'll come get you."

She gave me a thumbs-up as everyone laughed. I kept an eye on the twins, who were running around the yard without looking at any of the adults or Ben.

While I ate a hot dog, Maddox and Leo both came up to me. "You're about thirty seconds too late," I informed them.

"For what?" Leo asked, confused.

"For a moment, I thought you'd come to corner me."

"Told you he'd see this coming," Maddox remarked.

"Dude, explain yourself," Leo demanded.

I shook my head. "I specifically said no questions today."

"Yeah, that was in regard to Allison, which we'll respect. We don't want to scare her away already. But I sure as hell won't be quiet around you."

"Since when are you so curious? I thought that was Gran's territory."

Leo pressed a hand on his left eye and then the right one, shaking his head. "Since you went from repeating that you'd *never settle down* to marrying someone and now apparently dating her."

"Exactly that," Maddox agreed.

"Listen, we don't want to intrude," Leo went on. "We just want to make sure that you have a solid plan and know what you're doing."

I swallowed hard as I took another bite of the hot dog. "I don't," I admitted.

"Fuck, I knew it," Leo said. "I told you this laissez-faire attitude would eventually bite you in the ass."

"Look, the original plan still stands. We'll stay married until she gets custody."

"And then what?" Maddox asked. "You'll just move out and go on with your old life?"

"Probably." But that sounded fucking awful. I didn't want to move back to the penthouse unless Allison and the twins came with me.

None of this made sense anymore.

"I hope it works out the way you want it to, without things getting messy," Leo offered.

"It will. Allison and I are both adults. We know what's at stake here. We know what we're doing." *Not.*

"You just said a few seconds ago that you don't," Maddox pointed out.

"I'm just not thinking that far ahead. We've barely heard from Hugo. The custody battle is ongoing. He's doing the brunt of the work, so Allison doesn't have to do anything, not even talk to Sophie and Bob. We'll see what happens."

"So, there's a possibility that you won't just pack up your life and move back to the penthouse as soon as she gets custody?"

"Everything's up in the air," I told my brothers. "Both Allison and I are fine with the way things are."

"As long you're both on the same page, that's perfect. It's all that matters. Forget all the excitement in the family," Leo said. "We have your back no matter what. You know that, right? In case Hugo needs any sort of character references or something."

"He didn't say anything about that. It probably wouldn't count much, though, coming from family."

Maddox weighed in. "It was just an example. You can count on us for anything you need. Same goes for Allison."

"Thanks." I liked that they had her back too.

"By the way... we have some news on Dad. I actually talked to him—told him we're not cool with him using the Whitley name," Maddox explained.

"I take it he wasn't happy?"

Maddox snorted. "He actually had the guts to ask for money in exchange for not using the name."

I rolled my eyes. "He's trying to *extort* us? He'll never change. I personally don't want to give him a dime."

Leo nodded. "That's the general consensus."

"You already spoke to everyone?" I was impressed.

"Yes," he said proudly.

"He probably did this on purpose to provoke us. So I'll just tell him he can fuck off. If he wants to use the name, it's on him," Maddox added.

"And to think Mom believed that he was sorry for everything. He sold her a sob story when they met in Indonesia a while ago." Leo shook his head. "Whatever. He's far enough away not to cause any real trouble."

I nodded. "I agree."

"Then we'll let you enjoy your hot dog," Maddox said.

"Thank you for your magnanimity," I said sardonically. "It was good catching up."

"That's not catching up. That's us finding out the bare minimum. Do us a favor: next time you want to throw a bomb like that, give us a heads-up so we can brace ourselves."

"Duly noted," I said before focusing on my hot dog.

After finishing it, I glanced around the garden. Allison was now chatting with Meredith, Natalie, and Zoey, laughing with them. I looked at her intently, trying to decipher her body language. She didn't seem cornered or in need of being rescued. At least I could count on my brothers' women to keep to their word and not overwhelm my girl.

Chapter Twenty-Nine
Nick

We stayed with the family until the twins got tired, and then we decided it was best if we simply went home. As usual, they fell asleep as soon as we put them in the car seats. We hadn't even left the street before Jack started to snore. It took me a while to figure out which of them was the snorer, but it was Jack for sure, though both of them slept with their mouth open.

I glanced at Allison, and she was smiling.

"You're happy," I remarked.

"I wasn't expecting your family to be so open and accepting about everything. They're good people."

"Very good people." I wondered if she knew exactly what my family imagined was going to happen with the two of us after she got custody. But there was no point discussing that now. Who knew how far in the future that was? And things could change between now and then.

Once we were at home, it took us no time at all to get the twins upstairs and into bed. We had a mutual agreement that if they fell asleep in the car, we'd just let them continue their sleep.

After we closed the door to their bedroom, I said, "You know, whenever I put them in bed, I always sort of feel like a real dad."

Allison tilted her head and brushed my cheek with her fingertips. "Nick, you are a real dad."

Her words shocked me for some reason.

"Does the thought scare you?" she whispered.

"Yes, and I'm not even sure why. It's insane."

She bit her lip. "I think it's normal, especially with your history with your dad. I mean, the thought that I'm the twins' mother figure scares the crap out of me too. But we're a good team."

That we were.

Without any further ado, I lifted her into my arms and carried her to the bedroom.

She giggled. "I see you have more surprises in store today."

"Yes, I do."

"Whatever shall we do now that we have the whole evening to ourselves?"

"I have a few ideas. I fist-pumped the air when I realized the twins were getting tired. I foresaw this exact scenario happening."

"You're awfully sure of yourself, huh?"

I grinned. "Always, Allison. You know that."

"It's true. I do know."

"I love our life." I didn't know where that came from, but it was exactly how I felt.

"Me too. I know it's crazy, but it's amazing."

"What we have means a lot to me, Allison."

"To me too. It's more than I expected," she murmured.

As usual, we were in sync. "Yes, so much more."

I wasn't good with putting it into words, not when I had no rhyme or reason for it, no explanation for how it came to be. But I could definitely show her. I made sure to close the door to the bedroom, turning the key as well.

"Oh, I heard the lock. You want to start with the sexy plans already?"

"Fuck yes. But—"

"I know," she whispered. "I have to keep quiet."

In the past, I'd always imagined that being married with kids was a nightmare for the sex life, but it wasn't. Quite the opposite. It was thrilling to always find that moment where it could be just the two of us. I loved the challenge of keeping Allison quiet while I overwhelmed her with pleasure. I loved every single facet of being married to this woman.

She immediately tugged at my shirt, taking it off. I walked with her until we reached the windowsill. I kissed her hard, smiling against her mouth when I felt her hand slide down my abs.

"What's this?" she asked, pulling back.

"What?"

"Your smile. You're laughing at me."

"I like your obsession with my abs."

"I love them. They're just perfection. I dream about touching them every time I'm with you. And when I'm not with you, I can't wait until I am."

"Touch me all you want."

I tugged at her earlobe with my teeth, then kissed slowly down the side of her neck.

"Nick, how can you turn me on so fast?"

She pushed her leg up my thigh. *Hell yes.* That was her telltale sign that she was ready for me.

"You drive me crazy, Allison. I didn't know anything like this was possible. That anything could feel so good." I straightened up, looking her in the eyes. "And I'm not just talking about sex."

"No?"

"No, although that's fucking amazing too."

"I quite agree."

I watched her intently before twirling her around.

She yelped. "What are you doing?"

"I want to kiss your back. It's been torturing me the whole day."

Her dress had zero cleavage, but it had a very deep V in the back. I kissed a straight line over her spine. Allison moaned, curving her upper back as she grasped the windowsill. She parted her legs wide without me even having to ask. She was preparing herself to be thoroughly fucked. It turned me on like hell.

I moved my mouth slowly until I reached the fabric. Suddenly I wanted to rip her dress apart so I had access to her whole body all at once.

"Take it off," I instructed. "Right now."

"O-kay."

Her voice was almost a stutter. I expected her to pull it over her head, but instead she pushed it off her shoulders. It immediately fell to her feet. That was fucking convenient.

"This is my favorite dress of yours," I declared.

"Why?"

"Because it's so easy to take off."

"Very interesting criteria," she murmured, then gasped and buckled forward once more as I traced my tongue over her left ass cheek.

Her skin was instantly covered in goose bumps. I teased her other ass cheek with my finger, then gave it the same treatment with my mouth. Her ass was a sweet spot for both of us. I liked worshipping it, and she got turned on whenever I had my lips on the cheeks. I alternated between kissing and licking each cheek and brought two fingers between her legs. I wasn't moving them, just pressed them right against her opening. The tips of my fingers were almost brushing her clit but not quite.

"Nick... Nick!"

She took off her bra instantly. By the way she held her arms bent at the elbows, I knew she'd grabbed her breasts. I loved how confident she was in her sexuality. It was more of a turn-on than anything else, even her delicious ass.

"Are you touching your breasts, Allison?" I growled against her skin.

"Yes."

"Your nipples too?"

"No."

"Rub them in a circular motion, both at the same time."

I knew the second she followed my instructions because she soaked through her panties. I moved my fingers over her clit in a circular motion to match what she was doing to herself. Her legs started to shake.

My gorgeous woman. So on edge already, so desperate for my cock.

I rose to my feet and got my own pants and boxers out of the way. Then I yanked her panties down, hearing them rip.

"Oh," Allison said, then giggled.

"Fuck. I wanted them out of the way."

"I gathered th-that."

Once again, she stuttered. I was going to make her stumble over her words even more.

I took my hand away from between her thighs, dropping the ripped panties next to us. Then I bent my knees so I could position my cock between her legs. I pressed the length of it against her pussy, and she cried out. I quickly covered her mouth with my hand.

"You need to be silent, Allison. Can you do that for me?"

She shook her head.

"Then I'll keep my hand right here."

I felt her sharp intake of breath as she coated my cock with even more wetness. This turned her on. I held my hand in place as I slowly rubbed my cock along her entrance, back and forth.

She was still frantically touching her breasts. I felt every moan against my hand. They were undermining my self-control. It was one thing to hear her approach the edge and lose control; it was another thing entirely to feel it.

Her breath changed and her groans vibrated against my hand. I was so damn hard that it was painful. I felt the orgasm tug somewhere deep inside me. It was building up. Allison started to tremble in earnest in my arms.

She wasn't only touching her breasts now. Her hands were roaming her whole torso, and then she reached back to caress her favorite spot: my abs. When she lowered one hand over my ass, trying to push me to move faster, I said, "No, Allison. Trust me to bring you over the edge, babe."

She whimpered in response but dropped her hands. Then she rose onto her toes and bent slightly forward. She was changing the angle, and she needed to brace herself. I knew she was close, so I stopped rubbing my cock along her folds. Instead, I gripped myself at the base and pressed the head straight against her clit. She rewarded me with one guttural groan after another. She was close to climaxing but still needed my cock buried inside her to reach it, so I pushed in slowly, just the tip at first, then an inch, then another.

I kept one hand on her mouth. With the other, I pressed on her upper back. She immediately took my cue and bent lower, putting her elbows on the windowsill. This was the perfect angle so I could reach her G-spot.

I pulled back and thrust again, moving faster with every push. Because I was still holding my hand on her mouth, I couldn't reach her clit from this position.

"Touch your clit, Allison. Right now."

She whimpered and lowered her hand. I felt her fingertips brush the side of my cock. I knew she was using her palm—that's how she liked the pressure on her clit best. Feeling her fingers on my cock while I drove inside her was fucking amazing.

I put a hand on her hip, needing the leverage as I slammed into her. When she cried out, I couldn't last any longer. I thrust and thrust and thrust until I filled her up with everything I had.

"Fuck," I exclaimed. "Fuck."

I put my mouth against her head, trying to minimize my own sounds, but I wasn't having much success. Allison pressed her own hand against mine over her mouth, probably in an attempt to keep herself quiet. We were both failing spectacularly. This orgasm was different from all the other ones I'd had with her.

Allison's legs were shaking so hard that even after we both came down from the cusp, she needed me to sustain her. I put an arm around her waist and straightened her up so she could lean against my front. Her head lolled to one side, as if she didn't even have enough strength to control it.

Slowly, she turned around. "I'm not sure I can stand yet."

"Then don't, Allison. Take all the time you need."

I wasn't doing much better. I felt like I couldn't trust my feet but simultaneously felt very grounded. Part of me was completely wrapped around her, almost like that part didn't belong to me anymore at all.

A few moments later, Allison turned around, and by the mischievous look in her eyes, I knew she wanted to jump into my arms, which meant she'd regained her strength.

But then Annie's voice calling, "Allisoooooooooooooooooooooooooooon!" broke the spell.

We both froze.

"Why do I feel like we're being caught doing something wrong?" I asked as she scurried to the bathroom. I quickly followed her.

"Maybe because we're sneaking around?" she said with laughter. She cleaned herself up quickly at the sink.

"I'll go check on them." She stopped in the doorway and came back, kissing my shoulder. Then she grinned. "I don't even know what to say."

I kissed her. "No need. Your body and that grin already tell me everything I need to know."

"Perfect. Less work for me."

She scurried out of the bathroom, and then a few moments later, I heard her turn the lock and leave the bedroom.

I cleaned up quickly, too, deciding to shower later. Allison was going to need my help battling the twins.

She seemed to have everything under control when I joined them in the living room, though. The twins were sitting on the couch, each holding a bowl of ice cream.

Given that they had just woken up, they didn't even look that grumpy.

I cocked a brow at Allison.

"They had a lot of healthy food at your grandparents' house," she said, then kissed their foreheads before sitting between them.

The view tugged at my insides.

"Nick?" Allison asked tentatively.

"Sorry, I spaced out."

"How about watching *Finding Nemo*?"

I nodded. "Sure, I've never seen it."

"What?" Annie asked. "Never? Not even once?"

Allison was fighting laughter.

"No, never," I replied.

"That's awesome." Annie had a huge grin.

I looked at Allison as I sat next to Jack, who was sleepy and rested his small head right on my ribs. "Why do I feel like this is a trap?"

She laughed. "I told them that we're only watching it this one time, because they've seen it a million times. But now they just found someone who hasn't see it at all. I guess it's your turn to watch it a million times."

"Then we'd better get started with the first time."

The movie wasn't half bad. Once it ended, it was clear the twins needed to sleep.

"Want to go upstairs? I'll read your bedtime story," I said.

I swear they both jumped off the couch right away. Allison and I took turns putting them to sleep. I didn't want to brag, but it seemed they preferred me to do it.

"Yes, yes, yes," Annie exclaimed.

"Then let's go up."

"I'll wait for you here," Allison said.

Nodding, I went upstairs with the twins. We chose a book together, and I sat down on Jack's bed, looking from Annie to Jack. They were both on their bellies, holding their pillow under their chin and looking at me with curious eyes.

"Are you two ready?" I asked.

"Yes," they said in unison.

"Then I'll start."

Kids' bedtime stories were some of the dullest things ever written. It was probably intentional so it wouldn't overstimulate them, but I genuinely had trouble not falling asleep myself.

A rush of affection went through me when Annie fell asleep first, then Jack. I kept reading a few more pages, knowing my voice soothed them, which filled me with a kind of pride that I hadn't experienced in business at all. How cool was that?

Once I was certain they were down for the night, I got up from the bed as carefully as possible and left their room.

When I came downstairs, Allison was moving around the kitchen.

"They're already asleep?" she asked.

"Yeah. Went out like a light."

"You're a toddler whisperer. They take much longer to fall asleep with me. I think they like your voice better. Actually, I think they just like you better." She smiled at me. "So... do you want to open a bottle of wine?"

"Sure, wife."

My brothers were right. Even though I'd been adamant that after she got custody, things would go back to the way they were, there was no way I would want to miss any of this. I knew I could visit them all the time, of course, but it wasn't the same. I didn't want to miss out on moments like this.

Could I just be Allison's boyfriend once this was over? I didn't think so.

I wanted more.

Chapter Thirty
Allison

Some days I could barely believe how much life had changed in the past few months. I felt like an entirely different person. I'd accepted a while ago that it was time to leave that version of me in the past. But I liked the present version, and I was immensely happy.

Which was why, as I drove into work on a gloomy Thursday morning, I was still singing at the top of my lungs. I simply wouldn't let anything drag me down.

So when Hugo called, I grimaced. *Crap.* Things couldn't work out perfectly, could they? I hadn't heard from him in a while, and he'd insisted that there was no point asking him for updates and that he'd call when he knew something.

"Hi," I said as soon as the call connected on Bluetooth.

"Morning, Allison."

"Any news?" I asked, but it was redundant. He wouldn't have called otherwise.

"Yes, the best of news."

I gasped. "Oh my God."

"They withdrew the custody plea."

"What does that mean?"

"It means they are no longer seeking custody."

"I can't believe it. They just gave up? Just like that?" *Why would they do that?*

"Not exactly. I found out that they weren't doing as well financially as they were pretending. Selling Jim and Nora's house would have gotten them out of the pinch they were in."

"Wait... they have money troubles?" I was absolutely shocked. Hugo had mentioned in the beginning that they were probably interested in the house, but I'd never believed it.

"Yep. And whoever gets the twins gets the house, remember?"

I blinked rapidly. "But that's not how it works. The house belongs to the twins."

"There are legal and slightly illegal ways to get around that if they wanted, and believe me, they wanted to."

"And they simply pulled back their request because you found out they have financial issues?"

"I made it clear to them that everyone would find out about their money problems and that they only wanted to get the twins in order to sell the house. Turns out, Bob and Sophie care about one thing most: their reputation. They agreed not to seek custody if we don't mention this to anyone."

"Thank you so much for taking care of all that. I'm speechless."

I couldn't believe anyone would be so callous. In all this time, they'd never once asked about their grandkids. I'd started to feel guilty, thinking that maybe because we were engaged in the custody battle, they simply wanted to ignore me and minimize interactions. But now I was starting to accept that wasn't the case.

"There is one small technicality, though. I need your signature on an affidavit that states that you gladly assume the custody."

"Of course. I thought I'd done that already."

"You did, but we need a new one."

"I'll drop by right now. My first meeting doesn't start until ten."

"Perfect."

His law practice wasn't very far away, which was great. I was bursting with joy as I stepped into his office, smiling like a lunatic. I could still remember all the anxiety I had when Nick and I first came here.

He smiled at me. "Allison, congrats."

"Congrats to you too. No small feat intimidating Sophie and Bob."

"There wasn't much intimidation required. They were scared shitless that anyone would find out they have financial troubles."

"Is there any possibility that they can file again later?"

"Technically, of course they could, but this would really go against them. Changing your mind shows that you're not committed. And if there's one thing a judge is looking for in a custody case, it's for a committed adult who has the children's best interest at heart."

I sat down in front of him in the chair that he pointed to. He already had the document there, ready for me to sign, and I did it without reading it.

"You can sign the other one, too, if you want, or you can take it with you to read it."

"What is it?" I asked.

"The divorce papers, of course, as promised."

I froze and immediately put the pen down. It felt as if it burned my fingers.

"Right, the divorce papers." My elation evaporated completely, and my stomach dropped.

"If you prefer, you can take it with you and read it. It's the same as the one I sent you months ago. No division of assets or anything like that. Each one of you walks out the same way you walked into this marriage."

My heart was pounding fast. I was going to throw up soon or faint or both.

"Do you have questions?"

"Is it not too soon to do it? Wouldn't it look suspicious if...?" If what? God, what was I supposed to say? I'd lost my train of thought completely. I tried to gather my wits, but I just couldn't. It felt like Hugo had punched me in the stomach and then dumped a bucket of ice on top of my head. Did Nick know about this? "I mean, if the divorce goes through so fast."

"We can wait. It's your call. I don't think it matters either way."

It was on the tip of my tongue to ask if he'd spoken to Nick about this, if he'd already signed, but I couldn't. I didn't even dare look through the files to check if his signature was there. I couldn't bear to see it.

Damn it. This was what we'd agreed on. I had no right to keep Nick tied to me any longer. He was probably anxious to get back to his freedom and his penthouse.

"Allison, are you feeling okay?" Hugo asked, his voice filled with concern.

"No. I'm not sure what happened."

"Maybe your blood pressure dropped. It happens when people carry adrenaline for a long time while waiting for an outcome. I'll make a strong coffee."

"That sounds good. Thank you." I couldn't even get up from the chair.

He disappeared behind me, and then I heard him turn on a coffee machine.

With trembling fingers, I looked through the papers. The signature page was blank. Nick hadn't signed yet. I felt as though a weight had been lifted from my shoulders, but then it dropped back down, and it was even heavier than before. It was probably because Hugo called me first. No way did he call Nick before, because he didn't say anything at the house this morning.

My thoughts were getting muddled again as Hugo handed me the coffee. I took one sip, and miraculously I did feel a bit better. Maybe this truly was just my blood pressure dropping.

"Are you feeling better?" he asked.

"Yes. I should probably get out of your hair."

"Stay another twenty minutes, just to be sure."

"Unfortunately, I do need to get going." I pointed at the divorce papers. "I'll take these with me. And I'll talk about it with Nick."

But even as I said the words, I realized there was nothing to talk about, was there? He and I were having a great time together. But we'd never, not once, even alluded to the fact that we'd continue after the battle was won.

"I wasn't expecting this to go so fast," I admitted.

"If they hadn't dropped the case, it would have lasted a while longer. As it is, they did us a favor. No judge will ever seriously consider them again if they change their minds. You really have nothing to worry about."

I realized on the spot why he was repeating this. He probably thought I wasn't 100 percent elated because I was still afraid they could come after me. But I wasn't—I believed him when he said they stood zero chance. All my thoughts were consumed with Nick.

"I'll put those in a folder for you," he said, correctly interpreting the fact that I was still too lost in my worries to even go through the motions.

"Do you have any plastic?" I asked, regaining some of my wits. "That's more flexible, and I can keep it in my bag."

"Sure." He opened a drawer under his desk and put the plastic folder on the table. With trembling fingers, I set the divorce papers in it.

I couldn't believe it. Divorce.

This is what you signed up for, Allison. Come on, don't waste the man's time anymore.

My hands were shaking even more as I shoved the folder into my bag and then rose to my feet. "Thank you for everything."

"No worries."

"Your invoice—"

"Forget about it. Nick has taken care of everything."

"But this is *my* custody battle, and I can afford to pay," I assured him.

"I know you can, Allison. But if Nick wants to pick up the tab, why not let him?"

Because I already owe him so much.

I'd discuss this with Nick.

"Right, I'm going to go, then."

"Sure. And let me know when you two are ready to sign those papers." He seemed to hesitate on the words for the first time, then frowned.

I nodded. "We will. Thank you."

I felt as if someone was squeezing my insides, especially my heart, and I was about to implode. As I left his office, that feeling only intensified. When I got into my car, I dropped my bag on the passenger seat. My eyes were burning.

Damn it, Allison, you've got custody. This is what you wanted. That's why you and Nick got married in the first place. You should be celebrating right now.

But I wasn't in the mood for that at all. Quite the opposite.

Chapter Thirty-One
Nick

I was ecstatic. I'd been in celebratory mode ever since Hugo told me that Bob and Sophie had canceled their case. I was going to celebrate with Allison tonight. I'd braced myself for a much longer fight.

I'd messaged Allison to congratulate her, but she hadn't replied yet, which wasn't such a surprise. I knew she had a full day. But tonight, once the twins were in bed, she was going to be all mine.

For tomorrow, I'd planned something bigger. It was Friday evening, and the twins were having another sleepover at my brother's house. The timing was perfect.

My day was even longer than Allison's. By the time I arrived home, she and the twins had already eaten dinner. In fact, they were already upstairs.

I took off my shoes and went right up the staircase, hovering in the doorway of their bedroom. Allison stood between their beds, instructing them to get under their blankets so she could read them their bedtime story.

"Hey! Congratulations," I told her.

She gave me a small smile. "Thanks. I still haven't processed it."

I kissed her cheek and then whispered in her ear, "Well, we can certainly process it after these two are asleep."

Allison nodded, but as I pulled back, I realized she was averting her gaze. Maybe she was just shy. I should have more self-restraint when we were around the kids.

I went to each of them, kissing their forehead. "Sorry I'm so late, guys."

"That's okay. Auntie Allison is gonna read our story tonight."

I looked over my shoulder at Allison. "Do you need me to do anything? If not, I can just wait for you downstairs."

Allison nodded. Something was off. "We'll catch up later, after I wrestle these two to sleep."

"What's wrestle?" Annie asked.

Allison laughed, but she still wasn't looking at me. Strange. Then again, we'd both had a long day.

I headed back down the stairs, opening the fridge and rummaging through it. Finding some leftovers, I heated them up and ate while sending some emails I'd put off all day. I set a bottle of champagne in the fridge too. This wasn't the one I'd planned to open for this occasion—I'd bought a Dom Perignon back when Allison and I decided to go forward with our plan—but it was back at the penthouse. This one would do for now.

After I finished dinner, I noted that it was already very late, and Allison hadn't come down. Did the twins not want to go to bed?

I headed upstairs and listened intently, but it was completely silent. As I opened the door, I almost chuckled but stopped myself in time. Allison had fallen asleep in Annie's bed. She must have been exhausted. Only one of her legs was covered, so I went to the master bedroom and grabbed a spare blanket from the dresser, putting it on her. It didn't make sense to wake her up.

Annie was nestled right under her arm. Allison had put her hand protectively on Annie's shoulder. I watched them for a split second before closing the door and heading back downstairs. I was certain Allison would join me eventually.

Only she didn't. When I woke up the next morning, I realized I'd slept alone. I glanced at the clock and groaned. I'd overslept too. It was already eight thirty.

I hurriedly took a shower and dressed before going downstairs to drink coffee. As I took the first sip, I noticed a stack of documents behind the toaster. That was strange. Allison never brought physical documents home. Had she forgotten to take them with her to work today?

I pulled them out and did a double take when I saw they were divorce papers. *What the hell?*

Putting down my coffee cup, I quickly scrambled through the pages. It was the same thing Hugo sent us months ago. Why would she have it here?

I frowned and immediately called Hugo.

"Hey," I said.

"Morning, Nick."

"Question: yesterday, when Allison was in your office, did you discuss anything besides the custody?"

"The divorce."

I exhaled sharply, leaning against the counter. "What exactly did you discuss?"

"I told her that the papers are ready to sign. She took the stack with her."

Fucking hell. I closed my eyes, opening them again. I'd completely forgotten about the divorce.

"Do you have any questions? Did you manage to talk about it?"

No, we fucking didn't. "Yeah, I do have one question. Wouldn't it be smarter to wait for a while?"

"Look, I'll tell you the same thing I told you in the beginning. No one's going to come after you for dissolving a marriage, you know? It happens often. And even if the other side did think it was suspicious, *they* are out of it, and no judge would take them seriously anymore."

I swallowed hard and started to pace the kitchen. "All right. Thanks for everything."

"The divorce papers are bulletproof. You don't have to worry about division of assets or anything like that. It's all covered."

I wasn't fucking worrying about that. "Thanks. I have to go."

"Sure. Anything you need, just call me again."

After hanging up, I turned around, glancing at the papers. Was this what she wanted, to go ahead with the divorce? Why wouldn't she, though? That was what we were planning all along. Now life could go back to the way it was before.

That sounded fucking awful.

I looked around at the living room. I liked it. Now the thought of living by myself in the penthouse seemed insane. Why did I think I needed so many rooms? Maybe I should just rent the place after all and find something smaller.

Fuck no! I didn't want to find anything else. I wanted to be right here with Allison and the kids!

My mind was racing a million miles an hour, but I couldn't put my thoughts in order. I couldn't make a plan; I was simply too blindsided.

But why, though? We'd agreed on this from the start. Since she'd brought the stack home with her, she probably wanted to move forward with it.

That was the right thing to do. There was no point wasting more time going over it, as I had a long day ahead of me. I left the house without even finishing my coffee.

My schedule was so packed, I didn't have time to call Allison. I needed this day to end so I could talk with her, make sure this was really what she wanted.

At five o'clock on the dot, I left the office so I could pick the twins up from daycare. Allison had a meeting at the opposite side of the city, so it made no sense for her to pick them up. I was going through the motions. I couldn't comprehend that this stage of my life was coming to an end.

They were ecstatic when I arrived. They were so hyped up about the sleepover, I could barely believe it.

"Best day ever," Annie said.

"What did you do?"

"We learned how to paint a tree." Her voice was full of wonder.

"That's great!" I looked at her in the rearview mirror. I didn't want to give things like this up: talking to them every evening, learning about their day, spending time with Allison after they went to sleep.

When had I started to enjoy this life so much? And why couldn't I see myself doing anything else at all? After all, I'd been single and dating for years, and it had always been fulfilling to me. But now it seemed hollow and not at all how I wanted to spend the rest of my life.

We arrived at my brother's house a short while later. Both Annie and Jack were so excited that it took me a while to get them out of their car seats. Then they bounced out of the car all by themselves and ran toward the front door.

Spencer must have heard us coming, because the door swung open. To my surprise, Gran was right beside him.

I grinned at her. "This is a surprise."

She put one hand on her hip. "Well, since the invitation to have them over at my house went unheard, I figured this would be a great opportunity to see them again."

"We didn't do it on purpose, Gran."

Although we kind of did because I'd voiced my concerns that Gran might have bitten off more than she could chew by suggesting having the kids, and Allison agreed. My granddad wasn't here, just Gran.

Penny and Spencer both opened their arms, and Annie ran into Penny's, Jack into Spencer's. Ben looked up at me with big eyes and held out his hands, so I picked him up.

None of the kids wanted to be held for too long, though. They demanded to be left to their own devices in the yard. It was convenient that it was narrow enough that you could see the whole area from the living room. We could keep an eye on them from inside.

"You seem tense," my brother said.

I realized I'd been massaging a spot under my right shoulder. I nodded. "Yeah."

"Problems at work?" Penny asked.

"No, it's not that. We got news. Jim's parents pulled back their petition for custody."

"That's wonderful news," Gran said. "Now poor Allison can stop worrying."

"Exactly."

"Fantastic," Spencer said. "Then why are you tense? Or is it not related?"

"It is," I admitted.

He frowned. "I'm not following."

Penny and Gran were sitting next to each other. They exchanged a glance, and then Gran gave me a sad smile. "This means it's time for the divorce."

I couldn't even bring myself to say yes. I just nodded and pressed two fingers on that fucking sore spot again. When had it clenched so tight?

"It's what we agreed on. And yesterday, Allison brought the papers home from Hugo's office."

"Oh." Penny sounded stunned.

"You've already signed?" Gran asked.

"No, we didn't have time to chat about it at all. I just found the papers this morning."

"You're having second thoughts," Spencer exclaimed.

I ran a hand through my hair, pacing their living room. I normally liked debating important decisions with my family. My thoughts had been a jumbled mess the entire day. Maybe laying out everything would help.

"I was blindsided. I think that's the problem. I'd completely forgotten."

Penny sat down on the couch. "How is that even possible?"

I shrugged. "Because everything was moving along smoothly. Frankly, I always figured it would take longer to get the issue resolved."

"You don't want to go back to the way things were," Gran said.

As usual, she had the ability to get to the bottom of things in record time.

"Exactly," I admitted. "I've always been good with the way my life is."

"But now, you've had a taste of something different, and you're surprised that you liked it," Spencer finished for me.

Penny clapped her hands together. "I'm sorry, but this is exactly how I was hoping things would turn out."

"All of us did," Gran added.

"Do you want a drink?" Spencer asked.

"No, I'm driving."

"Well, I need a drink for this conversation." He went to the kitchen and poured himself a Scotch.

"I don't understand. What's the problem?" Penny asked.

"You're not sure what Allison wants," Gran said.

I felt like my brain was about to explode. "Exactly."

"But you two are very close," she continued. "Anyone could see that."

"It's one thing to be close—"

"And another to want to stay married," Spencer cut in.

I looked straight at my brother. I had an inkling that he understood exactly what went through my mind. Penny and Gran both seemed to watch this through rose-colored glasses—which wasn't bad, but it just wasn't my style. Spencer could put himself in my shoes easier.

"My guess," Spencer said, taking another sip, "is that you'd like things to stay as they are."

"Yes!" I was perplexed by my family's ability to see right through the muddled thoughts in my mind. Then again, perhaps it was easier to have perspective if you weren't in the situation.

"That's perfect," Gran said.

"Is it? I mean, I've lived my whole life being happy as a bachelor."

"You think this might be just a phase?" Spencer asked.

I shook my head. "Not exactly, but it's all happening very fast."

"That's true." Gran nodded. "But I think that deep down, we all know what we want and where our heart is. Sometimes it's more useful to turn our mind off and let our feelings guide us. Sometimes the mind can get in the way of our own happiness."

Hell if that wasn't true. Today, I'd driven myself insane for no reason.

Gran was right—I did know what I wanted. Why the fuck was I fretting like this? I was always decisive. Always went after what I wanted. And I knew exactly what I wanted to do.

I rolled my shoulders and felt the tension between them disappear. "Right. Well, it was good chatting with you."

Penny pointed at me, grinning. "You have a plan."

"Yes, I do."

"This is fascinating," she murmured. Gran just beamed at me.

Spencer finished his glass before saying, "Don't let us keep you from it."

I nodded. "I'll see myself out."

After leaving their house, I checked the clock. I knew that Allison's business meeting would last for another hour. I had just enough time to grab that bottle of Dom Perignon from the penthouse.

It was fantastic how clear things seemed now after talking to the family. I should have done that first thing in the morning.

I drove straight to the penthouse but didn't bother going into the garage, as it would take too much time. Pulling into the temporary parking that was reserved for taxi drop-offs, I jumped out and hurried inside the building.

The doorman greeted me. "Mr. Whitley, we haven't seen you in a while."

I nodded. "Can you keep an eye on my car, please? Make sure it doesn't get towed. I just need a few minutes upstairs."

"Sure. You can count on me."

I threw him the key and then headed up.

Frances came here regularly to bring me clothes, but I hadn't been here in a while. When I stepped inside, I looked around. It almost seemed like a hotel, like it didn't belong to me at all even though I'd lived here for five years. I went to the fridge, grabbing the bottle of Dom Perignon. It was the only thing inside. After that, I took one last look at the living room.

The only way I would return here was with my family. With Allison and the twins.

Chapter Thirty-Two
Nick

Allison's car was already in the driveway when I arrived. Perfect. The champagne was still chilled. I could put my plan in motion immediately.

"Allison," I called as soon as I stepped into the house.

"In the kitchen." Her voice sounded so soft.

I headed straight there and then stopped in my tracks, taking her in. She was wearing yet another one of those very conservative suits that drove me insane with desire. It was bizarre how much they turned me on.

"How were the twins? I called Penny, but she didn't pick up, just texted me that all was well."

"That sums it up."

Her eyes fell on the bottle. "What's that for?"

I set it on the counter. "I kept it especially to celebrate."

"I noticed there's another one in the fridge."

"This one was at the penthouse. I just stopped by to grab it." I leaned into her. She looked down at her feet.

She was avoiding my gaze again. Damn it, what if she *did* want a divorce?

Then I'd simply win her over because that was not happening. I wanted this woman to be my real wife more than I'd ever wanted anything else in my life.

She looked up at me as I glanced at the toaster. The papers were still behind it.

"Want to talk about those first?" I pointed to the folder.

Her shoulders drooped. "You saw them, right? I mean, I brought them home because..."

I waited, hanging on to every word. I wanted to know.

"Yes?" I prompted when she didn't continue.

"I don't know. Hugo had them ready, and he sounded as if I should sign them on the spot. But I figured that we should talk about it first."

I took a deep breath. This was the moment of truth. I couldn't postpone it. As much as I wanted to spend the rest of my life with Allison, I needed to know how she felt.

I touched her chin, but she was still stubbornly looking downward, so I bent my knees until I was level with her eyes.

"What do you want, Allison?" I asked.

She licked her lips. "What do *you* want?" For the first time since I'd met her, she sounded afraid.

If she needed me to make the first step, then I'd do it.

"I want us to tear those fucking papers to shreds and forget about them. Forget about the divorce. Everything has changed, don't you agree? I love you so fucking much that I couldn't even imagine not being married to you. You and the kids—it's all I want, Allison. For you to be my wife for the rest of our lives."

"Nick, are you serious?" Her eyes were full of uncertainty.

"Yes. Fuck yes. I've never been more certain of anything in my life."

She closed her eyes, and I sucked in a deep breath. If she said this wasn't what she wanted...

But then both corners of her mouth tilted slightly up, and I felt a sense of relief wash over me.

"It's all I want too. When he mentioned the divorce, I was dumbstruck. I didn't know how to react, or what you'd want." She opened her eyes slowly. They were full of tears.

"Jesus, babe, why are you crying?"

"Because I never saw this coming," she whispered. "I never figured that I'd fall for you for real... or that you'd reciprocate."

"You have no idea how much I love you. *I* had no idea until I saw those this morning, and I immediately thought, 'Hell no.' I have everything I want with you and Annie and Jack. This life we have is perfect. *You* are perfect. I love you more than I ever thought I was capable of, Allison."

"And I love you too. I love the way you love me. I wasn't sure of it, even though I could feel it in my bones. And I love the way you love the little ones."

"They're part of us."

Allison put her arms around my neck, jumping up on me. I caught her by the ass and set her on the counter, spreading her legs. A ripping sound startled both of us.

She burst out laughing, dropping her head back. "Yeah, this skirt needed that. It had it coming."

"I fucking love these suits of yours. They turn me on."

She gasped. "What? But that's the opposite of what they're supposed to do."

"That's perfect. No one else can fantasize about the same things I do."

"Hmm, you can't dictate what others can fantasize about or not."

"Yes, I fucking can." I took a step back with great difficulty and said, "Let's open the bottle. I want to celebrate with my wife that we get to keep our kids."

Allison leaned forward and tugged the collar of my shirt, pulling me closer to her. Then she kissed me.

I let her take the lead, liking the hungry way with which she devoured my mouth. But then I groaned. I was starting to get hard, and I wanted us to open the damn champagne before I completely lost my head. But then I had another idea.

I stepped back, grabbing the bottle and an opener, and wiggled my eyebrows. "Come on. You grab the glasses, and we'll take the party upstairs."

Her pupils dilated, and her mouth opened in a delicious O. "Nick Whitley, you always manage to surprise me."

"And I promise to do that for a long time to come."

Instead of letting her come down from the kitchen counter, I put the bottle back and kissed her harder than she'd kissed me before. My need for her was growing stronger by the second. I removed her suit jacket, touching her waist before moving to her breasts. I needed her naked now.

I lifted her into my arms, deciding we could pop the champagne later. Right now, I wanted to feel as close to this woman as humanly possible.

I carried her up the stairs and directly into the master bedroom. When I laid her down on the bed, I spread her legs wider. The skirt ripped even more.

She laughed. "You're determined to make this skirt unwearable, huh?"

"Fuck yes. I told you I could keep you naked with me all the time. I'd be the happiest man on the planet. But I'm happy enough knowing you're my wife forever."

She smiled at me and propped herself up on her palms, putting them a few inches behind her back.

"Then let me make it easy for you." She reached to her side and lowered the zipper. I yanked the skirt down the next second.

"I fucking love this blouse. All buttoned up." I took a step back. "Take it off for me."

She straightened up, bringing her hands to the bottom of the shirt. She glanced up abruptly. "Where do you want me to start?"

My cock pulsed. I liked how she craved instructions.

"At the top."

She immediately moved her hands to her neck and undid the buttons quickly. I didn't interrupt her or tell her to slow down because I didn't have enough patience for that. Instead, I decided that I needed to speed this up even more or I was going to explode.

With each inch of skin she revealed, I became even harder. I took off my pants and boxers. A sly grin appeared on her face. She could sense my desperation, but I didn't want to hide it from her. I didn't want to have any secrets from this woman. Ever. I didn't take my eyes off her as I undressed myself. She kept my gaze, too, right until she blushed violently and looked away.

"Allison, I want you to keep looking at me." I didn't know why I needed the eye contact so much, but I did.

Her eyes widened after I took off my shirt. That look was everything. She still had her panties on, so I yanked them down. I wasn't gentle about it, but at least I didn't rip them. Then I leaned over to unclasp her bra, freeing her breasts. My cock was hovering over her belly. I grabbed myself at the base, drawing a circle around her navel with the head. Then I lowered my erection, changing the angle so I was drawing the circles on her pubic bone. I touched her clit on every circle. She undulated beneath me, moaning. I lowered my cock from her clit down to her entrance, coating myself in her wetness.

"I love making you wet. I love knowing that you want me, too, so damn much."

"Yes. Yes, I do."

I kept moving in the same place between her entrance and her clit. I couldn't get enough of this. When she was wet enough, I decided that I wanted her in another position, so I straightened up.

Her eyes flew wide open, and she immediately touched her breasts. Glancing at my cock, she licked her lips.

"No, beautiful. I want to be inside you already."

Her sly smile told me how much she wanted that as well.

I sat on the bed and put her on my lap. "I want you like this. Take as much of my cock as you need."

"Oh."

I wanted her to be in control of her pleasure, at least in the beginning. I also wanted to be in a position in which I could move.

She grabbed my cock with one hand, and I dropped my head back, groaning. I expected her to sit on me the very next second, but instead she pumped my cock up and down.

I opened my eyes, looking at her. "Allison," I warned.

She licked her lips again. "You teased me enough. It's my turn now."

While she moved her hand, she also rubbed her clit over my crown.

A tremor shook my body. "Fuck!" Watching her take her own pleasure this way was almost too much.

"Oh my God, Nick."

"That's it, babe. Take whatever you want."

I wanted to drive inside her more than I wanted to take my next breath. But I wanted her to have her orgasm too.

She climaxed right away. It took me by complete surprise. Allison, too, judging by her wide eyes. I caught only a glimpse of her gorgeous face before she hunched forward, resting her forehead on my shoulder.

She hadn't even finished coming when she lowered herself onto me all at once. My vision blurred for a few seconds. Then she stilled and stopped moving. I put a hand on her back, feeling every shudder of her body. This was exquisite. Feeling her orgasm was a surreal experience.

Then she started moving up and down. Her pussy was still pulsing, but my woman was already chasing her next release. She was desperate for it, and I needed it just as badly.

I wanted to watch her come again before I gave in to my pleasure. I knew she needed my help to get there, so I took my hands off her waist and put my palms on the mattress. Then I lifted my ass just a few inches off the bed so I could easily move. I thrust upward, meeting her halfway. Her eyes flew open, because I'd slammed into her with more force than I'd planned.

"Nick!"

I fucking loved this position. I looked between us and saw my cock sliding in and out of her, her breasts moving up and down right in front of my face. We were both desperate. I pressed her clit on every thrust. I saw her body change as she neared another climax.

When I almost couldn't keep mine at bay for any longer, she said, "Nick... Oh my God." She touched her breasts, dropping her head back and crying out so damn loud that I could swear the windows rattled. Her cries were almost animalistic, as if she was no longer in charge of her own body.

I felt my cock thicken, and then energy shot through me. I came the next second, forcing myself to keep my eyes open and frowning with the effort because I didn't want to miss any part of this. Not the way her body moved or the way her head lolled from one side to the other.

She wrapped one hand in her hair, tugging at it. With the other one, she pulled her nipple between two fingers. The sight alone was enough to intensify my climax. I didn't think it was possible to feel even more pleasure, but the orgasm simply didn't end. Not while she was still riding out her own.

When I felt her body relax and saw her eyes focus again, I finally came down from the cusp. I put my ass back down on the mattress and held her close to me. She was shaking. A second later, I realized that I was too. Our bodies still had so much adrenaline, and I knew it wasn't just from the fantastic fucking. We both had a lot of pent-up tension.

Feeling her hot, ragged breaths against my shoulder was exquisite. Once they calmed down completely, she straightened up her back and looked at me with a sassy smile.

"This was magnificent. The only thing missing was the champagne."

I laughed. "I'll bring it up here."

"Or we can drink it drink downstairs."

"Nah. We've got more plans with it, babe."

"After all, we do have all evening and all night for ourselves," she whispered.

"We have our whole damn lives. I promise to make you scream like this every time."

She put a hand over her mouth and giggled. "Oh my. I was loud, wasn't I?"

"Yes, and I fucking loved it."

"Hmmm. All right, I accept that you'll have your way with me for the rest of our lives on one condition."

"And what's that?"

"We get that bubbly here ASAP."

I laughed. "That's easily arranged. But I have a request too."

"I'm all ears."

"I want us to have a real wedding."

Her breath caught, and she put a hand on her chest. "What?"

"Yeah."

"I mean, ours was beautiful," she murmured.

"But I want one where we allow ourselves to feel what we're feeling," I said. "Does that make sense?"

She nodded. "Yeah. Yes, it does." Then her face exploded into a grin. "Oh, Nick, this is the best idea you've ever had. When do you want to have it?"

"I don't know. But we can debate it some more over champagne and orgasms."

She grinned. "Yes, we can."

First Epilogue
Allison

"Are you ready, Auntie Allison?" Annie asked. "I can walk in front of you. I'm a big girl."

"I want to walk too," Jack said.

Nick and I decided to have our real wedding on the anniversary of our first one. There just seemed something magical about the twelve-month mark. The twins were big enough that I could trust them to walk with the rings, although I couldn't really trust them not to fight all the way.

So much had changed over these past few months. Nick and I were closer than ever. Once we'd decided that our marriage was real, we somehow became even more in sync, especially when it came to raising the kids. I'd already told Derek that I was ready to take on an M&A whenever the company decided to acquire a new venture. He was glad after I'd turned the last one down. And Nick was going to open the very first gym location in Texas next year.

In between all of that, we'd also organized our wedding. Of course, the Whitleys helped.

The ceremony was taking place at Maddox and Gabe's hotel. The party was inside the restaurant, and the vow renewal ceremony was in the gorgeous forest adjacent to it. Nick and I had been thinking forever about where to have the event. One day I came here with his family for a picnic, and I completely fell in love with those old trees.

I was currently waiting for Mom's sign that it was time for me to walk out. She and Dad had insisted that they had to travel for this occasion. They did seem much healthier than ever before. True to his word, Nick flew us out to see them with the kids after we got custody and all the paperwork was filed and official. Now Nick was talking about adopting them too.

God, I loved this man so much.

Mom poked her head in. "All right, everyone's ready, honey. Annie, Jack, you're coming with me," she told the little ones. "And your dad will walk with you."

I nodded as a knot formed in my throat.

Dad stepped into the room a moment later, looking at me with tears in his eyes. "You're so beautiful, my girl." I was wearing a gorgeous dress. This one was red with black accents on the hem. Neither of my parents had expressed any surprise that I was wearing something like this.

"Thank you, Dad. I'm so happy you're here."

We walked behind Mom and the twins. I'd been given a hotel room to get ready in on the ground floor. All we had to do was literally walk through the door into the yard. Then we'd step into the common area where the pathway to the forest was. Dad was walking very slowly, but that was okay. There was no need to hurry.

"I'm so glad you found happiness, my girl."

"Me, too, Dad."

"You, Nick, Jack, and Annie are a beautiful family."

A lump caught in my throat. "Yes, we are. But I miss Nora so much."

"We all do. But we have these two little ones to remind us of her."

I leaned my head on Dad's shoulder, soaking in his warmth. He used to be a strong man when I was a little girl. His arms always made me feel safe. And even now in his old age, and although he was frail, he still made me feel that way. It was the most wonderful feeling in the world.

We could hear the twins bickering even though they were quite far in front of us, and that made me smile.

"They remind me of you and Nora," Dad said. "You two used to fight all the time too."

"I remember that. Even when we got the exact same toy, we fought over which one was prettier." I squeezed his arm. "I'm so glad you and Mom could make it."

"We wouldn't miss this for the world, baby."

When we reached the forest, I gave a mighty sigh. Initially, I figured the ceremony would be small. Then I remembered how many Whitleys there were. My friends Violet and Danielle did come this time. They apologized profusely for missing the ceremony last year. I didn't want to hold a grudge, but it would take me a bit to get over that.

Nick was already waiting at the end of the pathway. There were benches on either side. The twins finally stopped bickering as Mom lowered herself to their level and told them to move slowly down the aisle. Then she sat down, beaming at us. She was right next to Helen, who had tears in her eyes. I truly liked the woman. I'd only seen her a handful of times over the past year, but it warmed my heart that she loved Annie and Jack as if they were her own blood.

As the music started, I only had eyes for Nick. He was wearing a gorgeous tux. The pastor behind him was a man similar in age to us. He was smiling from ear to ear. What a difference from the previous grumpy officiant.

Nick looked me up and down shamelessly as I approached. Fortunately, the trees were tall, and the light between them was a game of shadows. I didn't think anyone could tell except me.

Jack and Annie stood on one side, as I'd instructed them a few times. They looked at us with big, expectant eyes.

I loved these two munchkins so damn much.

Nick leaned in, kissed my cheek, and whispered, "You're fucking sexy and gorgeous."

I instantly blushed.

The pastor cleared his throat. "Shall we begin?"

I nodded, as did Nick. The whispers among the guests died down.

"We're gathered here today to celebrate the one-year anniversary of Allison and Nick's wedding." He'd been a bit surprised that we wanted a vow renewal only a year after the wedding, and his voice still held a bit of amazement. "These two love each other so much that they decided the anniversary deserved to be celebrated in style."

Someone whistled—I thought it might be Leo.

"Without further ado, I'd like to ask Nick to say a few words."

Nick beamed at me, wiggling his eyebrows lightly.

Oh, he wouldn't dare put anything dirty in his vows, would he? I mean, I wouldn't put anything past this man, but still, my parents were in the audience... and his mom... and his grandparents.

"Allison, last year when we walked into city hall, I knew it was more than just signing papers. At least for me."

Out of the corner of my eye, I saw the poor pastor frowning. I could see how someone would be extremely confused by that if they didn't know the details.

"All I wanted was to make you happy. That's all I want today as well—to see you content, happy, in love with me," he added, as if there could be any doubt. "I promise to make you the happiest woman for as long as I live. To be the best husband and the best father figure to Jack and Annie."

I heard little sighs of surprise from the twins—they probably hadn't expected to hear their names—but they thankfully remained silent.

"The three of you changed my life completely. Even though we started out on this journey with an entirely different goal. I couldn't be happier with how things turned out, with the life we have together now. I love you."

"And I love you," I whispered.

Nick looked at the pastor and nodded.

"Now, it's time for Allison's vows," the pastor said.

I swallowed hard, pushing a strand of hair behind my ear, only to remember that it was pulled back in a bun.

"Nick, I've never loved someone the way I love you, with all my heart and every cell in my body. It's as if my soul had just been wandering around all this time, waiting and waiting. I'd never realized that. Then, when you came into our lives, I didn't realize it in the beginning either," I confessed. "But as we spent more time together and I discovered what an amazing person you are, I fell for you completely, and—" My voice cracked, and I stopped for a moment to collect myself.

Nick squeezed my hand, and I managed to continue. "And I know that I will fall more and more in love with you every single day. Every time I think my love for you can't grow more, you prove me wrong, and I can't wait for every single day for the rest of our lives. I know it's going to be epic."

"Hell yes, it will," Nick said, and the crowd laughed. The pastor just smiled.

I'd debated making my vows longer, but I knew I couldn't do it without bursting into tears.

"You two are clearly more in love than ever," the pastor said. "I hope we'll see each other again whenever you feel the need to renew these vows. I wish you both a very happy marriage and a wonderful life along with these two children. Are you ready to give the rings?" he asked the twins, who nodded enthusiastically.

Even though we had rings already, Nick insisted that we needed new ones. I couldn't disagree with him. This time, we both obsessed over it—well, me more than Nick. When I showed him the five-hundredth option, I could practically feel his eyes glazing over. He very eloquently told me that he'd be happy with whatever I chose. We decided on platinum wedding bands that had a simple design along the middle—interlaced leaves.

"Repeat after me," the pastor said, and I heard confusion slip into his voice once again. We'd told him exactly what we wanted him to say for the ring exchange.

"With this ring, I take you to be my wife," he said, and Nick repeated after him in a strong voice. As he put the ring on my finger, I could feel our bond grow stronger. Logically, I knew it was impossible, but that was how I felt.

Then I took the ring from Jack, and the pastor said, "With this ring, I take you to be my husband."

"With this ring, I take you to be my husband," I repeated. My voice was a mere whisper.

"I now pronounce you husband and wife."

I grinned as Nick tilted closer to kiss me. "I think we completely confused him," I whispered.

"Yes, we did," he said right before kissing me. To my surprise, it was a much, much tamer one than the one he'd given me at city hall a year ago. Then I felt him grab both my hands, putting them on his shoulders. I immediately wrapped my arms around his neck, and then he deepened the kiss.

Oh, I realized his strategy. He'd wanted my arms to cover us up. Then he kissed me shamelessly, tongue and all, until I nearly forgot we were surrounded by our families.

When we finally paused, I heard clapping and realized everyone was already on their feet. Someone was whistling again. I was right; it was Leo. The pastor was also clapping and smiling.

I felt something tug at my dress and glanced down to see the twins looking up at us with big eyes.

"We want to ask you something," Annie said. I crouched to their level, as did Nick. The two of them looked at each other. "We talked to Gran." They referred to Nick's grandmother as Gran just like he did. "She helped."

"What is it?" I asked.

"We know Mommy and Daddy loved us very much and that they're up there." Annie pointed to the sky.

"But you're our mommy and daddy too," Jack said.

Annie frowned at him. "No, Jack." She then quickly looked at us. "We're *asking*."

Oh my God, my heart was melting.

Nick cleared his throat and said, "What do you want to ask, Annie?"

"Can you be our mom and dad?"

Oh my goodness! I'd been doing so well, but now I was certain that I'd simply burst into tears. These two were adorable.

I pulled both of them into me, and they put their little hands on my shoulder and my back. Then I felt Nick encompass us all in a bear hug.

"Yes, we'll be your parents," he replied.

"Yes," I added, but it was strangled.

They both shouted, "Yay!"

When they pulled back, Nick and I rose to our feet. I noticed that his eyes were glassy. He kissed the back of my hand, interlacing our fingers. "Our life is so fucking epic every day, just as you said, babe."

"I know," I whispered.

Our guests were clapping as they came to congratulate us. Even though we'd already done this last year, it had a completely different meaning right now, and I soaked up every hug. I didn't overthink anything; it was simply blissful.

Helen waited until the very end. "My darlings, you two certainly know how to keep me on my toes. I'm very, very happy for you. You're such a wonderful little family."

"Thank you, Mom," Nick said.

"Not to put any pressure on anything, but I'm ready to move to Boston anytime you tell me that you need help with the little ones—or with any more little ones you're planning."

I started to laugh. "No pressure," I whispered.

Nick kissed my temple. "Bah, don't listen to my family. They have their own ideas and timelines."

"But they work, don't they?" Jeannie said, then hugged us.

"I have to say they do," I replied.

As the twins launched themselves at my mom, Nick said, "Ready to start celebrating?"

I beamed at him. "Yes. I can't wait. This will be a day to remember."

Second Epilogue
Nick

Five Years Later

"Jack, Annie, come on guys. You can't show David how to climb there. He's only two."

Jack and Annie looked at me with fake-innocent expressions.

"Okay," Annie said.

"Let's all go to the living room."

The penthouse was full today. The entire family was here, and in the past few years, quite a number of kids had made our group even larger. Allison, the twins, and I moved back to the penthouse three years ago when she got pregnant... with twins. I had the whole place redecorated to make it fit for kids, and I was amazed at how many things weren't childproof.

David and Dina were following Annie and Jack everywhere. Those two took their roles as older siblings very seriously, although sometimes they tried to lead the younger ones astray. I still wasn't sure if it was on purpose or not.

My woman was in the living room with the clan. She was sitting right next to Mom and talking loudly. Dina ran into her arms, cuddling against her. Our little girl loved cuddles more than any of our other kids.

I liked that Allison and Mom were so close. Mom had kept her promise. Leo and Tori got pregnant a year before me and Allison, and Mom moved to Boston after Tori gave birth. Maddox and Cammie had a baby girl at the same time our twins came, so Mom had her hands full. In the beginning, neither of us knew how it would work with the rest of our brothers, but thankfully they accepted Mom into their ranks too. Not only that, but they made her feel welcome. I hadn't expected anything less from Gran, Granddad, and Gabe, but even Jake and Colton were treating her with kindness.

"Here's your drink, Helen," Colton said. "Your favorite."

"Thanks. You make the very, very best margarita," she told him.

"I learned some tricks from Gabe."

Zoey had a little boy in her arms who was six months old. Colton immediately took him from her, burping him as he walked through the living room. It was a kids' wonderland out here.

Spencer and Penny welcomed a baby girl, too, two years ago. Ben doted on her as much as the adults did.

Jake and Natalie now had four kids in total. I'd once asked Natalie if they planned on having any more, and she said, "We're thinking six is a nice number." I didn't think she was kidding.

And Cade and Meredith were expecting their first child soon. Gran was over the moon.

I watched Allison head to the kitchen and followed her there. In my experience, whenever one of us went to the kitchen, they definitely needed support.

"Hey, gorgeous woman. What are you doing in here?"

She looked over her shoulder and smiled. "You have a sixth sense. I was just wondering when the food is going to be here. Some of the little ones are already starving."

"Then let's raid the fridge!"

She laughed. "You always have a solution, huh?"

"You know it."

She opened the door to the fridge, and I hovered behind her, kissing the back of her head. "I love you so damn much," I told her.

She melted against me. I used every opportunity to tell her this, and her reaction was always the same.

"I love you, too, baby," she whispered back, shimmying against me.

I never knew which side of her I would get: the sassy one or the romantic one. Both were great, in my opinion.

As we started to get things out of the fridge, Spencer, Cade, and Maddox joined us.

"You're taking out food! Great survival instincts," Maddox said.

"Yep. I think Ben is getting ready to raise hell if he doesn't get something to eat. And the rest aren't going to just stay calm while he does it," Spencer added.

"And to think, when you bought this penthouse, you thought you were going to have it all to yourself forever," Cade teased, taking out plates. Everyone dropped by regularly, so they knew where everything was.

"I definitely don't mind being wrong," I assured him.

We routinely hosted sleepovers, taking turns in the family. That way everyone got some free couple time. And besides, the kids loved sleeping somewhere else. It was one big adventure for them.

Dina started crying, and Allison sighed. "I'm going to check on her."

"Sure. We've got this covered," Spencer said lazily, waving her off as she headed to the living room. Since he'd been the first one among us to become a father, he was a pro at every stage. "It's a good thing you like to host here. Although, I do think Gran is getting jealous that she doesn't get to host as many things as before."

Gran and Grandpa really had gotten way too frail to host anything lately. They were very glad to come wherever we asked them to, mostly here at the penthouse or at Spencer's house. I had a feeling that Gran was secretly relieved that she didn't have to deal with us all at her house anymore.

The rest of my brothers came in, too, and Spencer chuckled. "Let me guess, everyone's offspring is preparing to throw a tantrum unless we shove some food into them?"

"You know it," Colton said. "It's like they have a timer or something."

"They probably do," Jake said.

For the next ten minutes, we prepped food for our respective kids. I had my hands fuller than others with four plates, but I'd learned the hard way not to make them share plates. Sharing *never* worked.

"Oh, it's good to see my boys like this," Mom said. I hadn't heard her approach the kitchen. She looked at me and then Maddox and Leo, then the rest of our brothers too. "You're all such amazing dads."

There was a quiet moment in the group before Colton replied, "Yes, we are."

The apples had fallen very far from the tree. Dad didn't end up using the Whitley name for the restaurant—he did something worse. He embezzled from his investor and was currently serving time. Karma had finally caught up with him.

"I'm very proud of all of you. Now, Nick, I think you need two extra pairs of hands."

"Took the words right out of my mouth, Mom. Thanks."

She grabbed two plates, and we all headed to the couches, where our ladies were already wrestling hungry toddlers.

We all made good teams with our partners. And wasn't that what life was all about?

I sat down between Jack and Annie. Mom and Allison were handling the other two. We very narrowly managed to avoid a tantrum. All the kids were surprisingly silent as the doorbell rang.

"That will be the catering company," Mom exclaimed. "I'm on it." She went to open the front door.

Mom had arranged everything with the catering company this time. Usually, Allison was in charge, but she'd had back-to-back meetings the entire week. She was no longer just CFO of the company—she was now the CEO. I couldn't be prouder of my woman. She was smart, ambitious, and went after what she wanted. I was happy that her hard work was being rewarded. As for me, I'd opened ten more fitness centers in the last few years. With Allison at my side, I felt like I was on top of the world.

"Your mom is awesome," she said.

"I know."

As the catering team came in, the kids got wind that more food was on the way, and no one was interested in the snacks anymore.

Just a day in the life of a parent.

Lunchtime was complete madness, but then everyone seemed to settle down once Allison and I announced that we were bringing the cake out. Annie and Jack were very proud to be celebrating their birthday. And I was too. I loved these two as if they were my own, which was why I was more than happy that I'd adopted them. They came straight to the kitchen island, and the whole family gathered on the other side.

"Ready to sing happy birthday?" I asked.

The whole room replied with a chorus of "Yes."

Both of them were ecstatic as everyone cheered for them, and Jack actually blew out his candle before the last person had stopped singing.

Then again, Leo had always been somewhat off-key, even during something as simple as "Happy Birthday."

For once, Annie didn't scold Jack, a habit she'd maintained over the years. Instead, she blew out her own candle too.

Gran was walking around with a smile. Her eyes turned a bit glossy as she came closer and said, "I'm very happy for all of you, raising your families with so much dedication. I'm happy to be here with you."

"Thanks, Gran." I knew why she was so emotional. For so many years, all of us were adamant that we didn't want families, that we absolutely didn't want to be fathers. Yet over the years, that had drastically changed. *We* had changed. And we owed it all to the amazing women we'd met.

"All right, everyone, who wants to blow candles out next?" Colton asked.

We'd made a deal with the kids. Everyone was allowed to blow out candles because apparently it was their favorite activity to do. So, at every birthday, every single kid got to blow out candles. It was always a long wait before we finally ate cake.

By the time everyone left, it was almost ten o'clock, and the kids were asleep. Allison and I were in the living room, lying down on the couch. She was on top of me, and I was rubbing her back without saying a word.

"Babe, are you asleep?" I whispered.

"Oh no. I'm just enjoying being on top of you. Feeling you up with my own body."

I laughed. "All these years later and my abs are still your favorite?"

"Definitely. Some things never change."

I kissed her forehead and then brushed my lips over hers.

"And you know what my favorite place in the house still is for sexy time?" she asked.

"No, what is?"

"The dressing room, of course."

That made me laugh. "You don't need to say it twice," I said, then slowly lifted us off the couch, carrying her in my arms. "Your wish is my command. Now and forever."

Printed in Great Britain
by Amazon